Acclaim for Girls with Hammers

"After reading *Cat Rising*, I—and I'm sure other readers—wanted more of the amazingly wise and down-to-earth Lily Cameron, owner of the all-female construction company, Girls with Hammers. And now we've got it. This book has all of the emotional complexity, humor, sexiness, and communal quirkiness of the first novel, but with unexpected twists and surprises, not the least of which is a well-read, lanky ex-con named Arlo. Like Faulkner—only less tortured—Chadwick is building her own Yoknapatawpha County!"

—Karen Essex
Author, *Kleopatra* and *Pharaoh*

"*Girls with Hammers* is a page-turning story of the important (new, as well as old) relationships in the life of Lily Cameron. The relationships between herself and her father, mother, lover, best friend, co-workers, and even future members of her family are all explored. Challenges are considered, losses are endured, growth is anticipated. The girls with hammers are separated from the women with hammers and the evolving characters continue to develop. This novel hits the nail on the head!"

—Emöke B'Racz
Founder, Malaprop's Bookstore/Café,
Asheville, NC

"There is much to admire in Cynn Chadwick's new novel, *Girls with Hammers*. Its breezy, comic tone; the engaging cast of characters and the quirky but easily recognizable world they inhabit. But it's Lily, its tough but tender heroine, whom we follow from page to page."

—Sebastian Matthews, MFA
Instructor, Warren Wilson College

"*Girls with Hammers* is an identity crisis wrapped in mystery and intrigue. Those who love a great story, and anyone who has ever crossed gender lines in the business world, will love it."

—Martha L. VanderWolk, MPP, PhD
Professor, Vermont College
of Union Institute and University

Girls with Hammers

HARRINGTON PARK PRESS
Alice Street Editions
Judith P. Stelboum
Editor in Chief

Past Perfect by Judith P. Stelboum

Inside Out by Juliet Carrera

Façades by Alex Marcoux

Weeding at Dawn: A Lesbian Country Life by Hawk Madrone

His Hands, His Tools, His Sex, His Dress: Lesbian Writers on Their Fathers edited by Catherine Reid and Holly K. Iglesias

Treat by Angie Vicars

Yin Fire by Alexandra Grilikhes

From Flitch to Ash: A Musing on Trees and Carving by Diane Derrick

To the Edge by Cameron Abbott

Back to Salem by Alex Marcoux

Lesbians in Committed Relationships: Extraordinary Couples, Ordinary Lives by Lynn Haley-Banez and Joanne Garrett

Cat Rising by Cynn Chadwick

Maryfield Academy by Carla Tomaso

Ginger's Fire by Maureen Brady

A Taste for Blood by Diana Lee

Zach at Risk by Pamela Shepherd

An Inexpressible State of Grace by Cameron Abbott

Minus One: A Twelve-Step Journey by Bridget Bufford

Girls with Hammers by Cynn Chadwick

Rosemary and Juliet by Judy MacLean

Girls with Hammers

Cynn Chadwick

Alice Street Editions®
Harrington Park Press®
An Imprint of The Haworth Press, Inc.
New York • London • Oxford

Published by

Alice Street Editions, Harrington Park Press®, an imprint of The Haworth Press, Inc., 10 Alice Street, Binghamton, NY 13904-1580.

PUBLISHER'S NOTE
This is a work of fiction. Names, characters, places, and incidents either are the products of the author's imagination or are used fictitiously, and any resemblance to actual persons, living or dead, business establishments, events, or locales is entirely coincidental.

Cover design by Jennifer M. Gaska.

Cover art by Julie Felton.

Library of Congress Cataloging-in-Publication Data

Chadwick, Cynn.
    Girls with Hammers / Cynn Chadwick.
        p. cm.
    ISBN 1-56023-475-X (alk. paper)
1. Lesbians—Fiction. I. Title.
    PS3603.H33G57 2003
    813'.6—dc21

                                                                2003006739

For my mom and dad

Editor's Foreword

Alice Street Editions provides a voice for established as well as up-and-coming lesbian writers, reflecting the diversity of lesbian interests, ethnicities, ages, and class. This cutting-edge series of novels, memoirs, and nonfiction writing welcomes the opportunity to present controversial views, explore multicultural ideas, encourage debate, and inspire creativity from a variety of lesbian perspectives. Through enlightening, illuminating, and provocative writing, Alice Street Editions can make a significant contribution to the visibility and accessibility of lesbian writing and bring lesbian-focused writing to a wider audience. Recognizing our own desires and ideas in print is life sustaining, acknowledging the reality of who we are, as well as our place in the world, individually and collectively.

Judith P. Stelboum
Editor in Chief
Alice Street Editions

Preface and Acknowledgments

Stephen King once said that we writers never ask one another where we get our ideas; because we know we don't know.

In a café in Hollywood, California, seated across the table from my friend Karen Essex, discussing our next book projects, I looked out the window and noticed construction workers tarring a roof. This is a hot, dirty, muscle-wrenching job. *"In the trades,"* I said, *"tar roofers are legendary. Mostly ex-cons,"* I swore to my skeptical companion. Suddenly, in that instant, in a way that writers cannot explain the magical moment that sends us leaping to the page, the entire story of Lily and *Girls with Hammers* flashed before me. It seemed to hover in the space above our table and somehow, perhaps because we were both writers, we each recognized it.

What tar roofers have to do with this story, I haven't a clue. But I do know that had I not been sitting in that coffee shop with my friend, watching guys smoothing thick black goo across a rooftop, this book would not be. And so these first thanks go to Karen Essex and the tar roofers of Hollywood.

I have dedicated this book to my parents, Harry and Shirley Chadwick, not just because they have been supportive (they have), but because they like each other. Because my father is smart and he believes my mother is smarter; because they make each other laugh; enjoy flea markets and antique stores; take long drives and short vacations (together not separate); because he likes to hunt and never invites her along (for which she is grateful); because she would rather be in her garden, which she never asks him to weed; because at night they fall asleep in opposite chairs with books open in their laps, and each morning when they wake up, they are genuinely happy to see each other; because, after fifty years of marriage, my parents remain each other's best friends.

Although the subject of this book is *girls* with hammers, I feel compelled to mention those men who have brightened my life (then and now): my Grandpa Chadwick who liked to take walks; my father; my beautiful, intelligent sons, Zac and Sam; my brother, Chris; my godfather, Albert Stansfield; the family men, Scott Clayton, Barry Mahoney, and Mark Manley; my friends and mentors, Dave Wills, Ed Katz, Adam Hall, Dick Hathaway, and in memory of Willis Conard Jr.

I can't imagine my world without the loving presence of my artist metalworker, Lana Garner, who makes me believe that everything is imaginable, anything is achievable, and nothing is impossible.

I offer gratitude for the endurance of those dear friends who are always there, no matter where *there* is: Lucy Nehls, Donna McDonald, Ro Hiley, Martha Vanderwolk, Irene Sherlock, Marcia Kenny, Laurel Joan, and Kat Williams who reminds me that *God don't like ugly.*

Thanks to my amazing editor, Connie Conway; Peg Marr, who makes sure the commas and the hyphens behave themselves; Judith Stelboum, for taking a chance; Julie Fenton, my Web mistress; Eileen Joy, who lent me a story; Paul Deamer, for his quick attention; Larry Chilnick, with his sound advice; and Rick Chess, for having faith. I am especially grateful to Dr. Cindy Ho for keeping me in my day job. Finally, I'd like to thank my students at UNCA for helping me to become a better writer.

One

The clatter from behind startled Lily. Whirling around, sliding her safety glasses from her nose to the top her head, she watched as Hannah stopped at the threshold into the house. Plastic grocery bags were sliding from her grips, deflating and gaping, losing oranges and kiwis across the floor into the disarray of the living room. Tentatively placing her foot inside, Hannah edged around the doorway, joining the produce in the hazy chamber.

Lily stood shrouded in a billowing cloud of chalky dust—half a foot taller than usual. In a futile attempt to clear the air, she swatted at the murkiness from her elevated position. The wall that had once divided the living room and kitchen was demolished, piled in layers, flat beneath her feet.

"What have you done?" Hannah gasped, forgetting the rolling citrus.

Swaying a little, reminiscent of someone maneuvering a river raft, Lily bounced the hammer that had delivered the final blow from palm to palm. A slow grin spread as she saw Hannah's eyes search the empty space that now exposed the sink and stove and the loud hum of the old refrigerator.

"Jesus Christ, Lily," Hannah finally muttered, stepping over and around a stilled kiwi, and making her way into the center of what had been their living room. Tools were scattered. A reciprocating saw lay motionless, its toothy blade pointed away from the destruction, distancing itself from Lily and the scene.

She glanced over her shoulder, folding her arms. "Cool, huh?"

The question itself seemed to snap Hannah's head around. "Are you out of your mind?" She reached out to the space that had once been wall—as if seeking evidence that it was gone—as if she were merely imagining its disappearance. "How dare you wreck our house?" This came as a whisper.

Lily's brow dipped. "Hannah, look at all this new space!" She turned, examining her own handiwork. "I made it better!"

But Hannah pushed past her and headed for the bedroom. "You just don't get it, do you?" Lily watched as the woman she loved knelt and yanked a suitcase from beneath the bed, lifted it to the mattress, and threw back its lid. Pulling open a drawer from the dresser that Lily had built her, Hannah began filling the suitcase with piles of underwear, then with handfuls of shirts and jeans pulled from the lower three drawers.

"Hannah, come on now." Lily approached carefully. "What are you doing?" She flipped down the lid of the suitcase.

Swiftly Hannah pushed it back up. "Stop it. I'm leaving."

"What are you talking about—*leaving*?"

Moving into the bathroom, Hannah began tossing toiletries, landing many of them in the suitcase, others on the bed. She emerged with a hair dryer and three bottles—shampoo, conditioner, and body lotion—which she dumped on top of her clothes. "I'm going to my sister's. I need a break."

"A break? From what?"

"From *that,* in there." Hannah thumbed over her shoulder. "From *you* and your manic behavior."

"Shit! Don't be psychobabbling me, now." Lily folded her arms across her chest.

The conversation appeared to have wearied Hannah already. Leaning up against the remaining wall, she closed her eyes and sighed heavily. With the back of a sweaty arm she pushed russet curls from her flushed cheeks. A tiny trickle of sweat slid past her ear. Finally, her blue eyes landed on Lily.

"Ever since Cat left for Scotland," she said, "you have been nuts."

Lily thought that this was a giant exaggeration, but she held her tongue.

"I know it must be hard not having your best friend around. I miss Cat myself."

Hannah raised her palm to Lily's attempted interruption, and presented evidence in defense of the theory and diagnosis; "In two months you have cleared the attic, basement, and barn; planted flowers in the yard; built and stained a chest of drawers; sanded and polished all of the floors . . ." Her hands fluttered. "Listen to me, I'm rhyming. I need a break."

"These are good things," Lily said. "What's wrong with rhyming?"

"Don't try to change the subject." Hannah's attempt at patience seemed to be thinning.

Lily suspected she was thinking that this was not the first time for this conversation. It was not even the second time. The last time it took place, Hannah said she was going to rent a jackhammer to pound through Lily's thick skull.

"Like what other things?" she said, buying time.

Hannah zipped the suitcase and pulled it upright. "Do you really want the litany again?" She made for the door. "You're not sleeping or eating. You can't sit still for a minute; you fidget constantly."

Lily dropped the screw she was fiddling between her thumb and forefinger.

"You haven't read a book since I don't know when." Hannah walked across the downed wall and kicked a kiwi out of her way. "When you're not *busy* (which sounded like *bizzzzeee*), you are zoned out in front of the TV watching *Gomer Pyle.*"

"*Andy Griffith,*" Lily mumbled.

"You've been seen," Hannah said this accusatorily, "hanging out at the freaking *mall!* Dropping in on our friends, unannounced . . ."

"What are you talking about?" Lily asked.

"You stopped by the Hoods' and offered to toss up the ceiling of the new house for Will?!" She paused for a breath before descending the steps into the yard.

Lily thought Hannah might go on about her visit to Will Hood, Cat's brother, but she didn't.

Hannah turned to look at Lily as they both strode toward the truck. The sun was beginning its dip behind the darkening ridge. The bowl of valley, in which their little stone house reposed, always became night before the rest of the world. "People don't just *toss up* ceilings, Lil." When they reached the Dodge, Hannah turned to face her. "And . . . we haven't had sex in over a month."

Lily's head dropped and she kicked at a loose stone. Peepers and night creatures were beginning to hum. The settling of feathered and furry bodies nestling into pockets of dry leaves, burrowing and lodging under black earth, was white noise unless you listened. But Lily always listened.

Hannah put a hand on her shoulder. "You need to calm down. Get a hobby, or find a new friend. And if you're missing Cat this much, then you should e-mail her."

"I'm not good on the computer," Lily mumbled, tears beginning. She didn't want to talk about Cat, or her own fidgeting, or a less than active sex life.

"I don't know what's going on in there," Hannah said, gently tapping Lily's head. "But, baby, it's getting in between us. You've got to figure out why you're engaging in these hypomanic behaviors and, right now, I'm just way too busy to be your shrink."

At this, Lily's back straightened. This wasn't about any psychohypomania syndrome that she supposedly had. And this wasn't about Lily alone, either, she decided. Cat's leaving was only a little part of why she had so much time on her hands. What else was she supposed to do with herself? Lately, Hannah hadn't only been way too busy to be her shrink; lately, it seemed like she had been way too busy to be her girlfriend.

Over the past year, since Hannah's appointment to the World Association of Children's Educators and Doctors—or *WACKED,* as Lily liked to think of it—Hannah had spent less and less time at home. Weekend conferences, late night meetings, and even a trip to Switzerland had claimed Hannah's presence. Lily recalled how just last night she'd found Hannah asleep at her computer where she'd been writing an article. Lily had noticed the title contained the word *Psychoanalytical.*

"Too busy to be my shrink!?" Lily finally burst out. "What makes you think I'm the one who needs a shrink? Maybe *you* need a shrink!" She huffed and backed away from the truck. "Ain't there some psychoblahblah term for workaholics? 'Cause that's what you are, Hannah Burns. And *that's* what's really getting in between us."

Hannah paused, then shook her head. "No, you are not throwing this back on me. True, I've been a bit busier since my appointment, but it has nothing to do with . . . *that* in there!" She raised her arms, helplessly, in the direction of the house.

"A *bit* busier?!" Lily's voice was rising with her words. "How about all the time busier? I have been trying to talk with you about that wall for the last three months."

Hannah shifted in her spot and looked to the ground.

"And you know what you said?" Lily stepped toward her and with a knuckle, lifted her chin so their eyes would meet. "You said, 'Why don't we make an appointment with each other to talk about it?' "

Hannah shrugged off Lily's hold and turned away.

"Do you remember that, Hannah?"

"I gotta go." The suitcase she'd been carrying landed in the truck bed and Hannah slid behind the wheel.

"God damn it," Lily yelled, and pounded a fist on the truck's hood as it backed out of the driveway. Swinging the vehicle around, Hannah headed it down the hill, face forward and windows rolled tight.

"I'll put back the wall," Lily said out loud, the promise a whisper. Massaging the side of her hand, she stood stiffly in place long after the taillights of Hannah's truck had disappeared around the bend. She then recalled that it was on this very spot that she and Hannah had decided to buy the house.

Lily remembered like it was yesterday. A man and woman in matching blue suits, who had been pounding the *For Sale* sign into the ground with a large mallet, had paused as the motorcycle reeled into the driveway. Cutting the engine, Lily whispered over her shoulder to Hannah, "When I was twelve, I swore to Cat that I was gonna live in this house."

In the moonlight, Lily stood back from the structure, mentally tracing all of its angles. She did this sometimes—stand back from her home, close her eyes and pretend she'd never ever seen it before. When she opened them, it sometimes felt as if she were seeing it anew, fresh, like a familiar stranger.

After Lily and Hannah had followed the realtors through the apple orchard and two barns, they had all entered the house built of yellow and cream river stone. The interior walls and floors were planked with warm pine. There were two fireplaces and a screened-in porch. In her excitement, Lily had excused herself to the realtors and rushed Hannah down into the basement where she was stunned to see rafters and beam supports as thick as the trunks from which they'd been hewn.

"Hannah," she had whispered, pulling her close, as if the realtors above could hear. "If you don't buy this house with me right now, I'll never speak to you again."

And that had been that. Lily toed at some gravel that had strayed into the grass when Hannah zipped out of the drive. She wondered why Hannah hadn't left her long before now. Who would have thought a carpenter and a doctor would've lasted this long anyhow? Was that what was really happening? Were they drifting so far apart through their work lives that the next step was just naturally out the door?

Shrugging the answer, she turned and stared up at the tin roof shining in the rising moonlight, where an owl had perched on its peak. It was a good house, she thought, a house that made you want to stay home sitting in front of a fire, sipping tea, and petting your cat. It was the kind of house that welcomed dinners with friends, gatherings with family, and babies asleep in cradles. Lily slid her palm over the smooth, cool river stone wall. She patted it, as she might have patted the flank of a healthy cow were she a farmer. It was a strong house that could withstand any storm: rain, ice, sleet, or snow, she was sure. But she was not as sure about how it might weather the storm that was now breaking between her and Hannah.

Before going back into its emptiness, she walked over to the work van. Across its side she noticed a long, jagged scratch scraping through the dark blue lettering of her logo, Girls with Hammers. Running her hand over the hash marks she recalled the two pine trees she'd skinnied through that afternoon. She'd been alone. Cat would have made sure she didn't skim a needle. But her new helper, Dolly, wasn't always available for work. Fiddlers sometimes played gigs till the sun came up. Today had been such an occasion. Lily yanked open the driver's side door and rummaged beneath the seat until she found a half-full pack of cigarettes.

Fuck it, she thought, lighting up and walking inside the house—*verboten*—she exhaled, dramatically blowing smoke all over the room before slumping onto the couch.

Taking a long drag, Lily focused on the great space opened by the mere removal of one wall. An illusion, somehow, she thought. She'd built up and torn down so many walls in her carpentry work that she really hadn't considered the true impact of such an act. If Hannah had been able to get over her shock, she'd love all this openness. Lily pulled herself up and got a beer from the fridge. Backing up against the sink, she observed the room again. From here it seemed even larger, windows at the far end expanding space, inviting the eye outside. She wouldn't put the wall back, that she knew. Hannah will love it when she gets back, Lily thought.

Hannah had never left like this before, not in fifteen years. And only once had Lily been away from home without Hannah, and not for vacation, either. She'd wound up in the hospital after falling from what her carpenter daddy called a buck-high scaffold.

In this particular case, there had been three bucks, or levels, twelve feet off the ground. She and Cat had been up on the top one together maneuvering a heavy concrete saw through a block wall. Too late they noticed the thick black hum of bees swarming, forcing the pair to a mad scramble down the steel framework. It had been the angry yellow jackets' assault on her neck that had caused Lily to jump, snapping her ankle on impact.

There had been a lot more times in the recent months that Lily'd had to fall asleep without the curve of Hannah scooping around her, but neither of them left because they were mad. Lily looked around the room. Maybe it *had* been shocking for Hannah to walk into this. It was pretty dramatic—she had to admit, but leaving seemed an awfully drastic thing to do. As it often had recently, Cat's voice sounded in her head, *"Unless it's the last freakin' straw, Lil."*

Maybe it *was* the last freakin' straw for Hannah. Maybe it was the last freakin' straw for herself, Lily considered. Maybe tearing down the wall was the only thing that she could think of to get Hannah's attention—because lately, even running around in her underwear was gaining no more response than, *"Aren't you cold?"*

Lily began picking up her tools and carrying them out to the van. She did this in many trips, one handed, as she drank a beer.

Get a hobby, Hannah had said, as if she was the one needing Lily to find something to occupy her time. Hobbies were for people who pushed paper around desks all day long—not for carpenters. Hannah wanted her to acquire a new friend. Acquire? What, advertise? Lily'd gotten Cat by beating up a playground bully when they were only five years old. She was pretty sure that as an adult you got friends in more civilized ways, probably in social clubs or at church. Like she'd ever be caught dead in either of those places. That wasn't it anyway.

Why was Hannah so keen on her getting a new friend? Did Hannah have a new friend? Lily reeled through the Rolodex in her mind, listing names of Hannah's new colleagues and acquaintances, finding none that she could finger as threatening, at least none that she could recall.

"E-mail Cat." Hannah's voice repeated. *"If you miss her that much . . ."*

Did she miss her that much? Was it Cat's absence that had made her so—she wouldn't use Hannah's word, *manic*—*driven,* she decided, instead. Sure, she missed Cat. Hell, it was like half of her own self, gone. Cat was the closest thing to a sister that Lily was ever going to get. Six siblings and not a damn girl in the lot. And you didn't spend most of your life hanging around with another person and not notice when she just took off to go a thousand miles away for a whole fucking year, especially if you'd worked together for decades. How could e-mail compensate for shoulder to shoulder? Talking every day about everything? It wasn't the same. A pang of guilt shot through Lily. She knew she'd been plain lazy about answering Cat's near daily e-mails.

Suddenly Lily ached to talk to her old friend, to tell her about this trouble with Hannah, to ask advice. But she didn't really need to hear in person, to know exactly what Cat would say about the whole thing: *"Christ, Lil, you knocked down her fucking wall. What'd you expect her to do? Dance on it?"*

But it's not that simple, she wanted to explain. It's not just the wall, or her own restlessness, it's not even just about Hannah's increased absence.

Then what, Lil?

Then—it's about dinner the other night. Their first in two weeks. Soft whispery jazz playing beneath the low lights of flickering candles, the carefully selected bottle of merlot breathing easy on the counter, and the silence that filled the table between them. Dense and urgent all at the same time, as if one of them didn't say something soon, the thickness would block each from the other. Lily felt clumsy in her attempts to engage Hannah, and Hannah's attention seemed to be elsewhere. It had gone to something more important, more imminent, more interesting to Hannah than this quiet little dinner with this boring little carpenter. Perhaps, the two had outgrown each other, Lily thought, or perhaps Hannah had outgrown her. And this thought made her weak.

She went downstairs to the basement to lock the door to Hannah's office and turn out the lights. It was a soft, warm space, she thought. If she had needed a shrink (which she didn't) and she hadn't been Hannah's girlfriend (which she was, since forever) she would want to have Hannah for a therapist. But then, she thought, she'd fall in love with Hannah and quit therapy when they became girlfriends, anyway. For a moment she didn't feel so sure about that, and then she was scared.

The computer was humming quietly on the desk. Its screensaver, a web of slowly moving constellations and shooting stars, was calming, according to Hannah. Lily sat down in the big chair and tentatively punched a key. There were two new e-mails from Cat in Scotland. Just as quick as that, Lily thought, like the person was in the next room. She skimmed through the first letter and slowed down through the second.

Cat's e-mails were always thick descriptions of misty landscapes and ruddy people, stories about her students: adolescent girls who followed her around as if she was an American princess: a flattery, Cat confessed, that she enjoyed. She talked about the family she'd tracked down and the castles she'd visited. And, although she was having the time of her life, she said she still really missed everyone back home. Then, ending every note were all the same questions: How's everything? Work? Home? Family? Weather? And on and on . . .

All of this reading just wiped Lily out. How could she respond to all of that? What was she supposed to say, anyway? Did she have to answer all those questions? This felt too much like math, making her temples throb. She had not the will, nor the way, to get into this cyber chatter, as she thought of it. Right then, she couldn't imagine trying to tell Cat the truth about what was going on with Hannah. She didn't want to write anything, not even *Hey*. No, Hannah, you're wrong, she thought, this is not the answer to my inner peace.

On a small piece of paper taped to Hannah's computer, written in pencil, she read,

It's never too late to be what you might have been.

George Eliot

Lily read it again, aloud, wondering why Hannah stuck it there. Was Hannah thinking that she'd missed something? That all those years becoming a psychologist weren't enough? That living here in this little place with Lily might have been settling? What more could Hannah possibly want? The notions sent a cold tingle across Lily's brow. The urge to snoop around Hannah's desk for more evidence of discontent had crossed her mind, but before Lily could slide the middle drawer open, the taped note again caught her attention. And then she wondered about it for herself.

It's never too late to be what you might have been.

What might she have been that she wasn't already? Ever since she could walk, following her daddy around in a pair of overalls and a mini hard hat, she'd wanted to be a carpenter. Since she was seventeen she'd wanted to be Hannah's girlfriend. From the age of twenty-two she'd wanted to be her own boss.

She was already, at thirty-five, everything she might have wanted to be. True, once, she'd thought she'd be a croupier. The fantasy had lasted four days of a seven-day vacation she'd spent in Las Vegas; on the fifth day, she'd lost everything plus her shirt in a game of black-jack, and that was the end of it.

She glimpsed her reflection in the mirror hanging across the room. Her hair looked scraggly, the long dark strands passing her shoulders. Wisps of bangs grazed her eyes, causing her to swipe at them. There were dark circles under those eyes, from nights of sleeplessness, and something new, a crease across her brow that, when she did relax her face, remained. She looked old, she thought. She was just now as old as her mother, Sophia, had been when Lily was born. She'd been the baby. It was risky to have babies much later than thirty-five back then. Now, Lily thought, fifty-year-old movie stars are having babies. Whew. She didn't think she would want that. She wondered if even now, at thirty-five, she might already be too old or too rickety to be hauling around a kid.

There had been a time when Lily and Hannah had talked about children—entertaining discussions about sperm donors, jokes about turkey basters, and some serious considerations regarding adoption. Somehow, those conversations dwindled and the pair seemed to be contented by their occasional stints as weekend baby-sitters for nieces and nephews and the children of friends. Lily thought about that—her contentment without children. Was she content or just resigned? There was not one inch of space for a kid in this life she and Hannah had created; that was pretty evident.

Lily wished she could say all this to Cat—write it down, call her up, have a cup of coffee with her, but all three options seemed equally impossible.

She looked back down at the screen and tapped against the keys, thinking. She didn't miss Cat in the way Hannah thought she did. Cat was her best friend; that would never change. And, for the first time in her life, Cat was following her own dreams. Lily was happy for her. Leaning forward over the computer keys, she pecked at the *reply* icon. She let the subject line repeat Cat's; *Hey, Lil!* greeting and shifted down to write her message.

Dear Cat,

It's never too late to be what you might have been.

George Eliot

She hit the *send* button and imagined the words flying across the mountains, over the ocean, all the way to Scotland. She looked at her watch. Cat was now, Lily thought, in the middle of a deep sleep.

Two

Hannah was wrong. Rather than spurring Lily on to discover or develop new interests, her departure plunged Lily even farther into the most odious of her secret hobbies—channel surfing. After that first sleepless night alone, she could not work due to sheer exhaustion from watching the *Home Shopping Network* into the wee hours of the morning. Not to mention running up a fat credit card bill after being seduced to believe, that among other items, she did desperately need that George Foreman Lean Mean Grilling Machine, to complete her life.

That next day she had left the job early, first dropping off her delighted helper, Dolly, with a full day's pay in her pocket, then stopping by the grocery store for two steaks and a bouquet of flowers.

Somehow she fully expected to see Hannah's truck back in its spot and maybe one or two of her therapy clients' cars in the driveway. Instead, "Due to an emergency," the note read, "clients should contact Dr. Burns at the phone number below." An apology for the inconvenience ended the neatly typed message taped to the back door. Lily tore it down and tossed it in the bushes. *Let 'em guess where she is.*

On the fourth day, Lily didn't even wake up until after noon. When she did, she immediately headed back to the couch with a cup of coffee and a full pack of cigarettes in her pocket, just in time to catch the whoops and bleeps of *Jerry Springer*. She held onto the clicker and let her rip: with lightning speed, riding her senses, she glided through the judges: all first named, as if they were your next-door neighbors, Judy and Joe, all deciding, who, plaintiff or defendant, was most pitifully stupid: soap stars gushed from behind poised palms, twisted hankies, and dark threats, and then, as evening drew in, she skimmed over *Survivor*. These were grown men and women, normally making sensible decisions in their lives, who were now agreeing to be dropped onto some godforsaken landscape to dart around disheveled, un-

shaven, cranky, selfish, conniving, and even sometimes naked, all for
the chance to score some cash. Late night, with a few quick flicks,
vying between *I Love Lucy* and her beloved *Andy Griffith,* she settled
on the redhead, who, Lily had decided years ago, was the uber-come-
dienne.

There had been a million phone messages. She hated whoever invented the damn machine and had forced her to live her life through
it. That's how it felt sometimes; all she or anyone else ever did was
play phone tag for three days just to get a job or to catch up on some
buddy's life. By the time you do catch up with the friend you're over
it. If she hadn't been hoping for one of those blinking signals to be a
message from Hannah, announcing her return, Lily would have torn
the freaking thing right out of the wall.

Dolly had left phone messages, as had a number of perplexed clients wanting to know where Girls with Hammers had disappeared to.
Lily just sat back and listened as the voices reeled from the machine's
speaker. Marge Hemphill had left a long frantic one about the leak in
her ceiling. The floor was a mess, she screeched, what should she do?

"Use a bucket," Lily had shouted from her spot on the couch, lucky
that she couldn't really be heard. But when it was Hannah's voice on
the machine, Lily jumped to retrieve it.

"Hey, hey, where are you?"

"You know where I am." Hannah's voice was tight. "What are you
doing home in the middle of the afternoon?"

Lily pulled the belt of her robe tighter and made an attempt at
smoothing her tangled hair. "Didn't feel good," she answered.

"Dolly called. She says you haven't worked all week. And that
you're not answering your calls."

"What is she—my mother? Anyway, how did she know to call you
at your sister's? What did you do, send out announcements?"

Silence. Lily glanced around the room. Even though she'd managed
to clean up the wall destruction mess, she hadn't managed to even
throw away an empty pizza box. There were a few empty beer cans, an
ashtray piled high with smoked up nubs, and beside the couch, on its
side, the hollow carton of a Ben & Jerry's Chunky Monkey that had
been her dinner. She'd better start cleaning up.

"Are you coming home?" Lily asked.

"No. I just wanted to make sure you weren't dead."

"What if I were? Would you come home, then?"

"Lil."

"I can arrange it . . ."

"I'm hanging up, now," Hannah said, after sighing. Then she was gone.

Lily stood staring at the phone, at its seeming emptiness now that Hannah's voice was no longer coming from it. God, she wished she could talk with someone about what an asshole she, Lily, was being. Cat would agree with her. Tell her right up front that she'd hit the nail on the head. *Suicide? Lil, do you realize what you just threatened? No wonder Hannah left. You're acting like a basket case.*

But it was her daddy's voice that followed, the voice she'd heard in the back of her head for her whole life, whether she was with him or not. *Now, darlin', you know it's time to pick up your tools and get back out there. No ifs, ands, or buts.* He knew what to say. Maybe she'd call him.

Later, not now. After *Survivor*. Tonight it was the one where everyone felt bad about booting off their new friends. She decided that she liked the mean *Survivor* better, and so instead clicked over to a segment of *Castles of Scotland*. She kept her eye out for Cat, just in case—but in the end she fell fast asleep. When she awoke the sun was on the rise and she was not. She was settling into another day of not feeling well, when there came a knock at her door. Groggy, resentful, she got up and shuffled across the room, opening it cautiously.

"Kevin?" She looked past her brother to see who else had come along. Every now and then, he'd drop by unannounced, on his way from a party with a girl or two. Usually well lit, he had more than once crashed on her floor. Surprisingly, it was Hannah who had put up with it better than Lily.

But, now Kevin appeared to be alone and he wasn't smiling his usual toothy grin. He wasn't smiling at all. "Come in. What's up with you? You look worse than I feel."

The youngest of her six brothers was a year older than Lily, but he'd always seemed younger, somehow. His manner was easygoing and his humor infectious. A photographer by profession, he could charm a smile out of his most sour subject. His dark good looks and thickly lashed bright blue eyes made him a hit with the girls. Kevin wasn't married.

Now, he pulled himself by the door jamb and into the house as if he were an old man. The look on his face was foreign to her. He appeared to be physically hurt, in pain, as if he might double over. But she could detect no signs of injury. Instinctively she reached for his brow, pulling back at his clammy skin.

"Kevin, what's the matter?"

It came in one breath: "Daddy's in the hospital. He fell off a ladder. I came to get you."

She steadied herself on the back of the chair beside her. "Is he OK?"

Her brother shook his head.

Lily whirled around, throwing off her robe. "You wait right there. Sit down." In the bedroom, she quickly dressed in jeans. Carrying her boots in one hand and leading her brother with the other, she made him give her the keys to his sports car. Still in her socks she floored the little two-seater and sped out of the valley.

At the hospital they quickly made their way to the waiting room where her mother, Sophia, was surrounded by three of her five daughters-in-law. Three more brothers were huddled, heads bent, talking in low whispers by the coffee machine. It was James, the eldest, graying at his temples, tie loosened at his throat—the lawyer brother—who broke free of the group and approached.

"Lily. Good, you're here. We've been waiting. No real word yet."

"I want to see him." She started to push past him.

"Wait. You've got to wait." James held her back. "They won't let anyone in right now." He raked his fingers through his thick hair.

"So what aren't you sayin', James?" Lily said. Her brother looked as polished as ever, she thought, only kind of paunchy. There was not as much to keep you fit in the lawyering trade as there was in carpentry, Lily had decided.

He said, "Nothing. We're all waiting, just like you, Lily. Daddy broke some ribs falling off the ladder. Damn fool at his age."

Lily saw the cinch marks letting loose the girth of her brother's belt; his once tight six-pack bulged over his pants. Yeah, she thought disgustedly, like a youngster such as yourself should have been up there instead. Jim Cameron could have run any one of them up and down that ladder, herself included. A few cracked ribs would be like a hangnail to her daddy.

It was odd that out of seven children, six of them boys, Jim Cameron only got one carpenter from the lot and that was his only daughter, Lily. His sons had opted for easier lives behind desks, cameras, and computers.

Lily went to her mother, who sat hunched over and barely listening as her children spoke, trying to distract and encourage her.

"Mamma." Lily knelt beside her. "Are you OK?" She thought to take her mother's hand but hesitated.

"I'm fine, dear." Sophia patted Lily's knee. "The doctor said it would be a while."

Lily remained squatting, looking just past her mother, but noticing the tiny lines taut around her mouth. Neither said anything. Sophia kept peering over Lily's head and she kept ducking to give her view. Not wanting to stand, not wanting to stay, Lily began to wobble on her weak ankle.

"Have you called Hannah yet?" Sophia offered a way out of their mutual awkwardness.

"No, but you're right, I should." Lily's knees popped as she rose.

"Just like your daddy," Sophia smiled. "Those bandy knees—snap, crackle, pop."

"Carpentry," Lily said, naming the cause. She left her mother's side and made her way to one of the pay phones lining the far wall of the lobby. Hannah's sister, Kelly, picked up on the other end and interrupted Lily before she could get out hello.

"Is your daddy all right?" Kelly asked.

"We don't know. How'd you know? Is Hannah there?"

"She's on her way to the hospital. One of your brothers called looking for you."

After she'd hung up, Lily wandered, not back to the circle of women surrounding her mother, but to the grouping of brothers with whom she had always felt more comfortable.

"Which one of you called Kelly's house?"

"Mamma said Hannah was spending time there," Ben the architect brother said, looking down, seemingly embarrassed by the knowledge that his sister's relationship was having some obvious difficulties. But the brothers wouldn't ask about it. In her experience, men only want to tell you what they know—and the brothers didn't know enough to tell and would never ask to find out. The other men shuffled and James looked at his watch. Lily picked at an old scratch across her knuckle.

Hannah and the doctor arrived at the waiting room at the same time. He was a young man, and stood awkwardly regarding the large number of family members that had risen to meet him. His gaze finally rested upon Sophia: "Mrs. Cameron . . . I'm . . . we were unable to stop the bleeding."

Hannah quickly moved to Lily's side. In spite of their estrangement, or maybe because of it, their hands quickly gripped tight.

The doctor looked as if he were about to cry. Jim had died quietly, he said, never having regained consciousness.

Lily felt the world go surreal. Her cheeks and fingers felt numb, as if she'd been out in the cold a lot longer than she was supposed to be.

No one moved. It wasn't like one of those moments where the room spins, somebody collapses, and the keening begins. It was just quiet, like a breath held in. Then the air became solid, thick, blunt. Kevin was the first and only one of the brothers to sit down. His elbows rested on his knees, hands dangling helplessly. His head was shaking no, but slowly, as if he were wishing it untrue.

The sisters-in-law made their way to their respective husbands. Lily sagged briefly against Hannah and then disengaged, making a slow walk to Sophia, now sitting alone. Her mother reached up to take Lily's hand, not hanging on, not squeezing tight, just holding. The group postured this tableau as the doctor backed and bowed his way out, like a Chinese waiter apologizing for the wonton being cold.

"James," it was Sophia's voice filling the stillness, beckoning her eldest, "you take care of the hospital business." She raised herself, never letting go of Lily's hand.

Turning toward the nurse, Sophia said, "We'll say good-bye to him now." Her eyes swept across the faces of her grown children, except for Kevin, whose back was turned where he sat.

"Time to rise, son," she said. "Time to go see your daddy." With Lily's hand still in her own, Sophia Wright Cameron led her family into the room where Jim, her husband of fifty years, lay as if in a deep and peaceful sleep.

Sophia stood still beside his bed at first, then leaned toward him, swaying slightly.

"You old fool," she whispered. "What have you gone and done this time? Climbing ladders alone at your age. What were you thinking?"

Yet her tone was soft as she questioned and then excused his vanity for behaving "like a teenaged boy," she murmured. With one delicate, blue-veined hand she caressed his cheek.

"It was a good life, darlin', a sweet and good life." She pulled herself straight again. "And, you remember, I'll be following you soon enough—so behave yourself," she said, her trembling carrying through her body to the hand held in Lily's. She bent again and dropped a kiss on his forehead.

Without letting go of her mother's hand, Lily bent too, kissing the same still warm spot; then she moved to make room for the others.

Hannah had come home. There had been no words, no apologies, no discussions about their recent separation and not an utterance about its cause. When they arrived late from the hospital, Lily had merely lifted Hannah's suitcase from the truck bed and deposited it in the bedroom.

In that next moment the pair went at each other with the desperate urgency of teenagers fumbling around the backseat of an old Ford. A ferocious want rose between them. Savagely pulling and tearing clothing; roughly yanking jeans off hips, buttons sputtering from shirts, shoes slamming walls and windows. They tore wild into each other. Animal-like utterances groaned guttural and throaty—bestial. Across backs and buttocks brutal nails raked and sharp teeth pinched soft skin, leaving reddening trails and angry marks. Frenzied mouths seeking, licking, sucking; tongues plunging deep into hot crevices, sliding along creases and folds, bruising splotches along pinking white skin, sending fierce convulsive waves through bodies unyielding. When they had finished devouring each other Lily rolled onto Hannah—spent.

In the quieting aftermath of their rapacious passion, as Lily lay listening to the slowing rhythm of Hannah's heart, she knew there remained a chasm between them. It was humming low beneath the surface, like a nagging static threatening to cut off a phone line. She just couldn't go there, now. Not on this night.

"Do you suppose that's why they have funerals?" Lily asked Hannah, curling tighter around her. "To keep you so busy that you can't even think about how miserable you are?"

"Probably part of it. But I think we have a need to mark time, to honor the life; to give people a chance to say good-bye. Amazing how primitive we are in this way," Hannah said, stroking Lily's hair. "We don't really know what else to do."

"Mamma didn't cry," Lily said.

"She will. So will you."

"I feel bad not calling Cat."

"No, Sophia's right. She would only try to move heaven and earth to get back for the funeral."

"Daddy wouldn't want Cat scuttling her life around for this—I know."

"No, he wouldn't."

"She's gonna be mad," Lily whispered as she drifted off.

The cars filled the parking lot of Eastman's Funeral Home, then wound all the way to Main Street, packed the lots of the First Baptist Church, Luden's Furniture Store, and finally the police station—everyone else had to park at the elementary school and walk half a mile.

Lily had no idea that her daddy had known so many people. She had only a vague idea of how she was related to most of them. She sat beside Sophia, greeting folks as they filed in to pay their respects.

With each approaching outstretched hand, under her breath, Sophia identified and then named the familial relationship. In less than a minute a piece, she encapsulated the lives of every mourner who came and went.

"Your great-uncle Hubert," she muttered out of the side of her mouth. "On your daddy's side, had business money in the sixties but drank it up in the seventies."

Lily nodded and shook the hands of these many sketchy uncles, spinster aunts, third cousins twice removed (one with several hairy moles), fatherless children, and, "dirty little secrets you don't even want to hear about," Sophia told her matter of factly.

"Here comes Jon-Paul, Minnie's boy. Went to New York City to try his luck at dancing . . . light in the loafers as your daddy would say."

"Daddy said that, Mamma?" Never having heard her father make this kind of remark, she was taken aback. "You mean just 'cause he looks gay?"

"Shhh," Sophia frowned then smiled as the young man made his approach. "They don't like to talk about it."

Lily stopped her eye rolling in time for Jon-Paul's handshake. As the day wore on, she tried to ignore those personal things her mother insisted on passing along as folks came and went.

"Second cousin Melanie," Sophia reported, as if for duty. "Pregnant in high school by that no account Billy Rutherford. Divorced twice."

And then, "Your third cousin, Iris Dutter. Lost her left breast in ninety-two and her husband in ninety-three. No connection."

Lily found herself wearying. "Mamma," she said, looking pointedly away from the woman's chest.

"Here comes a fourth cousin, Jake Bendy. He's not right. Not since that cow kicked him when he was nine. Head injury. If you talk to him he'll sing 'Dixie', and we can't have that today." Her mother patted Lily's knee, assuring her that a mere quick nod to Jake Bendy was in everybody's best interest.

Lily was glad that Mamma's mind was occupied with things other than her buried grief. But Sophia's preoccupation with the sordid details of these lives felt akin to going through someone's underwear drawer. . . . Lily guessed there was some morbid fascination involved. She, on the other hand, was not even mildly interested in the whacked out Jake or the Amazonian Iris.

At the cemetery, the sea of mourners stretched across the landscaped acreage and all the way to the knoll at the far end. The two missing brothers had flown in from California with their families, all of them looking suntanned and smart in their cool outfits—the kind you could probably only buy in California, Lily figured.

Her friends had come: Cat's brother, Will Hood, holding his baby son, Stryker, had hugged Lily with his free arm and said, "Jim Cameron's the kind of father I'm aimin' to become," and his wife, Marce, beside him, cradling Stryker's sleeping twin, Mary Kate, had gently cupped Lily's cheek with a soft palm and kissed her forehead. They had brought along Cat's girlfriend, Melissa.

"Have you talked to Cat?" Lily asked her.

"She left a message the other night. But I couldn't bring myself to call her back," Melissa said. "I don't think I could have pulled off the secret."

Lily nodded. "I'll call her when this—" she gestured to the surroundings—"is all over."

Other friends and neighbors, Delores and Matthew, arrived with Delores' aging mamma who pulled Lily into her large breasts and squeezed until Lily thought she might suffocate. "A kinder man you couldn't find," Mamma said. "You be good like your daddy, Lily, and you won't go wrong."

"Yes, ma'am," she managed to gasp.

Even Dolly, Lily's helper, had taken the day to pay her respects. "I'm gonna go up to Craggy and play the fiddle for your daddy this afternoon. Did he have a favorite?"

Lily thought for a second, then asked, "Do you know 'The Parting Glass'?"

"By heart," Dolly said.

Lily then noticed that all the fellas from Dizzy's Lumberyard were there and before she could stop it, big old Dizzy Sr. scooped her up and held her tight as he cried into her shoulder, "I knowed your daddy since we was boys," he choked.

She comforted him, "He always said, 'Dizzy's like a brother, he'll do you right.' That's why I do my business with you."

It seemed that every tradesman in the county and beyond was there, each looking similarly uncomfortable in his shiny suit and slicked down hair. Lily noticed that some, the ones she knew best, had shaved close, leaving tiny pricks of dried blood where their styptic pencils had missed. Quite a few had even removed the chew from their cheeks, making them even more uncomfortable and nearly unrecognizable.

All the carpenters who'd ever worked for Jim Cameron were scattered throughout the crowd. There must have been twenty-five or thirty of them; the ranks of the current employees numbered around ten. The company had doubled its size since Jim had inherited it from his own daddy when he was twenty-three years old. But recently, Jim had begun to subcontract some of the work to smaller companies. He had told Lily, "I'm too old to be managing so many boys. Subbing lets you hire the boss and then you only have to tell one person everything once."

Pappy Adams was there. Lily saw him swiping at his eyes with the heel of his hand, first his right cheek, then his left. He'd been working for Cameron since he was a boy of fifteen: now he was a man of fifty. Pappy's Christian name was George, but the twelve children he'd sired had given him the title. The dozen kids and Mrs. Pappy, who looked amazingly like a kid herself, flanked him, as he stood in his own grief.

There were others, many others, more than Lily could take in. Her teeth were buzzing from it all, she swore. And in one small moment, standing away from the crowd—as if the few feet of emptiness around her were some kind of barrier, protecting her from the collective dis-ease of the mass—she allowed herself the memory of her father's big hand covering her much smaller one as he guided her first cut. She might have been six years old. The circular saw had eased smoothly down the exact middle of an eight foot two-by-four. Nearing the end, maybe because the saw had never once veered off her chalk line, her

father had let go, in the same way that other fathers let go of the back
of the two-wheeler for that first solo ride.

It was all finally over. *Over, over, over,* Lily chanted in her head as she
stepped inside the house, Hannah behind her. There was a growing silence between them which had begun in the car. Lily had allowed herself the quiet space to zone out—not think, not feel the hole that was
widening in her heart—the one that had been filled by her daddy. But
she and Hannah had lived together for over half a lifetime. She knew
the difference between the kind of easy quiet that comes because there
is no need for words, and the quiet that looms to keep out words. This
silence, Lily knew, was of the latter kind. She flopped back onto the
couch and watched Hannah poised at the doorway, keys fumbling in
her hands. Lily crossed her arms behind her head and tried to slow her
rapidly increasing breathing. Her body was bracing for the blow. It
was coming; this she could have felt even without seeing it in Hannah's eyes, but it was there as well.
    "You got something to say?" Lily finally asked. "You gonna do it
from the doorway?"
    "I need some more time away," Hannah started, faltering on every
word. "Things . . . aren't suddenly different just because Jim died . . ."
As if realizing the callousness of her remark, Hannah tried again, "I
mean, the problems are still here . . . Lil . . . you are still manic and . . . "
    Lily jumped to her feet. "Yeah?! And you are still not around
much." She paced a circle and then stopped, "Come to think of it, I
could barely tell the difference between you living here and you living
at Kelly's. So go ahead. Go on back. I sure don't need you being here
for pity's sake." She went to the bedroom. "Go ahead and make it
worse, Hannah." And with that she slammed the door.
    Hannah's walk down to the driveway was slow, Lily could hear,
leaning against the door jamb, listening to the waning footfalls. The
click of the truck door being opened felt like the cracking of her ribs.
Lily concentrated, waiting for a shuffle of feet indicating a turning. A
hope for the sound of retracing steps—a change in directions, a
change in mind. Then the door slammed, a key turned, and the grum-

bling engine started up. In spite of herself, Lily kept up her hopeful wait, even as tires crunched, gears shifted, and the rolling sounds of a distancing vehicle dissolved into the night.

She remained in her spot for some time. Waiting, she thought, as much for Hannah's return as she was for her own tears. She had not cried, not as Hannah had promised. Not for her daddy's passing or even for her mamma's pain. She felt hollow and lonely and yet no tears would come in the wake of her own angry grief. Here she stood, alone, the first great love of her life gone—on the night of her own daddy's funeral—and still she could not conjure a droplet.

After awhile and a couple of beers, Lily wandered down to the office and sat in the big leather chair. She lit a candle and her cigarette and opened her tattered address book. Reaching to her throat, she grasped the silver thistle hanging from a chain around her neck. As she smoothed the charm between her fingers, she closed her eyes and re-called her tenth Christmas when her daddy had given them, Cat and herself, the identical necklaces.

Still so familiar, even now, was the feel of her hand clasped with Cat's, as the pair had made their way through a forest of legs to the Cameron kitchen. They had been about to sneak a second helping of Granny Cleaver's red velvet cake when Jim had called from the parlor, detouring them into an empty corner.

Lily saw him now, as she had then, from her child's vantage: head tilting upward taking in the length of him. He had been a tall man, with long limbs, fingers, toes, and even ears. A shock of light brown hair bounced above his brow, and his crooked grin might have been that of a teenage boy, rather than a grandfather.

He had slowly squatted between the little girls, and Lily recalled the vivid mingling of cherry tobacco and sawdust that was her father's scent. His face had been smooth, carefully scraped by the straight ra-zor he had always used. He told her once, "A man oughta be able to shave clean with a hatchet, my old daddy used to say."

Her memories now layered and overlapped and blended together as she rested before calling and breaking the sad news to Cat.

Lily hadn't had a chance, in the days since he'd died, to remember him.

A hike through the woods meant her three steps to every one of his long strides.

"Do you see that twisted limb?" He had pointed to an old poplar tree. "That's an Indian sign."

She listened, rapt.

"In the old days . . ."

She could hear his voice now.

"Indians tied up the saplings to mark the path they'd come."

Imagination now curled her into a ball on Jim's lap while he read from a worn copy of *The Jungle Book*.

Another frame had her seated across a chessboard from him.

And then behind her closed eyes she watched as he puffed away on his pipe, seated in his big leather chair.

Finally, with the little thistle tumbling between her fingers, she came back to the original memory of that Christmas when she had stood feeling shy, as her daddy dropped the first small box into her palm and the second one into Cat's. Each thistle had been clasped around their necks as Jim declared Lily and Cat his favorite little girls.

Lily had never minded sharing him with Cat, who'd been orphaned before she could worry about it. Jim was as close as Cat was ever going to get to a daddy and Lily dreaded telling her that she'd just lost another. This was Lily's last thought before dialing Scotland.

She lifted the phone and punched in the string of numbers that would connect her to Cat's voice all the way across the ocean. She waited as strange beeps and whistles zipped and clanked along the way. Lily figured it would be around five o'clock in the morning over there and she was glad that the sun would be rising, rather than darkness falling, as she gave Cat the news.

If you were to have asked Lily to recall the words of this conversation, she would have come up blank. There was no conversation, really. As soon as their voices had connected there were no sentences; no detailed chronology of events, no guilty explanations, no blaming; there were only a few words, some memories spoken aloud, and then, together they cried and talked until the sun pinked over the banks of the Clyde River that Cat could see from her room, and the shadows turned the tall pines black beyond Lily's orchard. They hung up with barely a whispered good-bye.

Lily didn't know how long she'd been sitting there at Hannah's desk. Minutes that felt like days. She vacillated between heaving sighs and jagged coughs and long stares at nothing. It was the *"You've got mail"* signal from the computer that stirred her from an empty daydream. She reached for the keyboard and prompted the screen. The message was from Cat, online, one last question.

> Once your daddy told me what he wanted it to say on his headstone—I can't remember anymore . . .

Lily smiled and hit the reply button.

> "Wherever I wander, wherever I rove,
> The hills of the Highlands, forever I love,"

she wrote. "Bobby Burns. We're all just a bunch of scattered Scots, ain't we, Cat?"

Three

What she had thought was, *over, over, over,* Lily realized, had just only begun. First, she was summoned to James' office with the rest of the clan for the reading of Jim's will. It seemed there were no real surprises, only small moments when smiles mixed with tears as James read, announcing the next thoughtful remembrance. Each of his sons was left a piece of his jewelry, all in perfect condition since Jim had never worn any of it. On the job he wouldn't even wear his wedding band: "Seen too many fingers yanked off by a caught ring," he'd explained.

He hadn't forgotten anyone: not child or grandchild, or in-law (Hannah included), not his oldest or newest friend, nor any of the men who had worked for him. After all of the personal mementos had been doled out, James took a breath, adjusting the glasses on his nose and looked to his mother.

"Go on," Sophia reassured him. "It's what your daddy and me decided."

Lily's knee was bouncing. She was anxious to get out of the office. Being this closed in with her family was making her antsy.

As James began to read the next part, the part about the family business, she was fidgeting with a string on her shirt, pulling at it and then twisting its fraying end between her thumb and forefinger. She was so absorbed in this task, so distanced from the reading that she didn't hear her name mentioned, didn't even hear the collective gasp of the family seated around her. It wasn't really till she felt all eyes upon her that she looked up.

"What?" she said, embarrassed to be the focus of so many.

"Did you not hear James?" Kevin asked.

Lily glanced at James, and then at her mother. She shrugged.

James said, "Why don't I read it again?" and proceeded to repeat the words; *I leave my business, Cameron Construction Company, to my daughter, Lily Nelda Cameron . . .*

No, she thought. Hell, *no.* She stared at her mother. "No," she said aloud. But they were all nodding, and smiling, getting up and coming over to pat her on the back. The brothers were all happy for her, their wives relieved not to have their lives shifted from their country club existences into the red-neck nail-banging lifestyle of their in-laws. Lily could barely believe their smug well-wishing and congratulations—as if she could possibly want this! Maybe they thought her protestations were perceived to have come from some place of modesty or perhaps overwhelming emotion rising because she was her father's chosen one, now. But her *No* had been the genuine response of a trapped animal; she did not want Cameron Construction, she never had. She'd just have to find a way to turn it down.

But it wasn't that easy, was it? You couldn't just say thanks but no thanks to your daddy's last wishes, could you?

"Mamma . . ." she started, appealing to Sophia who only nodded and smiled.

"You'll be fine, honey," she said to her daughter. And then looked straight back at James.

After the rest of the family, including her mother, had left James' office, Lily stayed seated in the chair directly opposite her oldest brother. They stared at each other and then James removed his glasses and pinched the bridge of his nose.

"I'm sorry, Lil," he said after a time.

"You knew about this?"

He nodded, leaned back and folded his hands across his paunch.

"Why didn't you tell me?"

"You know I couldn't do that." James' tone reflected his patronizing manner—the one he used on everybody.

James had been born an old man, she'd once overheard Daddy say to Mamma. She had been on her daddy's shoulders, watching James grumpily shake off a younger brother's enthusiastic greetings upon his return home from college, one summer.

Lily had probably only been about five years old, but could still recall the picture she had imagined—that of a baby body carrying an old man's head. This alone could have been enough to keep her distant from this strange brother, but the span of intimacy had widened further as she grew older and James grew grumpier still. The first time Lily had heard the word, *curmudgeon,* she thought of him, even though he could have been no more than thirty.

"Why didn't somebody ask *me* if I even wanted this?" She finally asked, breaking from her thoughts.

"Maybe he knew you wouldn't want the business. Maybe he wanted all along to give you what he'd worked so hard for—so *you* wouldn't have to work as hard as he had. But he didn't have to see that look in your eyes."

"What look?"

"The one like someone just shot you. The look you've got now."

Lily slumped back in her chair. "I would have rather he'd left me his old wool scarf."

James nodded and shuffled papers, dismissively. "Well, he didn't and that's that." He said this as if he were finishing up a meal. One more swipe across the mashed potatoes and he'd be done, not full, but done.

"I haven't worked commercial construction in over a decade."

"But you know how."

She scowled. "I haven't looked at a blueprint, haven't bid a job—in I don't know how long."

"Ben can help you brush up," James said, mentioning their architect brother, the only other sibling who might have been considered to take over the family business.

"Why didn't he give it to Ben?" Lily looked at her brother, helpless.

"Ben's got his own firm; he doesn't have time to run a company the size of Cameron. It would have been a burden."

"God damn it!" Lily jumped to her feet. "I've got a firm, too. Nobody considered reminding Daddy about that when ya'll got your heads together?" She slapped her palms flat onto James' desk, and leaned over at him. "How am I supposed to run *two* companies?"

James flinched but then got that lawyer look on his face. The flat one, Lily thought, that somehow always distanced him from everything. She guessed it made him a good lawyer. Skinnying slick clients out of sordid situations was James' specialty. It was well known in these parts that if you got yourself into a conversation with the government or the cops or even the IRS, James Cameron was the man to do your talking for you. But she didn't appreciate him pulling that snake face on her—not family. It wasn't right.

She stood with her fingertips pressing into the desktop and met her brother's cool bearing. "I am not giving up Girls with Hammers." A heaviness was pressing on her shoulders. Dread. She could feel she was already puttin' the dread on the whole thing.

James might have been as handsome as his father but he wasn't. He was soft and pudgy where Jim had been lean and firm, and his eyes were sly. Her father wore a tan year round. James' skin was white, shiny white. His fingernails were clean and manicured.

Like her own, Jim Cameron's nails had always been ragged and beat-up. Lily imagined the palms of her brother's hands to be as smooth as a baby's butt. Nothing like the rough knobs of callous she would feel against her fingers as they nestled in her daddy's big hand.

But it wasn't this physical difference between father and son that struck Lily as she looked down into her brother's dark eyes. There had been enough similarity between the senior and junior Cameron men that any stranger could tell they were related. The real difference wasn't on the outside, anyway; it was on the inside. That big soft heart had timed an easy rhythm within her father, but had not replicated itself in James. His heart, Lily imagined, was clenched like a fist, begrudging its very own cadence.

"Mamma needs you to do this," James said. It was all James needed to say and he knew it and Lily knew he knew it. She deflated into the chair.

He pushed some papers around his desk. "You won't have to worry about the accounting. Mamma's been taking care of that part for years, and she'll keep on doing it. I'll take over doing the contracts etcetera, if you want. Pappy'll be right there beside you . . ."

Lily tuned out the rest of his rattling. She'd been whupped. She was about to become the last thing she'd ever wanted to become. *It's never too late to be what you might have been.* Was this it? If so—what a joke, she thought, disgusted at the words now. She had no idea what *she might have been.* "What a fucking joke," she now said aloud, startling James in the middle of his ramblings.

She took the weekend to recuperate. Mostly she slept, which didn't make her any less tired on Monday when she went to finish up her last GWH job. When she returned home that evening—feeling as if she'd been wrung out—there were a billion blinking messages on her answering machine. Like a child in a pout, she threw herself into the chair beside the phone and punched at it, rattling the receiver from its cradle. The new order of communication, telephone tag; she hated it. She barely listened to the messages as they clicked on and off: dentist office reminding her about her appointment, client whining, Dolly wondering about work, client happy, client begging, Sophia wishing her well on the new job, client worrying, client canceling, Hannah checking in . . . "Where are you now?" Lily called to the hollow voice echoing from the machine.

Tomorrow, she had reluctantly agreed with James, she would go out to the Cameron job site and assess the situation. Not till then, she told him, would she make her final decision. It was the fourth or fifth message that caught her attention. Pappy's voice sounding distressed.

"All four a those Whitley boys is leavin'. Gave notice today. Tommy Ledford and another fella got hired on over to the Bly site. We're down six men from ten . . ."

Lily let the rest of the messages play out. She closed her eyes to the pressure that was building behind them. This was exactly what she couldn't deal with, workmen quitting, Pappy calling *her.* It made her want to cry. Or drink a lot of beer. She picked up the phone and dialed Dolly's number.

"I'm gonna need four or five more helpers by tomorrow, Dolly. Can you help me out?" She waited. Her phone call had half-interrupted band practice in Dolly's living room. Lively Irish music still jigged in the background, making her smile in spite of her agitated state. Dolly laid the phone down, leaving her hanging while she went to ask if any of the musicians were interested in doing a carpentry gig. Lily heard the instruments quiet down.

It was taking a long time and there was low murmuring, and then Lily heard Dolly's voice pleading, "Just do me this favor, will ya?" and then there was another stretch of humming. Come on, Dolly, she thought, make it simple—yes or no, work or no work. Lily tapped a pencil against her teeth. Finally the music resumed and Dolly lifted the receiver.

"Micah and Laura say OK," Dolly said.

"Good," Lily started jotting on the note pad, then stopped. "Who?"

Dolly repeated the names.

"Now, how'm I gonna remember these names? Not to mention Daddy's fellas. Only one I know is Pap; the rest are strangers to me."

"They end in *ah*," Dolly said, "Mic*ah* and Laur*ah*."

"*Ah*," Lily nodded and then wrote them all down. Two ahs, she thought. Easy.

"I know two other girls who might be interested," Dolly said.

"What are their names?"

"Jenny and Jennie, with a Y and an IE. They both play the tin whistle."

Unbelievable, Lily thought, but said, "See if you can get 'em for tomorrow. I'll be pickin' ya'll up between seven-thirty and eight, and tell 'em to bring lunch."

The rest of her night was spent returning phone calls to neglected clients, rearranging work orders and estimates, placing all the Girls with Hammers paperwork to the left of her desk and all the Cameron Construction stuff to her right. It was this pile that rose all the way to her shoulder. It was this company that would demand all of her time, she knew. She placed her palm on the smaller pile with the blue and white Girls with Hammers logo on its letterhead. She loved that logo: two stick-figured girls with stick-figured hammers poised midswing above a giant stick-figured nail centered between them; the company name arched above and across like a rainbow. She and Cat had picked it out together. The logo was on their ad in the phone book and on the side of the work van. She wasn't giving it up. She picked up the phone and dialed James' number. Now *his* machine picked up.

"I'll do it, James," Lily said, "on one condition. Cameron becomes part of Girls with Hammers, not the other way around. That's my final offer, James." She hung up, feeling both better and worse.

The next morning, three messages were blinking away when she stepped out of the shower. They were all from James who was clearly pissed. Controlled but pissed.

"I need to speak with you immediately," the first one said.

"Call before you leave for work this morning," the second one ordered.

"Don't you do anything rash without talking to me first," the third one warned.

She deleted all three while she brushed her teeth.

There had also been a message from Hannah, left some time after Lily had gone to sleep. The voice was soft and loving and gentle in its missing of her. She had saved it.

It had taken some time, but Lily had fashioned a bench seat the length of the van by setting a pine plank atop two overturned mud buckets and fastening them together with screws. This would have to do, she decided, till something else could be figured out. Her first stop was, as usual, Dolly's. What made it unusual was the presence of the two *Ahs* (as they'd become in Lily's mind) climbing up and into the van. Introductions were made in the rearview mirror as they settled themselves along the bench. The one good thing, Lily thought, was that they each had different color hair.

One was a redhead, well, an orangehead really, Lily thought, watching the bounce of two tufts of frizzy fuzz escaping from beneath a baseball cap. And another little itty-bitty thing; what little hair not shaved from the head of this one was dyed a particularly bright pink.

All at once they were chattering, literally. Dolly sat beside her in the same quiet way that she had for the past six months, yet now behind them was this noise. Not the natural noise of a work van: swaying tools, knocking steel, a rumble of shaken lumber; these were girlie-voices that giggled. One of them was particularly high and another was unnervingly low. Lily wondered which *Ah* possessed it. And then hands rummaged in paper bags, food began crunching in between words, and someone sucked on a straw, straining the final drop from the bottom of a bottle. The rasping echoed through the van.

When Lily picked up Jenny and Jennie—the black and white (respectively) tin whistle-blowing-couple (*girlfriends,* Dolly confided)—the crescendo of voices behind her raised in such cacophony that Lily felt as if she were being muscled out of the van along with the comfortable quiet that usually accompanied her work mornings.

Her temples were beginning to throb and her toes were getting hot. When Lily got agitated, the tips of her toes would burn, sometimes so bad that she'd have to yank off her boots and plunge her feet into the nearest water source. One time, after they'd run out of gas on the top of an isolated mountaintop, Cat had poured a whole Mountain Dew onto Lily's fiery toes.

She looked at her watch now to see that it was only twenty minutes past eight. Those chatty musicians in the back were gonna wear themselves out before noon, she worried. As she turned the van onto the Cameron job site, she looked over and noticed that Dolly had shifted in her seat, turned to face the group, and was grinning with the rest of them. Lily rolled down the window, conjuring Hannah's voice, hearing the words repeating, like a mantra, *"Easy, baby, easy."*

Four

This job was a double-whammy, Lily thought to herself, as she approached the site. Both renovation and new construction were happening simultaneously on this soon-to-be bed-and-breakfast. The rambling three-story structure sat on a two-hundred-acre farm that had originally belonged to the Galway family, for whom the town was named. The place had been abandoned nearly a half century before. The rotting barns had caved in on themselves, and the creaking house had given way to the creeping kuzu that had knitted around it like a tailor-made sweater. Nearly everyone had forgotten about it, James had told her: Then one of the Galway heirs, a Charlotte lawyer named Malcolm, had decided to turn it into a B & B.

Cameron Construction had been hired to restore the house to its original beauty, and to build an addition doubling its size. There was also remodeling being done on the outbuildings; the springhouse and chicken coop would be returned to their original functions; the other four buildings were being converted into artist studios, to be rented by the week. The van kicked up a cloud of orange dust as Lily swung around the driveway and pulled in front of the house. When they came to a halt, she jumped out and strode around back, unlatching the van's doors. The girls tumbled out, shading their eyes from the sun, and craning their necks to get a look at the pitch of the roof covered by a blue tarp. Lily too was looking up as Pappy approached.

He didn't look as old as you'd expect a *Pappy* to look. His hair had grayed and had even thinned a bit on the top, but his mischievous blue eyes danced when he spoke and you might take him for a man in his thirties rather than his fifties. But today, those eyes were not dancing. They were dark and serious. Taking her aside, he bent, keeping his voice low.

"Another one of the boys quit," he said slowly. "They don't like the idea of workin' for a woman—no offense."

Lily stomped. "Damn it, Pap. How'm I supposed to run this job with less than half a crew?"

"Some think the job might fold and no more'll come in, on account of your daddy goin'."

"What kind of loyalty is that?" Lily looked up at him.

Pap shrugged and then squinted over her shoulder. "Some can't adjust to having a woman on a site. It ain't natural to some." He shuffled, scuffing his feet, stirring dust.

"And you, Pap?"

He scuffed some more.

"You, Pap?!" She could hardly believe her ears. "You'n me, we've worked together before. You know how I operate. You know I run a good crew, just like my daddy did."

He looked around and then at her. "Word has it you're gonna keep your company's name, Lil." He nodded at the big blue-and-white Girls with Hammers logo on the truck.

Lily planted her feet. "What if I am?"

Two other Cameron carpenters had wandered over to listen. The first, upon hearing this news confirmed, threw down his tool belt and walked off the site without so much as a look back. The other, a young man with a long skinny yellow braid down his back, spat as he went by. "I ain't workin' for no woman," he muttered.

Lily relented, looking at Pap silently, begging him to stay. She followed his gaze across the yard to the circle of young women, half sitting, half lying on a grassy patch under a big tree. The two Ahs were blowing cigarette smoke rings toward each other. They appeared completely nonplussed by the situation.

"That what you call your crew?" Pap gestured with his chin.

"What about it?"

"Any of 'em ever do carpentry before?"

Lily shrugged.

Pappy shook his head. He unbuckled his tool belt. "I know'd you since you was a bitty thing and rode in your daddy's truck." Now his eyes did dance some. "Your head only just poked above the dashboard, but you'd be jumpin' up and down, clammerin' to get outta that truck and onto the site. I remember once I found you napping in a pile of sawdust. When I picked you out, you said, 'Pappy, I love sleepin' with the wood.' You was only four or five."

Lily looked down at her shoes. Then she adjusted her own tool belt, just to avoid Pappy's eyes.

"Your daddy added extra cinch holes to that ol' tool belt just so you could lug it around. That hammer was longer'n your legs. Used to nail everthin' to everthin' . . ." He stopped himself and turned away. "I got another offer down the road, Lily." He looked embarrassed. "I loved your daddy like a brother . . . but I got young-uns at home . . ." he trailed off.

She wouldn't argue. She wouldn't force Pappy to say what everyone had been thinking—that Lily Cameron was about to run her daddy's construction company into the ground.

Pap put his hand on her shoulder. "Good luck, gal," he said and got in his truck and drove away. Lily watched till the dust had settled. Then she turned back to the women under the tree. They were a sorry-looking bunch, all dressed up like they were ready to play a game called carpentry, each now fiddling with a tool. Laura was twirling a hammer around her finger like a six-shooter and Micah lay on her back, arms stretched above, holding a long level in her hands and squinting as she swayed it back and forth, floating its bubble in search of an even plane.

"Stick 'em up!" White Jennie was standing in the overgrown driveway, pointing the nail gun at Black Jenny's back. None of them seemed terribly concerned about getting on with work. Just fooling around, Lily thought. With the exception of Dolly, none really appeared to have done much carpentry. Lily couldn't avoid this fact any longer. Not now.

"Knock it off!" she shouted at White Jennie. Lily strode across the lawn and grabbed the gun. "You could kill somebody with that thing!"

Then she paced around in a circle, stopping every few steps to glance at the roof of the building. The girls watched her; she knew they were watching her. Finally, she walked over to them, shaking her head at the way they were all flopped across the ragged lawn. Before she could open her mouth, Dolly grabbed her arm and twisted her around, back toward the house.

"What?"

Rising up from a shady corner on the old porch, a long form slowly unfurled. Straightening, but still shadowed, the figure reached and stretched, then dropped his arms and gave his shoulders a fast shrug. He jumped the missing porch step to the ground and came across the yard toward Lily and the girls.

"Who—" Lily began, then stared as he approached. He was young, in his early twenties, maybe. She wondered why she hadn't noticed him there before. He was wearing a bright white T-shirt that hugged his lanky muscular frame. *A long drink of water,* her mother would have said. A long drink of *hard* water, Lily thought. The next thing she noticed was that he was especially clean. His blue jeans were creased down the front to folded cuffs, and his well-worn Red Wings had been recently polished, she could tell. Not a speck of dirt on him. His tidiness was suspicious.

The girls in the grass were suddenly at attention: three shot upright, and two actually got to their feet. Lily looked back at his eyes. Approaching her, he didn't look away.

"Who the hell are you?" she asked.

He had a scattering of freckles across the bridge of his nose, and an off-center cowlick that shook loose a shock of dark hair from his neat trim. He didn't answer Lily, but came within two feet and stopped in front of her. He smelled fresh, she thought, like cucumbers and watermelon. But what was he doing here—on her job site?

"I don't mind working with girls with hammers," he said, smiling shyly, his voice soft and low, unhurried. There was a hint of a mountain accent that Lily couldn't place. Warily she took his extended hand.

"You don't, huh?"

The boy grinned and shook his head. "Nah, I was raised by a passel of women. I'm used to girls."

By this time, her crew (Lily used the word loosely) was gathered in a semicircle, slowly closing around the two. Micah and Dolly vied for an empty patch of grass which brought them a foot closer to the stranger. She noticed that it was Laura, with the red hair, who was least interested, standing back, away from the group, seemingly indifferent to the newcomer. But Lily could see that her indifference was merely a façade. The redhead's eyes searched and devoured every small detail about the fella before them, and of this Lily was sure.

"I'm Arlo," the man-boy said. "Arlo Halsey. Pleased to meet you." His eyes swept including them all in his pleasure.

Lily introduced herself and waved the others to do the same; she couldn't be trusted to remember which was which. After the niceties, as she called them, were over, she beckoned for Arlo to follow her toward the house.

"You're not from around here," Lily told him.

"Nope. South Carolina," he said.

"How long you been working for my daddy?"

"Few months," he said, again not offering more.

She had to look up to look him over. He was nibbling a stalk of sweet grass and when he noticed her scrutiny he stopped and grinned down.

"Like what you see?" he asked.

His boldness startled her and she looked away embarrassed and then felt a pang of anger, the kind you get when you trip over a rug and you pray nobody saw you.

"Why don't you show me what's been going on around here," she said, and turned to walk ahead, forcing him to follow her into the torn-up house. Lily's eyes adjusted to the dim light, and the awkwardness between them seemed to dissipate. She began to feel like a detective walking into the aftermath of a murder scene. This would be the first time she was seeing the project herself. The only eyewitness, behind her, could be of some real help.

Everything was in some stage of destruction or construction. Ceilings gaped, wires hung limp, upright studs divided space that could no longer be considered rooms. Half the floor was missing; the other half was lined with new joists. Obviously, the place had been gutted and it looked as if each of the ten ex-Cameron carpenters had been right in the middle of his work when he walked off the job. Make that nine; Arlo was now naming the men at each workstation.

"Pappy had Bill and Wesley hanging the Sheetrock up the stair-well, before . . ." Lily suddenly stopped and lit a cigarette. "What were you doin'?" she asked.

"Me?" Arlo's brows shot up. He looked pleased by her interest. "Well, I did just about everything."

Lily looked around and took a drag, then offered Arlo a smoke.

"No, thanks." He waved the pack away.

"What are you, a runner?" she asked, knowing her father would have shifted a new hire around to every station till he showed what he could really do.

"I guess that's what you'd call it," he said, shrugging. He pointed up the stairs, then down a corridor, as he explained how he helped wherever he was needed that day.

She noticed how he talked with his whole body, each word empha-sized by a matching expression on his face, a flinch of muscle in his arm, chest, or jaw. A slow current of energy seemed to hum through him.

She'd been a runner more than once in her life, herself. You got to see how all the parts fit together. Assuming the guy was any kind of carpenter at all—and considering what she was stepping into—if she could have picked one Cameron carpenter to stick around (other than Pappy), she would have picked the runner.

This was the first miracle of the day, Lily decided. In light of the sit-uation, she needed all the miracles she could get.

"All right, good, then. You're my new job foreman. I'll need you to take me through everything, down to the last hammer swing."

Outside, the girls had resumed their places beneath the tree; all five were now smoking, Lily noticed, as she stubbed out her own cigarette. Arlo was making his way back to the porch, swinging his long body up onto the platform again. Lily threw open the back doors to the van and began barking at her new crew. "Grab a tool belt, a hammer, some gloves," she yelled, like a field officer ordering her men to arms.

What she hadn't noticed, until she saw the rest of the girls notic-ing, was Arlo. He was yards away, off to the side of the house with his back to the women, on a smooth-packed square of dirt, skipping rope like some boxer in a gym. The sound of rope zinging, as he whipped it faster and faster, ricocheted off the surrounding hills.

She jogged across the yard and around the jumping figure. Arlo didn't pause and continued to stare straight ahead while Lily made certain to keep away from the zip of the whip.

"We got work to do, now," she said.

"Ten-o-clock," Arlo said, not missing a skip. "Ten-and-two." His words timed his cadence. "Every-day-I-jump-at-ten-and-two."

Lily stood staring for a long time and when it became apparent that he wasn't going to quit she demanded, "How long?"

"Fif-teen-min-utes."

"Fifteen minutes?" Lily looked to her watch. Better than half the morning had slipped through her fingers. She was paying five pretend carpenters twice minimum wage to lie around smoking cigarettes and playing with tools, goddamn it. "The whole mornin's gone," she complained loudly to him.

"By-law," Arlo huffed, "law-says-work-ers-get-fif-teen-min-ute-breaks."

Clearly taking this in, the crew began to move less quickly. Black Jenny dropped her hammer and tool belt and squatted by the broken porch step to light another cigarette. White Jennie leaned in beside her and massaged her shoulders. Laura and Micah looked to Dolly for direction, which didn't come.

"What are you all waiting for?" Lily turned on them. "We've got work to do."

"Well, if it's the law . . ." Dolly defended.

Defeated, Lily made her way to the big tree where, alone, she propped herself and smoked another cigarette as she watched Arlo jump. This was turning into a bigger nightmare than she had feared. She had just spent time and money on nothing.

It was no use. Arlo had stopped jumping, but any of the momentum they'd had that morning was gone. Finally, Lily gave up and herded the crew into the back of the van, telling them to be prepared to actually work tomorrow. She asked Arlo, who was obviously without a vehicle, if he needed a ride. When he said no, she pulled away without another thought. It wasn't till she'd nearly reached the highway, some four or five miles away from the job site, that she wondered whether he was just being polite and didn't want to inconvenience her, or if he meant to walk. But where was there for him to walk to? They were out in the boonies. Between here and town was nothing but woods full of snakes and fields full of cow dung. At a crossroads, Lily noticed two old paint-peeled signs. The first, whose faded red arrow pointed right, invited people to Bubba Q's Bar and Grill. A tipsy-looking bull waving a beer bottle was dancing with a martini-sloshing, bug-eyed bass, smiling as only a fish might. Surf and Turf, the sign promised, All You Can Eat Buffet!

"Kind of cannibalistic, don't you think?" Micah with the pink hair said.

"Listen," Laura said, with a disgusted look, "if people didn't *eat* living creatures, we wouldn't be subjected to idiot advertising."

"Oh, I don't think you can really make that correlation," Jenny's voice boomed. Hers was the deep base that Lily had noticed that morning.

The sign below this one was nearly hidden by a tree branch. It read, Don't let your worries kill you. Let the church help—and then the name, Victory Vision Missionary . . .

"Oh, that's a beauty," Micah said, following with a seeming nonsequitur. "Hey, what about that Arlo guy?"

"Cute," somebody sighed. Lily, driving, couldn't tell which one.

"He seems sweet," White Jennie said. "And . . . that *body*."

Seated next to Lily, Dolly rolled her eyes.

Black Jenny said, as if this small detail had any real significance, "He's got a chipped tooth."

Laura grunted and leaned back against the tool boxes, catching one of her powder puffs of frizzy hair in the teeth of a coping saw. She yanked, freeing herself but leaving behind a few curly red strands. "Something about him," she said and sucked on her cigarette. "He's got a past."

"What do you mean, *he's got a past?*" Micah demanded, her face heated up, matching the pink of her hair, Lily noticed in the rearview mirror. "Who doesn't have a past?"

"I mean he's got a sketchy past that he doesn't want to talk about," Laura said.

"Oh, come on . . . he told us about his family. He said he's from South Carolina. How much does a person have to give up in the first conversation?" Dolly swiveled in her seat.

"For all we know, he could be a rapist or a drug addict."

Micah jumped in, "There is no way that a drug addict would or even could jump rope like that . . . the guy is a hunk . . . let's face it."

"Maybe he's an ex-con," Laura trumped. "Those guys keep in shape. It's all they got to do."

"If he were a criminal, what's he doing working on a construction site?"

"Criminals work lots of places, honey," White Jennie said, patting Jenny's knee.

"Maybe he's even worse," Laura fanned the flames of speculation, if not suspicion.

"Worse like what? He's mostly a kid," Dolly said. "Hardly old enough to have gotten in that much trouble."

"Oh, like rapists and murderers have age limits."

Lily slammed the truck to a halt. The girls clung to their seats and each other.

"Enough!" Lily said. "We don't know anything about this fella—except that without him, we're sunk. He's the only one who knows anything about this job and we need him." Her voice dropped a notch. "I need him."

The girls eased upright in their seats. None looked at Lily.

She said, "You all keep your opinions to yourselves," but she was looking straight at Laura —her spongy orange hair vibrated with the truck's rumbling idle. After that, each girl retreated into her own silence. Lily threw the van into drive and headed out onto the highway. Mountain greens and blues blurred by and Lily felt the shifting weight of the personalities behind her. As the wavering cityscape shimmered in the horizon, she pressed down on the gas pedal. All she wanted to do was dump this crew and head home to her own nice cool valley.

It was on that final leg of the drive when Lily finally allowed her mind to scan the events of the day. Laura was right, she thought, surprising herself, there *is* something sketchy about that Arlo. She didn't know if it was as ominous as Laura was making it out to be. She didn't figure him to be a murderer or anything so sinister, but he wasn't giving up his history very easily, and that made her own suspicions rise. People who keep their hands close to their chests are either hiding or bluffing, Lily thought. In the case of Arlo Halsey, she hadn't decided which it was yet.

As she pulled into her driveway, Lily wondered which way Arlo might have turned when he reached that crossroads: left, toward the bar with the tipsy bull, or right, toward the church that promised to help kill you.

Five

Two beers couldn't do it. Lily didn't think that even a six-pack could wash away the stress of the morning. She was whupped and pissed when she walked through the back door. Not until she'd hit the blinking message button on her machine, did she ease up on herself. She heard Hannah's voice saying she'd be by for dinner.

"I want to talk," she had said. Then the recording ended abruptly, and Lily imagined that the machine had cut off Hannah before she'd had the chance to say how much she was missing Lily. Maybe, Lily decided, Hannah was just about to say, "I want to come back home, baby. I can't live without you."

That's wishful thinking, Lily heard Cat's voice. *Like these things just ever go away on their own. They don't, Lily.* And then she wasn't sure if that was Cat's voice or her own.

Stepping into the tub and spinning the shower head to *pulse,* Lily let the hot water beat down on her shoulders, neck, and the top of her head. While the drumming stream felt good on her muscles, it was a flimsy substitute for a massage. Lily imagined Hannah's hands on her, working magic fingers into aching places that only she knew how to find.

Smiling in the steam, Lily felt the kneading heel of Hannah's palm rubbing a clutch of sinews loose in her shoulders. Lily listened, almost hearing the familiar tenderness. *You hung a ceiling today, didn't you, sweetie?* she might say knowingly and add kisses to the sore spots. Or if the knot were lower down her spine, the question might come with a gentle reprimand, *Were you carrying mud buckets today, Miss Lily? You remember what the doctor said.* And then she might apply a playful swat. Lily grinned in a flash of a passing memory, when once Hannah had teasingly whispered, *Do I have to spank you?* And this notion sent a familiar shiver through Lily, reminding her of all the ways she hadn't been feeling lately.

By the time Lily had towel dried her wet hair and slipped into some shorts and a T-shirt, she had convinced herself that it was time for Hannah to move back home. She was even further convinced that this was the cause for Hannah's phone call and pending arrival.

As she stirred the vegetables around the hot pan, she heard the sound of Hannah's truck pulling into its spot in the driveway. Lily went to the door and stood watching her get out. Unaware that she was being observed, standing in front of the truck's side window, Hannah pushed and primped at her hair.

Seeing this action sent such a longing through Lily that she nearly wanted to leap off the porch and just grab Hannah and hold her forever. Instead, she backed up into the house, wiped off her hands, and patted down her own flyaway strands.

In the next second Lily was at the door, disarming Hannah of a package she was carrying.

"So, I made dinner and cleaned up." Lily spread her arms wide, showing off the shining room, as if Hannah had somehow been expecting something else. "I've been thinking, baby," Lily came closer. "I want you to come back home, now, tonight. I'm ready."

When Hannah didn't respond, Lily pulled back. "What's the matter?"

"Let's go inside," Hannah said quietly. "We need to talk."

They sat together on the couch.

Lily's knee bounced in time with her jumping nerves. "You don't *want* to come home?" she asked.

Hannah shook her head; reddish curls bounced the way they always did with every move she made. "Lil," she started and Lily interrupted.

"You're breaking us up, aren't you?"

"No, I'm not breaking us up," Hannah started.

"So you're coming home?"

Hannah leaned over and placed her hand on Lily's knee. She steadied her and spoke softly, "Lil, you need to listen to me."

Her tone stopped Lily's fidgeting.

"I have an opportunity—to go to Amsterdam."

Lily pulled back. "Amsterdam?"

"The Association has appointed me their representative to work on an international project—family welfare. It's important work."

Lily stared at Hannah who suddenly seemed professionally distant, like a doctor giving a diagnosis, rather than a partner giving notice.

"It's a big deal, Lil. You should be happy for me."

"Oh, I'm delighted for you, Han. Just wonderin' about us."

"We need this hiatus, Lil." Hannah looked at her.

Lily gnawed on the inside of her cheek. "Hiatus, huh? That's what you want to call this? Not a separation? Not estrangement, abandonment, not divorce?" Lily watched Hannah shutting down. Her shoulders straightened, chin lifted, her eyelids lowered, cloaking pupils in shadows. "What am I supposed to do while you're gone? Sit around hoping you'll be ready to be my partner when you get back?"

"Lily, this is not about us. This is about something that I need to do for me." Hannah ran her fingers through her hair, entangling her pinky before wrenching free. "Maybe it's coming at a time that is about us, but I want this chance, Lil. I want to see what kind of difference I can make in the world. Maybe, right now, that supercedes how we're going to be together . . ."

"Or—*if?*" Lily's words were bitter.

Hannah's rigid form sagged and she pressed a shaky hand against her mouth. "Or—if. I guess a lot of that has to do with how long or even if you are willing to be in the waiting."

And then, Lily saw tears had begun their race down Hannah's cheeks. "How long?" she managed.

"Six months." Hannah swallowed.

"Lots of things can happen in six months."

"Yes, but does it have to be for the worse? Can't lots of good things happen, too?"

Lily thought that this could be true, but the ache that accompanied the idea of Hannah's absence made it so very hard to name just one. "Everything is changing," Lily said. "Seems like all this couldn't happen in such a little bit of time."

"In six months," Hannah ventured hopefully, "we're going to know a lot more about a lot more than we do right now. That's the only truth I'm willing to consider." Hannah reached out to Lily. It was a lover's beckoning. "I don't know what anything means, Lil, but I do know that these shifts have already happened."

Taking Hannah's hand, Lily knelt. She pressed Hannah's palm against her lips and then wrapped arms around her waist. Together they wept and Lily could feel tiny kisses being placed in her hair. Finally, she leaned back and wiped wet strands from Hannah's cheeks. "So, I guess we'll just have to be in the shifts," she said.

Lily tucked beneath her covers. She would not fight this. There was some big cosmic lesson she was supposed to be learning from all this crap going on in her life. God must think her one dense student if a disappeared best friend and a dead daddy wasn't enough—yanking the one and only lover out of the picture surely clinched it. The Almighty was one hard-ass son of a bitch, she decided.

Tossing from one side to another and finally landing on her back, Lily couldn't figure out why she hadn't gone out like a light the minute her head hit the pillow. She was cried out—wrung out, really. Hannah had stayed for dinner, and for the first time in a long time, the two chatted easily. Only when one would look across the table at the other and tears would well, was she reminded of their consensus decision—they'd be in the shifts as best they could. They parted with a kiss, the first gentle one in months.

Kicking her feet beneath the covers, and punching a pillow much harder than necessary, Lily's mind settled on the other reason she was tossing and turning. She grumbled out loud, the way she would otherwise have grumbled to Hannah, *"Where does he get off telling me how to run a construction company?"*

She was referring to Malcolm Galway, whose phone call she had mistakenly picked up without thinking, shortly after Hannah had left. She hadn't even had time for a smoke when Malcolm began his whine about the abilities of those now entrusted with the restoration of his family *estate* (the word he used). He even had the nerve to question her integrity when he demanded to know, "Are you sure they are trained carpenters? Patrick, my partner, heard through the grapevine that you hired a bunch of *women* bluegrass musicians to work on my ancestral home!"

A lot he knows, Lily thought. They're *Celtic* for one. And for another, anybody can be trained. In this case, it would happen on the job, that's all. And for another, women could do the same as men. She hoped.

Her arms crossed under her head and stared at all the little glow-in-the-dark stars that she and Hannah had glued to the ceiling by jumping up and down on the bed. They had laughed hard that day, even after knocking their heads together and springing painful tears, they had still laughed, because that was the one thing that they did the most of anyway.

If things hadn't been so screwed up, Hannah would be here right now, listening about that little pussy Malcolm Galway and his prissy little partner Patrick, and their subtle mutual misogyny—so much for a united queer nation. Asshole, she decided, obviously has no understanding of carpentry or loyalty to a sister. Gay guys—they want you to turn a ramshackle broken-down farmhouse into Tara from *Gone with the Wind,* and then want a bunch of straight guys to do it. Like any straight guy'd even spend half a second on the line listening to that little creep's bellyachin'.

Lily began to drift into a dream that included herself skipping rope along the ridgeline of the Galway Bed-and-Breakfast, keeping time with Arlo, who was suddenly jumping beside her. She could see down into the yard below, the way you can in a dream. It was filled with people. She recognized the upturned faces of her new work crew, all of whom were smoking cigarettes and looking up, watching with curiosity. A scowling James, whose left arm wrapped around their mother, Sophia, was also down there, but shaking his right fist at Lily and Arlo, demanding their descent. A few steps from him stood Hannah, smiling. She blew a kiss. The Galway boys, as she'd come to think of them, were waving, frantically. Finally, on the outskirts she could see Cat standing at the back of the crowd, slouched against a tree. She grinned and raised Lily a *two thumbs up.* Simultaneously, without word

or signal, Lily and Arlo reversed their ropes and began jumping backward.

Over the next few days, Arlo walked Lily through the entire project; from basement to attic through renovation to new construction,
and then out to the barns and sheds. He covered everything and Lily
took copious notes. While this was going on, Dolly was in charge of
teaching the crew how to use the power tools, measuring devices, and
levels.

Twice, she'd heard Dolly shout out her own words, *put a little greeeze
to that wheel.* Lily imagined this was directed at Micah, who, in the
band, played the guitar, which didn't seem to require much strength.
It showed. Not like Dolly on the fiddle who had some wicked biceps.

Lily was beginning to know these girls. Not that she did a lot of
asking, it was just that they all talked and talked. There didn't seem
to even be a need for an ear within hearing distance to keep them
yammering on and on at nobody—about nothing, as near as Lily
could tell.

Micah had had a boyfriend, but they were always fighting, and he
had just moved out. She said she didn't know if she was going to keep
working it out with him or any man, and that she'd been seriously
considering becoming a lesbian.

White Jennie and Black Jenny had met in college and had been together for five years. They were in love, as Lily understood it. White
Jennie's father was gay and her mother had remarried an artist. They
were both fine about her being a lesbian, she said. But Black Jenny's
family did not share these feelings. Her lawyer parents could have
handled the lesbianism, they said, if she hadn't gone and added salt to
the wound by taking up with a white girl. *"They freaked,"* in Black
Jenny's words.

Laura, not surprisingly, Lily figured, had given up on both genders,
swearing, "I'd rather have sex with myself." She'd said this and then
sucked really hard on her cigarette.

Arlo was helpful, seemingly able to anticipate her questions before she could even pose them. But his rope jumping irritated her. It distracted the entire crew. At ten and two exactly, the whole bunch of them would lay down their tools. Only, instead of jumping rope, those girls would flop onto the lawn, light up cigarettes, and settle back to watch Arlo. Lily might pace around the yard, blowing furious puffs of smoke into the air and checking her watch every two minutes, but nobody much noticed. Arlo, with his back to them, was oblivious to it all.

Once or twice, she thought about the dream she'd had; wonder what it had meant—if dreams actually ever *meant* anything other than late-night indigestion.

During lunch, while all the women sat in the shade sharing food and talk, Arlo hunkered down under the porch where he kept his backpack. Sometimes he'd eat, sometimes not, but always, he would read.

"What's that book?" Laura wondered one afternoon, aloud. "Probably a Hardy Boys mystery, right?"

Micah arched an eyebrow. "Actually, he told me, *On the Road*."

"Oh, he's *soooo* predictable," Laura looked smug, as if the evidence for her case against Arlo was mounting. "I told you he is probably a druggie . . . Kerouac . . . smokin' weed and shootin' horse."

"Who's Kerouac?" someone asked, but Lily couldn't tell which voice it was.

Micah continued, "He said that he found Kerouac's untraditional style inspiring, but he wasn't totally convinced that it had not sprouted out of sheer laziness for fictional conventions."

"He said that?" Laura demanded to know. "He said *fictional conventions?*"

"Just like that." Micah nodded.

"I'm skeptical that he would even recognize a fictional convention if he walked into one and Henry James himself was passing out name-tags."

Black Jenny laughed and asked, "Why do you care so much about this boy?"

Without answer, Laura huffed and stomped off to the outhouse, leaving the rest chuckling.

"What's up with that chick?" Micah wanted to know.

"She's being an asshole." White Jennie waved her cigarette dismissively in the direction of Laura's exit.

Lily walked away from the bunch, then turned back and tapped her watch. "Break's over," she said, loud enough for Arlo to hear, as well. The boy/man, as she sometimes thought of him, was a dang curiosity, sometimes sweet and accommodating, more often distant and wary, and every once in a while, just a little bit rebellious, as if he was testing her limits, see how much she'd put up with, but that might just have been a story she was telling herself. All in all, by the time she got home nights, she more often than not felt whupped by it all. One night she'd been so harried and tired by her day that she'd fallen asleep in bed with one of her boots still on.

Just as it was all getting nearly impossible for Lily to handle, Hannah had come home—at least for a visit before she had to leave for her trip.

"Too much is going on," Lily said to her, after they had made love and were now curled around each other in the big bed. Hannah would be leaving by the weekend. "This job is going to do me in," Lily said. "Trying to get all these nutty girls and Arlo to work together, I feel like Henry Kissinger."

"This Arlo, he sounds a bit odd. Don't you think?" Hannah asked. "I mean, what do you all talk about when you're on the job?"

"The job," Lily said. "You can't shut him up about the job, but the minute you ask him something personal, he clams up." Except this morning, she thought, but didn't say.

This morning she and Arlo were passing by the old milk barn when he had paused, raising his nose in the air. She stood watching as he closed his eyes and seemed to take in a deep breath.

"Smell that?" he had asked, nearly whispering.

Lily sniffed the air, catching a drift of cut pine, as it floated from the miter saw in action behind them.

"New milk," Arlo had answered, not waiting for hers. "Like when I was a boy, worked on my granddaddy's dairy farm." He grinned his crooked grin. "Kissed my first girl behind a brown Jersey named Bessie." He had tickled himself and jostled Lily's elbow saying, "That'd be the bovine's name, not the girl's."

Lily hadn't been able to suppress her smile.

"Where does he live?" Hannah asked, bringing Lily back from her morning memory.

"I don't know. Says he walks to work, but I've never seen him. He's always there before we get there and stays to clean up after we leave, so I really can't complain."

"How old is he?"

"I'm guessin' twenty, twenty-three. Sometimes he reminds me of an old man. Then he's like a teenager. The other morning he hid the Red-Ah's coffee mug . . ."

"Lil, you should really learn their names."

"Yeah, I know. I'm workin' on it," she continued. "He sets the mug on the kitchen counter and when Laura goes after it, he jerks on the string and makes her chase it down the hallway."

Hannah laughed. "That *is* kind of funny."

"She cussed him out bad."

"What'd he do?"

"He just laughed. She doesn't like him, though, not one bit. So while the rest of us laughed, she pretty much sulked."

"At least it sounds like you're enjoying yourself, sometimes?" Hannah ventured, hopefully.

"Sometimes." Lily nodded, but then other thoughts clouded this morning remembrance. "James came around yesterday. Struttin' in like he's the boss of everything. Starts poking around, looking for something."

"Looking for what?" Hannah wondered.

"I don't know. Evidence of me screwing up. Who knows!"

"That might be stretching it. With James, I suspect it has mostly to do with control."

Lily pulled away a little and straightened her pillow. "I'm thinking, maybe we should cut our losses. It'd be a burden off us all."

"You mean sell the business?" Hannah propped herself up.

"The relief I feel when I think of only having Girls with Hammers again—whew! Never knew how much I loved having my own little business, till this."

"Well, that says something."

"On the other hand, this is a challenge. Biggest job I've had on my own. Lots of thinkin'." Lily said this as if the idea interested her. "It's gonna require everything I ever learned and then some." She looked over to see Hannah smiling at her, a tender look that seemed to make all of this much easier.

"What about the crew?"

"Bad News Bears. That's what Arlo calls 'em."

"Oh dear."

"One screwed another one's shirt to a wall."

"Oh, no!" Hannah let out a sharp laugh.

"And the two Jennies *rearranged* a whole ceiling."

Now Hannah was laughing outright.

"To give it an *alluring* pattern."

"Oh God."

"Worst though was Dolly and Laura somehow managed to hang a set of French doors upside down," Lily grinned and then laughed. "You should've heard them cussin'; hadn't heard that kind of language since I was on my apprenticeship."

"Sounds hilarious." Hannah hiccuped, still giggling.

Lily sat up, pulling her knees to her chin. Hannah waited.

"But, I'm scared, Han. Last time I was scared like this was when I thought I was never going to see you again. And I'm not even talking about this time—I'm talking about being scared like I was when I thought you'd never speak to me again. It was so long ago, but it feels like yesterday."

Hannah's look changed slightly, going sad. She covered one of Lily's hands with her own and murmured something Lily couldn't quite catch.

They had been young, and their relationship brand new, when Lily's lie about her age had caused their one-and-only temporary breakup, till this last almost one, at least.

"You're not even of *legal age*!" Hannah had yelled through tears and rain before turning to leave Lily standing on the street corner after a meddling waiter (as Lily called him) had carded her when she tried to order a Brandy Alexandria. She was only seventeen, but had told Hannah that she was considerably older.

Now they held each other in the bed. "That night," Lily said, "standing on the corner, rain beating down on me like I deserved it, I thought, *I'm so scared*."

"And that's how you feel now?"

"Yeah, especially when I think of everything, all together, in order. Like Cat going and Daddy dying and now you leaving." Lily tried a small smile. "Feels like a lot of loss all crammed into a pretty little piece of time, you know?"

"Yes, I guess it really is. We don't seem to be able to control when we're prepared to handle our challenges. I guess if we were, they wouldn't be challenges. We've got a lot of things to accomplish these next months. I, for one, am going to try to be positive about it. I mean, there's a reason that your daddy left you this company. There's a reason you have to deal with it now."

Lily nodded. "That's how I feel when I think about that stupid old James, and it makes me mad enough to think, *I'll show him*. I'll just make this company *work*.

"Well, that would be rather satisfying, don't you think? James being made to eat a little crow couldn't possibly be bad for him. He's probably had rare occasion to taste it."

"Oh, I'd find it highly unlikely that James has ever even gotten a spoonful near his mouth. He was barking orders at me today: work schedules, employment applications, Social Security numbers—he was demanding. All that crap I've suddenly got to deal with. Give me my little two-girl operation any day."

"It's a legal thing for James; everything's got to be copacetic," Hannah said. "Lawyers."

"Yeah, well, I don't have time for *legal things* while I'm working a job. Then he's wantin' to know when the outbuildings would be finished, and why wasn't the kitchen done. Man, he was pissin' me off."

"You didn't hit him, Lily?" Hannah sat up straight.

Lily grinned, "No, but I wanted to." She reached for a curl of Hannah's hair and wrapped it around her finger. By moonlight, Hannah's skin nearly glowed. She's beautiful, Lily thought, and then she kissed her shoulder.

"So what did happen?" Hannah asked.

"It was sort of weird. That Arlo, he suddenly appears from around the corner and tells me that one of those girls needs me. Says she's cutting molding backward. So, I go. Glad to get away from James for a minute, anyway."

Hannah settled against Lily's shoulder.

"I see Arlo; he's got a hold of James' arm and starts walking him around."

"James?"

"He's looking all attentive *and* listening and nodding his head!"

Hannah ran her fingers along Lily's arm.

"Ten minutes later," Lily was grinning now, "Arlo's easing James into his big snotty Caddy and waving him good-bye! Then he walks this kinda slow walk back and says to me, 'Mr. Cameron's the kind of fella who likes honey on his bread.'"

Now Hannah was laughing again. "Seems like Arlo knows just how thick to spread that honey, too."

"Seems so, don't it?" Lily said, pushing her down onto the bed and pulling back the sheet so she could see how all of her looked in the moonlight. And then she began kissing; small kisses, butterfly kisses, Lily called them, fluttering along Hannah's forehead, across the bridge of her nose, lingering upon lips, edging the ridges of her neck; teeth skimming branches of collarbone, cheeks smoothing over soft breasts and belly, trailing strands of hair. Tongue-slicked kisses slid between toes, behind knees, leaving imprints on each pearl along the string of spine. Lily, eyes closed, memorized every inch of skin—this skin she would miss touching—losing her senses and her mind in the task.

Two days later, Lily put Hannah on a plane to Amsterdam and found herself really alone for the first time in her life. On the way back to town, she glanced at a billboard outside the airport. It was black with thin white letters centered, asking,

> Feel alone? Give me a call.
>
> God

When Lily was a kid, her mother would drag her brood to church every Sunday. Trying to keep six boys and one little girl clean for the fifteen-minute walk to the steepled white clapboard building was a near impossible task. It wasn't so much the boys who gave Sophia trouble, but little Lily in her black patent leather shoes and white ankle socks didn't have a chance along that dusty or sometimes muddy road. By the time the lot was in the pew, Sophia would be spitting into a white hanky trying to wash the dirt from Lily's face and hands and knees.

The fuss Lily would make about getting all dressed up just to get dirty was met with Sophia's one and only response, "God only likes little girls who are clean and who wear dresses to his house."

Most of her life Lily had been trying to figure out how to be the kind of girl God wanted her to be. Obviously she still hadn't gotten it right. Now, as she reflected on the billboard message, it seemed that God might have backed himself into a corner with all his rules, because, like Lily, they were both apparently quite alone.

Six

Both Lily and Arlo jumped at the sound of the scream reverberating through the cavernous shell of the new construction. They ran through the old building; again, the scream echoed. Arlo pushed ahead of Lily and rushed the room where the other girls had gathered and pinned themselves along the wall. Laura was plastered in a corner, staring, wide-eyed. Lily, following her focused gaze, landed on a scrawny blind possum, snout raised and sniffing the fear-filled air.

Arlo let out a hoot.

Laura scowled, but her eyes never left the animal. In a half-assed attempt, showing Arlo that his hoot was not justified, she pulled back her foot and swiped a kick at the creature. Before the steel toe could meet the pink snout, Arlo scooped up the critter by its tail and carried it away, muttering, "Sorry, old boy. You know how gals can be."

"He thinks he's so smart," Laura muttered, pulling away from the corner, leaving a fuzz of spongy orange hair stuck to the newly mudded drywall.

"Oh, he's all right," Micah said. "I didn't see any of us running and grabbing that big ugly rat," her tone admiring. "If you had had your way you would have kicked that poor little thing halfway to kingdom come. At least he has compassion."

"Oh, he's a regular Doctor Doolittle, all right," Laura said. "Don't you wonder how he got to be such pals with wild animals? Think he lives with them?"

Her eyes skimmed everyone, who didn't say a word, including Lily.

"Never mind," Laura said, disgustedly. "Anybody know where he's from? Where he lives? How's he get here, anyway?"

"He walks," Lily answered. "Didn't we already go over all of this?"

"From where? I looked him up in the phone book—he doesn't exist."

"Why?" Micah jumped to his defense, her cheeks matching the pink of her hair. "Just 'cause he doesn't have a phone?"

"Yeah, well, I checked on the Internet . . ."

"On the Internet? You?"

"I looked him up," Laura said. "You can do that. It's easy. I mean, if any of you were ever in a newspaper or anything, you could be found."

Lily watched as the girls gathered around Laura, intent on her words. Lily found herself equally as curious.

"I discovered something out about that Arlo Halsey. Plus, I think it's just the tip of a very cold iceberg."

"What the hell are you talking about?" Micah was getting mad, Lily could tell.

"Just that rescuing girls from rabid animals is something of a practice for Mr. Halsey."

"What do you mean?"

Laura was warming up. "Back about ten years ago, over in Hickory, a couple of boys, one by the name of Arlo Halsey, saved some little girl from being mauled by a Doberman."

"Shoot," Black Jenny said, "who'd bother to put something like that on the Internet?"

Laura smiled slyly. "*Crime Catchers*. Seems those two boys had been breaking into houses in that neighborhood when they rescued the girl. Got in big trouble over it, after all!"

"Oh, for God's sake," said White Jennie, rolling her eyes. "What were they? Ten? Twelve? Big news, Laura. Maybe you should call *America's Most Wanted*."

"Go ahead, make fun of me," Laura shot back, "but you-all are gonna be sorry when it comes out we've got a rapist on our hands."

The familiar sound of rope slapping dirt came from the distance.

"And what about that?" Laura asked, thumbing over her shoulder toward the sound. "Who jumps rope like that?"

"Habit he picked up in the Big House," Micah said, laughing.

"Well, I think he's nice," Dolly said. "Told me his mother played the banjo. And two of her sisters play the fiddle and guitar. They had sing-alongs on their front porch when he was a boy," she smiled. "He was especially fond of the fiddle. Said it made him want to weep."

"Oh, brother," Laura scoffed. "He knew just how to play you, didn't he?"

"Stop now." Black Jenny put her hands in the air. "We don't know anything about this guy. So far, he's not done a thing out of line, except play a few jokes and skip rope." With her hands on her hips, she fixed her gaze on Laura. "*God don't like ugly.* That's what my granny'd say."

Lily extricated herself from the group. She agreed with Black Jenny and the rest—Arlo had been nothing but a hard worker and a gentleman. But the same questions that had come out of Laura had been rolling around in her own mind. What *did* they know about him?

Out in the yard, distracted by these thoughts, Lily tripped and landed spread eagle in a pile of sawdust. Rolling over, she felt around herself, doing a body check and finding that mainly it was her right elbow that had caught the blow, leaving a small scrape. Otherwise, she appeared to be intact.

The villain that had tripped her, she saw, was a piece of tie-down rope carelessly looped around a bundle of two-by-fours. Lily tugged at it, pulling the knot loose. The sound of Arlo's jumping came to her. Standing, she wrapped a rope end around each hand and then jumped, sending sawdust and woodchips flying. She moved outside, skipping her way into the sun. Across the yard, she saw Arlo turning his rope, whipping it around his body. The space between his feet and the earth opening only just enough to let the rope slip between, on each jump, precisely timed. He was fast, Lily thought.

Without a word, she brought the rope to the patch of softer dirt beside him. He slowed some, the look of surprise showing on his face. Removing her outer shirt, leaving her in tank top and jeans, Lily tentatively twirled the rope over and under. She did it a few times, getting the hang of it, not lifting her eyes from the ground. She tripped once, but then found a comfortable pace. Arlo had slowed and joined her cadence. Once they were in sync, Lily finally dared a glance and saw him grin.

Later that afternoon, it was a quick thunderstorm that sent them all running for cover under the porch. They huddled, smoking and watching the hard gray rain beat angrily, sending steam rising from the hot ground.

Laura had been itching to yank Arlo's chain, Lily could tell, ever since her humiliation of the morning. She wasted no time.

"Hey Arlo, me and the girls went out last night. We wanted to invite you but you're not in the book."

"No, Laura, I'm not. Don't have a phone. Haven't had much of a need to call anyone lately." Arlo propped his knee up on a ladder rung. "But I appreciate you thinking of me. Where'd y'all go?" This question he asked of the group. There was an awkward silence, during which all eyes landed on the ground all at once, Lily noticed. None of them wanted to add to Laura's lie.

"Actually, it was another bunch of girls, not them," she gestured to the discomfited group. "I wanted to introduce you."

Whether this was true or not, the collective sigh signaled relief that no one would have to reveal their loyalties, at least for the time being.

Laura continued, "Did you say you were from South Carolina?"

"Mostly. Around Greenville."

The answer seemed somewhat offhand—almost too casual, Lily thought.

"Know anything about it?" he asked, not looking at any of them, just fixing his eyes on the rain. "My mamma was a Macon. We lived here and there among the Macons most all my life."

"Thought you said you were raised by six women?" Laura turned on him, pointing accusingly with the hot tip of her cigarette.

Arlo let his grin sweep over the girls as he said, "I didn't say those Macons were men, now, did I?"

The women shook their heads. Micah, closest to Arlo, placed her hand on his shoulder saying, "Of course we believe you." She threw a look at Laura.

"Greenville, huh?" Laura tried again. "I could have sworn you said Hickory."

"Hickory? Heck no," Arlo said.

The women, breaths caught in time, waited; Lily saw they were too embarrassed to want to hear Arlo get caught in a lie. All except for Laura, who now cast her baited line.

"Not Hickory, huh?" She looked genuinely confused.

"Nope, don't recall ever mentioning Hickory."

"Never even been there?"

Arlo raised his arms in a long stretch. He laughed, dropping them again. The space was starting to feel real cramped, Lily thought. She wished the rain would stop.

"What's funny?" Laura asked, suspiciously regarding Arlo's sudden mirth.

"Oh, Hickory's funny. I had me some adolescent trouble over there one summer. Heck, almost forgot about it, till now."

The faces of his audience riveted on him.

"The summer I was turning twelve, I got left with my great-aunt Maybelle over in Hickory, while Mamma went to work up north—in Ohio, I think. Anyway, I remember being happy 'cause I got to stay with my cousin, Duane, who was two years older and like a big brother, you know?"

Simultaneously they nodded, all except Laura. She sat, propped against the cement foundation, blowing smoke like a steam engine from her nose.

"Well, Duane, he was a sucker for baseball cards," Arlo explained. "Had a fine collection, probably worth millions by now. Anyway, that poor boy had his heart set on a mint condition Reggie Jackson down at the Pawn and Go. Every day we'd walk to that store; every day Duane would hang over the counter till the owner chased us out. And every day we'd sit on Aunt Maybelle's front stoop just trying to think of ways to get that card."

Lily could tell Arlo was warming up to his story by the way his hands were flying everywhere. He was a jittery fella when he got excited.

"So what happened?" escaped from Laura, who leaned in, forgetting to flick the long ash of her cigarette.

"So then one Sunday after church, Aunt Maybelle takes me and Duane to visit Miz Crockett, a poor half-blind old lady, who was, if I remember right, mostly just lonely."

"Oh . . . sad," Micah whispered.

Laura groaned. "Pul-leeze. Should we get out the violins for this?"

"While we were there," Arlo went on, ignoring her and speaking now mostly to Micah, "Duane snatches a silver candy dish and stuffs it in his jacket pocket."

"Oh, no. Why'd he do that?" Dolly, silent until now, moved closer to Arlo.

Lily thought, *What the heck is happening, here?* But she didn't comment. She was interested herself in the story.

"Well, in that moment he thought he'd pawn it for Reggie Jackson. But, later, he'd come to his senses and decided to return it. That's when it happened."

"*What* happened?" Laura asked sarcastically. Slowly, Arlo turned his eyes on her.

"As we were about to return the dish to old Miz Crockett, the police caught us trespassing in a neighbor's yard, and when they searched Duane, well, there was the candy dish. Mostly, it was an embarrassment for Aunt Maybelle."

Lily jumped in before Laura had a chance to quiz him further. "Shoot, that ain't nothin'," she said. "One time, me and Cat snuck into this old bachelor's house. Didn't touch anything except his dirty magazines. But then he came home unexpectedly and we ditched behind his couch."

"No!" White Jennie exclaimed. "How long were you there?"

"So long that it got dark and we had to pee."

"You're kidding?"

"I swear. Finally we just had to crawl out. The three of us stared at each other for a long time. Like we were in a movie."

"What'd he do?" Micah asked, easily distracted from Arlo's tale.

"Said something about *stupid girls not being feminine* or something."

"That's Nietzsche," Arlo clarified. "*Stupidity in a woman is unfeminine.* Nietzsche said that."

They all stared at him.

He shrugged and asked, "So then what happened?"

"Well, nothing," Lily finished. "We scrammed outta there!"

The whole group, excluding Laura, laughed.

A minute later Arlo excused himself and headed into the rain. "Nature calls," he mumbled, breaking into a jog through slowing drizzle, toward the soggy woods behind the house.

"So, Miss Smarty-Pants," Micah turned on Laura, and for a minute, Lily thought there might be some fur about to fly. "How's your Internet investigating working for you, now? Did you happen to notice that he didn't even *mention* saving that little girl from that dog? Oh, yeah, Laura, you are really onto something here!"

"You all just wait," Laura said, finally flicking an ash over the edge of the railing. "I have a feeling about this Arlo character, and it isn't a good one."

"Uh-uh, Laura," Black Jenny muttered at her. "Like I said before, *God do not like ugly*."

Seven

"We're bringing in subcontractors," James said, across his desk from Lily and her mother, Sophia. "These are professionals who'll get the job done fast." He glanced quickly over his glasses at his sister.

Lily smoothed the brass cartridge in her pocket. Now empty and hollow, it had been discharged, plowing steel through concrete at the pull of a trigger. She squeezed it between her thumb and forefinger, nearly cutting a circle into her own flesh. She'd been summoned here. James' secretary had called and arranged the meeting. He'd prefaced the particulars with a report of the company's business and then announced changes he'd be making to improve efficiency.

And it wasn't just Lily who was being lectured. She watched her mother's hands worrying a handkerchief into a tight twist as James described how the payroll and bills, Sophia's responsibility for the last forty years, would be turned over to his accountant.

He smiled, looking like Lord Bountiful. "Mamma, you can just relax. You won't have to be bothered with any of this anymore."

"I'm *not* bothered," Sophia began. "It keeps me busy."

"Mamma." James lowered his glasses and tilted his head. "You deserve this. It's high time you retire now. You've worked long and hard. You let Lily and me worry about Cameron Construction."

"What will I do?" Sophia said, more to herself than to James. She looked at Lily, the question repeating in her eyes. Lily touched Sophia's arm, tried to smile at her mother. The truth was that James was really pissing her off. She watched her brother's face, the way he sucked in his cheeks before he spoke, like a trumpeter in some king's court making ready to blow out the next pronouncement. Who did he think he was, making all these decisions for everyone else? Nevertheless, she sat quietly with her mother to hear the rest.

"We've hired Prestige Electric to finish the wiring," James said after a litany of other changes that had, up until that moment, not been infringing too much on Lily's workspace, but this news caused her to sit forward.

"But I'm workin' with Bess Pratt," Lily said. "She and I have worked together, on and off, for over five years. James, you know she's good; she did the lighting around your pool deck, remember?"

"She's a small operator," James dismissed. "We need a company with a crew. Time is money, Lil."

"I've already called Bess about the job."

James looked up from the papers on his desk. "You sign a contract with her?"

Lily frowned. "Hell no, I don't have to sign contracts with folks I've known most of my life!"

"Nothing to worry about, then. We're not obligated."

"The hell we're not." Lily made to rise and Sophia's gentle hand pulled her back. "My word is my obligation! Jesus, James, Daddy never signed contracts with his subs. His word was enough, and so's mine."

As if preparing to address a child, in his most patient tone, James put down his pen, slid his glasses from his nose, and sat back against the soft brown leather of his chair. With a look, he included Sophia in his lecture.

"This is not nineteen-fifty. This is not the Old South where everybody is related to everybody. We have moved into the twenty-first century, ladies. We've got more Yankees and Floridiots living here than we do natives and we can no longer do business with a handshake. Sad, but true," he finished. "Look, we do not want Daddy's business to belly-up, now, do we?"

They sat quietly for a few minutes and finally Sophia shifted in her seat. "All right, James, we'll try it your way," she said. And then she stood.

Lily looked up, surprised by her mother's words. She started to protest, but Sophia's hand on her shoulder again stopped her. Lily sat back, and then, as her mother's fingers eased, she slowly rose and stood as well.

"That's a fine decision, Mamma," James said, a little awkwardly. He seemed startled by her sudden acquiescence, but only for a moment. Lily could see his confidence recovering by the way James was straightening his already straight tie, as if he'd expected this win.

Sophia exited James' office so fast Lily found herself skipping across the parking lot just to keep up.

"That smart-alecky snot," Sophia was saying about her own son as she and Lily reached the car. Sophia, who had on the way over relinquished the driving to Lily, was now clicking the keypad on the Explorer, and sliding in behind the wheel.

"Who does he think he is? Retire? *Me?* How dare he? I'll teach that fancy-schmancy lawyer a thing or two. I don't care if he is my first-born."

Lily just sat and listened as her mother ranted and then screeched out of the driveway.

"Where do we get a whiskey in this town?" Sophia asked as she wheeled the big SUV out onto the highway. "Right now, I mean."

Lily coughed, but tried not to look stunned. Sophia? Whiskey? At eleven o'clock in the morning?

"Just point me. We need to strategize."

She had never once been in a bar with her mother. Lily had always suspected Sophia had probably never seen the inside of bar in her life. What her daughter did know for sure was that Sophia had never before been in a dyke bar, ever. When it became apparent that she really did want a whiskey, Lily guided her mother toward the river and OzGirlz.

Housed in an old converted brick sawmill, OzGirlz' back deck hung over the river, and it was here, among the ficus and palmetto trees, that Lily and Sophia sat across from each other beneath a large, dark green umbrella.

"Got your cigarettes?" Sophia asked, barely noticing the baby-dyke waitress with the ring in her nose who took their order of nachos and two margaritas. Sophia, having changed her mind from the whiskey, had told Lily that she'd always wanted to try a margarita.

Lily reached into her pocket, embarrassed. She didn't think that her mother knew she smoked. She had pretty much quit since she started jumping rope with Arlo, but when James' secretary called demanding a meeting, well, she had bought some on her way. Tentatively she passed them over. Sophia smacked the back of a pack like a pro, like she'd been at it for the past fifty years.

A cigarette scooted out and she leaned over Lily's lighted match, then inhaled long and sat back to exhale. As if suddenly realizing she was somewhere she'd never been before, Sophia surveyed her surroundings, her head tilting back toward the overhanging trees that shaded the big deck. Then she craned over the railing, gazing down at the river rushing beneath them. Bouncing in the flexi-chair, she finally brought her eyes to meet Lily's.

"Nice place," she said.

"Mamma," Lily started—her tone shadowed—what dare she say? As she lit her own cigarette, Lily realized that before her sat a stranger, even though it was her own mother. She found herself at a loss for words. This was not uncommon with Mamma, Lily realized, sadly. They'd spent a good many years trying to find a place in each other's lives. But it was tricky when there was a whole part of Lily's life omitted from every discussion. What had she been thinking bringing her mother to a dyke bar? It wasn't exactly something that they talked about.

Dyke, lesbian, queer (hell, even *bar*) were words that did not enter personal conversations between Sophia and Lily. As a matter of fact, the very omission of the descriptors made these mother-daughter talks mostly impersonal. As Lily watched Sophia sip and savor the salty concoction before her, she thought about how really impersonal their communications had become over the years.

Lily had lived with Hannah most of her adult life, and had been in love with her since the last remnants of adolescence. But so that everyone could be *comfortable* Sophia and Lily had, perhaps unconsciously, used safe words to construct a suitable story which cloaked the true nature of the relationship between Lily and Hannah.

Words again were key to the lie. It had begun with *roommates,* then, *companions,* once or twice *partners* slipped out, but this was conveniently conjured into a *business* relationship, somehow. But never, even almost twenty years later, had either mother or daughter named out loud the truth about Lily and Hannah—*Girlfriends* with a capital *G*.

Sophia had always been kind to Hannah. She even seemed to like Hannah better than most of those other daughters-in-law. Especially, James' wife, Rebecca, who, Sophia once confided, was only after his money. She must know, Lily thought. How could she not?

Daddy knew. She knew he knew because he always asked after Hannah, or sometimes sent strawberries from his patch—just for Hannah—because he knew how much she loved them. And once he gave Lily an extra hundred bucks to buy a ring for her birthday. Lily thought of other ways that Jim had let her know that he was OK with her being a dyke. Even if he didn't come right out with it.

Once, she recalled, passing by his reading chair, he'd lifted his glasses and his nose from the open book on his lap and stopped her.

"There's a detective in this book," he started, in his own awkward way, "who's a *lesbian* and so is her *partner*."

Lily'd been so startled by this that all she could do was stand there.

"I'll let you borrow it when I'm through." Jim slid his glasses back in place. "I think you'd like it."

She might have thanked him. She couldn't remember.

And now, here she was with her mother, sitting in a dyke bar trying to act like it wasn't.

"Don't look so surprised," Sophia said. "Where do you think you get your gumption, anyway?"

Lily didn't say anything. They both knew that she'd been her daddy's girl. They both knew that she'd loved wood like he did, loved building and working with her hands, just like him. What Lily didn't know, and was about to find out, was that Jim, a generous man, hadn't had much sense for business and making money. People liked him was all. They respected his work—so there was always business.

"Not from your daddy. I hate to tell you. Too simple," Sophia was saying. "Trusted too many people. In that way your brother is right,

Lily." Pausing long enough to savor another sip of her first margarita, she said, "That's cold, but I like the salt."

Lily sucked on her straw, draining her own glass.

"That's where I came in," Sophia continued. "Who do you think paid the bills? Ordered the materials? Hired and fired the men? Who do you think had to go after those fellas who didn't honor that handshake contract in the same way your daddy did?"

Lily nodded slowly. Although she never liked thinking about it, it was her daddy's overly generous nature, she remembered painfully, that had sometimes caused late-night murmurings between her parents. No yelling (Sophia and Jim had never yelled) but low taut voices came as thin whispers through clenched teeth, reaching Lily's young ears via the heating vent in the wall. The subject had always been the same—always about how much of everything—time, money, labor, tools, and even materials—were given away by Jim. And then Sophia's voice resounded in Lily's head. *Did you forget you've got seven babies of your own to feed, James Lee?*

And this was why Lily, she hated to admit, sometimes resented her mother. But now her mother's voice had shifted. Frustration had been replaced by something else Lily noticed as she listened. This voice of her mother's was growing stronger by the syllable.

There was a surprising element of defiance in Sophia's next declaration: "I've taken care of Cameron Construction for the last forty years, I'll not be forced out of it by some punk lawyer."

That's what she really said, Lily would later write Hannah in her nightly e-mail. *Punk lawyer.*

Their second round of margaritas came on the house, delivered by Ruthie, the owner of OzGirlz, a large older woman with spiky gray hair and silver rings on every finger, who pointed out all the carpentry work done by Girls with Hammers over the years.

"Best carpenter in the land," Ruthie said, patting Lily on the shoulder. "And they're women," she added, as if this were the most important part.

"Does that really matter?" Sophia asked.

"To me it does," Ruthie said. "To a lot of people in this town, it does. Most men carpenters don't listen when women tell them what they want."

Lily's mother nodded and laughed.

"A lot of single women feel safer having a woman carpenter coming into their house," Ruthie added with a slight air of superiority.

"I can imagine."

"They're neater. Clean up after themselves."

"I'm sure that's true."

Ruthie grinned and leaned in conspiratorially. "And, let's face it, girls are just lovelier to have around."

Lily gagged on her icy drink, but Sophia nodded wisely, ignoring her. "I know. I raised six sons; they stink."

It seemed clear that the margaritas were having their effect on Sophia. Lily'd have to drive her mother home; that way she didn't have to object to Ruthie's offer of another free round.

They munched on nachos for a while, then Sophia broke the silence.

"What do you want, Lily?"

Lily looked up at her mother. *Want? For dinner? For the rest of her life?* Sophia's tone had not been specific, as if any "want" might be addressed here. She's wondering about *me, that's what,* Lily thought. *My mother wants to know if I'm happy or fucked up.* What she wanted, Lily knew, was to tell her mother that she wished she could just have Hannah back, and Daddy, and even Cat. She wanted her life back.

"Cameron Construction? Or Girls with Hammers?" Sophia finally clarified. "Because, we both know that you can't have both."

"Mamma," Lily started.

"Be honest."

Lily looked at the woman seated across from her. She would be seventy in just a year. Her once-dark hair was now streaked and pulled back on top of her head in a loose bun. The creases on her brow and at her eyes had deepened since the death of her husband, Lily decided, but there was something in those eyes that Lily had never seen before. She didn't want to use the cliché *spark,* but in fact that's what she saw. It was as if someone had lighted something in Sophia Wright Cameron that had been dormant for years, perhaps always. You could see it now, in her eyes.

Her mother was looking at her, no more questions in those eyes. "We've got to get you *back* Girls with Hammers, don't we?" she said. "And we're going to have to do it in a way that gets you everything your daddy wanted you to have from the business. Just not the worry and not your brother James riding you all the time."

"What's he up to anyway, Mamma?" Lily asked. Her brother had always been arrogant and patronizing to them all. Lily had decided a long time ago that James thought he was better than the rest of them, especially Mamma and Daddy. But lately his own self-importance had him acting as if he was some lord and they were his serfs. He was guarding his territory like a pit bull, pissing on every bush and blade of grass his stream could reach. It was as if he was just waiting to catch Lily or someone in the family stealing his say-so over the business—as if he even *had* any say-so!

Sophia squinted, looking off into the woods beyond the river. She shook her head, "I don't know, but I don't like it."

"Sometimes I feel like James is itchin' for me to run this company into the ground," Lily admitted.

"You mightn't be far off on that one. If it looks like Cameron Construction is going to go belly-up at your hands, well, James has a strong case for buying you out for nearly nothing and selling it off for twice its worth."

Lily sputtered. She'd never thought about that. Even James wouldn't be capable of something so cold as that. A brother betraying his sister?

Oh please, she heard Cat's voice. *Think about all the Bible stories and fairy tales just filled with sibling rivalry and treachery, for God's sakes, Lil!*

"What'll I do, Mamma?" Lily asked, deflated.

Sophia patted her hand. "It's what *we're* going to do, darlin'. *We.*"

They began to sketch out a strategy on the back of a paper napkin. Lily would continue to work with James' subcontractors while Sophia got in touch with Houston Wilder, a lawyer and old family friend. A while back, Sophia told Lily, Wilder had been muscled out of the Cameron business by James.

"Your brother kept talking about how he could do all the lawyer-ing now," she explained. "Your daddy and I were swayed by his talk about saving the business money, but mostly James piled up a bunch of trumped-up evidence of Houston's ineptitude. We had lost a law-suit, as I recall." Sophia's eyes clouded over. "Your daddy tried so hard to defend his friend, you know. But James was just so *slick*." She sat back, suddenly angry. "Now he's downright slimy!" she declared.

And this too, Lily would relay to Hannah. *Called him slimy. No kid-ding.*

Sophia stuffed an extra ten-dollar bill into the check folder. "All your daddy ever wanted was for you to be happy, Lily," she said.

They walked to the parking lot.

Lily backed the truck out and headed toward home. For a while they drove in silence; then Lily said, "Cameron Construction is never going to make me happy, Mamma. But Daddy built it, and I know he wouldn't want to see it die."

"Then we'll fix it so that everybody wins."

"Even James?"

Sophia smiled at her daughter. She was pretty sober. Lily suspected Ruthie might have watered down her mother's margaritas. "No, maybe not James. He's too big for his britches. At least with his mamma, he is. Maybe this time James'll get a reminder of where he comes from and what's important."

"A kick in the tail," Lily said, and watched her mother's grin widen.

"I've got just the boot to do it with." Sophia laughed. "Do you re-member that song your daddy used to sing to you when you were a little girl?"

Lily looked over at her mother.

"He'd pick you up and carry you around on his shoulders."

"He changed all the words." But she joined in as her mother softly sang.

> If I had a hammer,
> I'd hammer in the morning . . .

Lily had pulled her mother's truck into the long, familiar driveway just as they finished singing the entire song for the second time. She parked the Explorer near the front door, same as always, where her mother liked to keep it *in case someone has to be rushed to the hospital,* she'd say, *and I'm the only one around to go.* Sophia enjoyed her status as matriarch of a grown brood. Even though her kids didn't all live nearby, she stood ready to come to the aid of any one of them if trouble threatened.

"Oh . . . dear," she said now, becoming aware of the fact that Lily's truck was home, parked in her own driveway, since Sophia had chauffeured them both to the morning meeting with James.

"It's OK, Mamma. I can use the walk. I feel like James got all over me today. I think I need to get the stink blown off."

"If you're sure, dear," Sophia said, looking to the sky. "No rain and plenty of light. You'll be fine." She said this as if reassuring herself, rather than Lily.

Lily looked at the old house where she had grown up. The white paint was peeling slightly from the second floor balcony that she used to climb down to sneak out in the middle of the night as a young girl. Over the hills and through the woods, if she ran fast enough, she would be tossing pebbles at Cat's bedroom window within twenty minutes of her escaping leap to the ground. It was a big old rambling farmhouse, with a wrap-around porch whose ceiling was painted sky blue. It was beginning to look a little worn out. She noticed how the back screen door was sagging a bit. She'd come fix it on the weekend, Lily decided. Maybe Sophia had underestimated the situation at Cameron Construction.

"Mamma," Lily started.

As if reading her mind, Sophia reached to cover her daughter's hand on the steering wheel with her own. "Don't you worry, honey," she said. "We're gonna make sure Cameron Construction gets strong again. That'll breathe new life into your Girls with Hammers." It sounded funny, but then Sophia *was* a little tipsy. But the iron was back in her voice again, and Lily knew her mother meant business. She was going to face off with James. She was not going to let him

railroad her and Lily into some inside job making reservations for estimates.

"You gotta be sure about this, Mamma," Lily said, giving Sophia
one last chance to get out.

Sophia was looking up at the house herself now. "I bet your daddy
is up there, watching and cheering us along right this minute," she
murmured in a half-whisper. Then she turned to look at Lily one more
time before climbing out of the car. Her eyes had that spark again.
"We'll fix that James Cameron and everything else that ain't working
right around here!"

For the first time in her life, Lily felt like she was a mamma's girl,
too.

Eight

It was a series of events that had led Lily to do what she did next, later on, making everything worse. Not just one thing and not even an accumulation of many, just a series, like a train careening in a forward motion, nowhere to go but where the rails lead. As if she had no will of her own, which she was beginning to think might have been true, it felt a little out of her control.

For sure, it had started yesterday with the confrontation with James, she thought, holding her red knuckles under the cold tap water at the sink. She packed a towel of ice around her hand and grabbed a beer to take to the couch. The fact was she didn't regret what had happened. Arlo's face appeared before her now, as clearly as it had risen those few hours ago just after she'd done what she'd done. *No regrets?* She imagined Arlo poking at her trying to make her feel guilty about it. But she didn't—just a little out of control. Her hand, now sore and nearly useless, wasn't helping her feel any less so.

Her day, she reckoned, had begun tightly wound and got tighter with each tick. What had happened had been inevitable, at least the first part of it.

Two shiny silver vans were parked at the site when she pulled up this morning. Across the side of each vehicle, Prestige Electric was painted like a gleaming bolt of golden lightening. She had cut the engine and sat motionless as she watched the electrical crew mill around. These guys were all dressed alike in matching uniforms: black jeans and navy blue T-shirts with that same flash of lettering across the back.

"Tidy, ain't they?" Lily said to Dolly.

A black leather tool belt snugged around each electrician's skinny waist. Neatly aligned in their right slots were silver tool handles that glistened in the sun.

"Looks like a TV commercial," Lily continued. "Like those Bug Guys . . . all clean in their spiffy outfits. The way they hold those dinky little sprayers that look more like flower misters than bug killers. Prancing like a bunch of boy toys off to water the pansy field. Ever have one of those guys come to your house?"

Dolly shook her head.

Lily stole a look at Dolly. She was a great listener, but she really didn't say much. Lily really didn't know what Dolly thought about much of anything, if the truth were told. She always just assumed that they were in full agreement, but now, as she dared another look across the cab, she realized that for all she knew, Dolly could be sitting over there making up a grocery list in her head. Either way, Lily thought, and continued to relate her exterminator experience.

"I *did* hire those bug guys one time. Found their big shiny ad in the Yellow Pages. So, this joker shows up—not in a truck with a bug on top, like the ad said, no, an old rusted out Pontiac pulls in, shocks shot and scraping sparks across my driveway. And the bug guy? Big fat and bald, chew stuffed in his cheek, dirty T-shirt with a hole right over his belly button. He's draggin' this monster canister that looks like an oversized fire extinguisher. Nothing like in the commercials. But these guys," Lily waved toward the robotic-looking electricians, "these guys really do look like an advertisement. Wonder if they can spark a wire?"

Arlo was talking to one of the men. He was pointing and grinning. Twice he glanced in her direction. Lily frowned back at him. She was developing a persistent beat in the back of her head, near the base of her neck. She was in no mood for this crap today, she thought.

Without a prompt, except for the fluttering in her middle, she recalled the e-mail message she'd had from Hannah last night. The news from Amsterdam just adding to this pooling negativity.

> Hi sweetie, great news . . . we got our grant money! We'll be here for another two months! Off to celebrate, just wanted to share the joy! Love, Hannah.

This wasn't the first bit of *great news* from Amsterdam. There apparently was an abundance of great news in that country. On a daily basis, Hannah managed to dash off these quick e-mails letting Lily know all about the great food, the great architecture, the great pubs and cafés, and parks and vineyards, and always about the great people she was meeting.

There was a brilliant sociologist, a lesbian, Hannah wrote. Her name was Heather and she was from Switzerland. She wrote at length about another amazing doctor from Germany, whose name was Hoerst (which Lily thought horrible), who escorted a group of them through an ancient castle that had once been in his family. Her work, Hannah continued to proclaim, had never been so rewarding.

And with each e-mail message, Lily had felt more and more distant from Hannah and their life together. Lily (hating to admit) had even begun to forget what Hannah looked like: not completely and not always, but sometimes, and that scared her.

Lily's grip tightened on the steering wheel as she thought about this, and tightened some more as she watched those electricians—the enemy—out there, just waiting to sabotage her at any moment. She couldn't get the girls in there and working until all the explaining and introducing was over. Arlo appeared to be taking care of the explaining part, but now she wished that Cat were here. Cat would have had those guys off her site within five minutes of demanding, "What the hell are you doin' here?"

Now, sitting behind Lily, it was only the two Jennies and Laura, all of whom were unusually quiet. The Jennies, she suspected, were having some kind of huffy fight. A bunch of deep sighing was going on back there. Great, she thought, domestic problems on the job. Meanwhile, Laura was immersed in a very thick book.

Earlier, when Lily had picked up Dolly, she'd been told that Micah had left town and that it was not clear when or even if she would return.

"What do you mean?" Lily had asked. "What happened?"

"It was *ugly*. Police were called. Domestic disturbance."

"Boyfriend?"

Dolly shook her head. "No, worse. Dyke drama. Micah's crazy Venezuelan girlfriend caught her in bed with some little hippie chick. The Latin nutcase had climbed in through the hippie chick's window and found them all cozied up."

"I thought she was straight? Micah, I mean," Lily said.

Dolly shrugged, "Wishy-washy. Can't make a commitment—not to her own sexuality, relationships, jobs, even her music. She'd be an awesome guitar player if she'd only commit, you know?"

"Seen it before. Lousy workers. I shouldn't have hired her."

But the new development brought the number of crew down to seven, including Arlo.

"Well, we ain't gettin' anything done just sittin' out here," Lily finally muttered. She jerked open the door. The others moved slowly behind her. It was going to be a long day, she thought.

They approached the house, and Lily noticed there was something familiar about the shorter of the two electricians talking to Arlo. Maybe something in the way his shoulders slouched and then pulled back in time with his nodding head. He was like a skinny hen, pecking away at flying bugs. She slowed in her approach as she watched him slap the shoulder of the taller man and then laugh. It was his laugh, high and grating as he threw back his head, which sent the hairs on the back of Lily's neck springing to attention.

She knew him now. He was older by about fifteen years, but not much changed. Scrawny guy whose once black hair had grayed to a jaundiced yellow color. His sideburns were as long as they had been when Lily'd first encountered him during her apprenticeship over in Greensboro. She recollected their entire relationship in a flash and then spit.

Jeremiah Glock had started picking on her the minute she'd stepped onto that first job site. He had put bugs in her sandwiches, locked her in the Porta-John, filled the pouch of her tool belt with Liquid Nails. But the final straw had happened on a Friday afternoon when Lily was leaving work. A stone had come flying at her windshield, sending a large crack through its middle. She hadn't actually seen anyone throw it, but Jeremiah, high atop a ladder with his back to her, was the only one in sight. That night she'd followed him to a bar and when the coast was clear, she'd slit every one of his tires. That next Monday, as she had stood off to the side, she merely listened while Jeremiah huffed out his story to the rest of the crew.

"Every last one slashed through—brand new Firestones—all four of 'em, ruint," he'd said, nearly incredulous. "Who'd a done somethin' like that, anyhow?" But when his eyes had landed on Lily, she could see recognition registering. He'd left *her* alone from then on.

But here he was again, these many years later—on *her* job this time. Lily had an urge to yell at him that she'd never regretted slicing up his expensive rubber.

As she joined the circle, she saw by Jeremiah's double take that he knew her. She watched as he tried to compose himself, then grinned and laughed a little, reminding Lily of the past, when they'd worked that job together in Greensboro. He stuck out his hand to shake. "Bygones be bygones?" he suggested.

Lily did not take his hand. Instead she turned and introduced herself to the taller of the two men, Bobby Dean. "Your brother James' wife, Rebecca, is my second cousin by marriage through Tommy Cobb," Bobby told her. "You know Tommy? From over in Acorn?"

James' words—*This is not the Old South where everybody's related to everybody*—ran through her mind.

"Can't say I do," Lily said politely. "But then, seems like I'm kin, one way or another, to just about everybody in this valley."

She had shown the Prestige crew around the site, making it plain what needed to be done, and then left them to themselves. It was her own bunch, she'd been annoyed to discover, that was in a collective funk. Not Arlo (never Arlo; at ten, just like always, he pulled out his jump rope and began his routine). But the Jennies had to be separated after Lily found them nose to nose ready to yank out each other's hair. It seemed, from what she could make out, that White Jennie had been cheatin' or at least flirtin' with somebody else and Black Jenny was ready to tear them both apart. She screamed this in colorful language over her shoulder as Lily set her to work in a distant part of the house.

Right in the middle of lunch, Lily's cell phone had gone off. It was Malcolm Galway, the owner of the bed-and-breakfast, extremely *agitated* he said because the Italian tile he'd ordered from Italy had arrived smashed *to little itty-bitty bits*. He was very *very* upset with this latest *disaster*. It was barely noon and already Lily's head was pounding.

The sun was making its late afternoon dip when Lily rounded the corner at the back of the house, carrying her circular saw. She jerked to a halt and backed up quickly. The nasally pitch of Jeremiah's voice had stopped her. He was smokin' and lyin', Lily could tell, with two other Prestige guys.

"Yeah, I really had her goin' back in those days," he bragged. "Once, I even went to her house when she wasn't home and boarded up her front and back doors." Snorting his final boast, "I used about a hundred screws on that plywood."

Lily's heart jumped twice. Of course it had been him! She hadn't put two and two together, back then, because months had passed since her tire caper. Now she remembered that it had been a late wintry afternoon when she'd pulled up to find Cat, her roommate at the time, half-frozen and pacing and stomping up and down the driveway. They hadn't even considered Jeremiah. More obvious had been Cat's madwoman ex-girlfriend who'd gone completely off the deep end and had been stalking Cat on campus and leaving threatening messages on the answering machine.

Lily poked her head around the corner and saw the other two electricians stubbing out their smokes and lazily making their way back into the house. When they had both disappeared, Lily waited and then looked around the yard. It was apparent that Jeremiah was alone as he sucked on the nub of his smoke. She put the saw down and wiped her hands. Then she simply charged him, knocking his cigarette from his grip and grabbing his shirt to lift and push him back up against the side of the house. She pinned him there, his only contact with the earth, the "tiptoes" of his boots.

"Listen, you little muther, how 'bout you and me have a little dance?"

He flinched as Lily's spit hit his face. She was bigger and stronger than he was and he dangled, like a rag doll, from his shirt collar twisted in her fist. Each time he struggled to be free, she pushed him harder into the wall behind him, forcing his chin back. "This time around, *you* get to wonder *what next?* Every day you walk onto this site, *my site,* you can worry about your tires." She had shoved her knee into his crotch. "Get it?"

He made something like a nod, and Lily dropped him.

Had it ended there, Lily decided, stretching out on the couch and finishing the last of a second beer, she might not have had any regrets. She might have been able to establish the rules without anybody knowing about it. But when that little prick had stood up, looked her in the eye and said, "Bobby was right; you got about three weeks before this job goes *belly-up*," something inside her had snapped.

Belly-up. James' words. "What the fuck are you talking about, asshole?" she asked, just before she saw her own arm pull back like the spring action on a kid toy and land a fist across Jeremiah's jaw. She actually heard her knuckles crack against his teeth, sending him stumbling backward into the house, sliding down into a heap at her feet.

"Piss ant," she hissed as he rolled over and lurched upright. Jeremiah wiped his hand across his bleeding lip, and then looked at her.

"I'm reportin' this to Bobby Dean," he said and ran off.

Lily turned as she heard a noise behind her. Arlo was standing in the shaded back doorway. How long he'd been leaning there she wasn't sure. By the look on his face, she was sure that he'd seen at least the last of what had happened.

"Feel better?" he asked, coming toward her. A long piece of grass dangled lazily between his teeth.

She scowled.

"'Cause, if you don't, I know where there's a puppy you could kick around."

"Shut up."

"Little yeller thing."

Her hand had begun to throb and she slid it between her left arm and waist, applying easy pressure. She turned and made for the open courtyard.

"Wait," Arlo called. "Let me see your hand." He caught up and took her arm. He grinned. "You're gonna have a bruise with this one." Already two of her knuckles were going blue. "Where'd you learn to punch like that?"

"Six older brothers," Lily muttered, then winced at a particularly sharp jab of pain.

"Here," Arlo took her good hand. "I know something that'll help." He guided her to a slip of a path in the woods, and dropped her hand. He seemed to fully expect her to follow, not looking back to see if she was there.

"Where are we going?" Lily had asked, a little wary. Even before Arlo could respond, the answer lay just before them. A small sunny clearing opened here, and through its center a rushing brook cascaded down a gentle slope. It wasn't wide, but large gray boulders edged and scattered the water. Along the far edge, forming a circle, were four such boulders ringing a deep pool. Arlo gestured for Lily to join him on top of one of the smooth slabs of granite. They removed their shoes and socks and rolled up their pant legs. The icy water nearly numbed Lily's toes.

"Here," Arlo said, taking her hand. "Soak it in there."

The cold soothed the ache in her knuckles and wrist. Lily looked down into the pool at their naked toes, hers and Arlo's, that seemed to ripple in the clear water. It was quiet out here.

Finally, it had been Lily who broke the silence.

"So, you were raised by a pack of Macon women across state lines?" She hadn't exactly been trying to make conversation. But she wanted the talk to be about something other than the incident in the courtyard. Throwing the spotlight on Arlo was the quickest diversion she could devise.

Arlo grinned and nodded.

"How about your daddy?" she ventured, noticing a quick darkening across his brow and then hidden as he cast his eyes to the water.

"To tell you the truth, I never have met my daddy. Last couple years, though, I've been traveling around looking for him."

"You don't know where he is? So, where you been lookin'?"

"Churches," Arlo said. "He was a preacher, Mamma told me."

"Shit, there must be a million churches in the South—one for every other acre. I'd bet my hat on it."

Arlo laughed. "Been to over a hundred of 'em. Every Sunday, I pick a new one. Good thing about it is, I don't need more than one clean shirt and tie and pair of shoes, 'cause I never go to the same place twice."

"You know his name—why not just make some calls?"

Arlo had chosen to ignore such logic. He leaned back on his elbows. A shock of dark hair fell across his forehead. His eyes in the sunlight seemed the same bright green as the water, clear and deep. He had a habit of smoothing his tongue across the edge of his chipped front tooth. This had often preceded words, Lily noticed, like a muse massaging his chin.

"My mamma told me," he had said softly, "that he was the most beautiful man she'd ever seen. Said, for the first and last time in her whole life, all she wanted was to lie beside DorrieBee Halsey for just one *damn* afternoon. That's what she said: *damn*." He raised his eyes to Lily. "Mamma hardly ever talks like that, but she did say it that one time in front of me."

Arlo's face, Lily thought, watching him, might have been beautiful like his daddy's. He was himself pretty enough to have women want to lie beside him, even only for one *damn* afternoon. Except, Lily had thought, he doesn't really know that yet. She had let herself admire his lanky boyishness, the way he straightened and unstraightened his body on the big rock. He was telling the story with his whole self. There was still that attractive awkwardness about Arlo. It was the kind of awkwardness that good-looking men get after pubescent pimples and pudge disappear, but before they recognize the handsome face in the mirror as their own.

In a missed sip, beer drained down Lily's chin and she leaped from the couch to the kitchen sink. Sponging the foam from her neck and chin, she rinsed the spilling suds from the sides of the brown beer bottle where the dripping liquid appeared golden, reminding her of the beads of river water sprinkling Arlo's tanned skin. And like this afternoon, she was again startled by a summoning of feelings she'd not had in decades.

In that earlier waning light, she remembered, as she had rested, dwelling in her admiration of the young man's lean and muscular body, she'd experienced a small rising within her, its familiarity nearly shocking her. The tingling in Lily's middle—or should she say below her middle—had been akin to the sensation that rose when she set her sights on Hannah as she'd step dripping from the shower, or climbing naked into their bed, or across a room, in that chance glimpse of witnessing her laughter among strangers.

How could this boy be evoking those feelings in her? Lily cupped a bowl of cool tap water with her palms and splashed the flushed heat from her face. Recovering quickly, she hated to think of how Arlo's innocent ungainliness might turn skillfully slick, just like the bad-boy preacher-daddy he had been describing. He had slowed in his telling, she recalled, as if he were remembering to get all the story's pieces in order, and in that moment, she recalled, his movements seemed to align perfectly with his words and emotions. Suddenly he was graceful, breathtakingly beautiful and mature, but not slick. Lily had wondered if she'd caught a glimpse of the man that he would become. The sudden crease in his brow, the shadowed thoughtfulness in his eyes . . . she wasn't really sure what it had been. But then the moment had passed. Once again, Arlo returned to the awkwardly nervous boy sitting on a flat, warm rock beside her, dangling his feet next to hers in the water.

Lily flexed her hand, spreading the ache nearly to her wrist. She picked up the almost empty beer bottle and went out to the porch. She set her gaze to the creek below, where small waterfalls splashed over big gray rocks. Was she attracted to a guy? Who wouldn't admire that body? He was young and charming. He listened carefully. Hannah was gone and Lily was forgetting her features and the sound of her voice—it was somehow safely natural that she'd have a little crush on the kid. But he was not a kid. That she also knew for sure and this new inkling, again, inflamed that heat inside her. There had been one moment that afternoon when she had wanted to reach across the distance between them, to touch that smooth bare chest, to feel its hardness, those muscles, and the soft skin stretched tightly across them.

God! What was she doing to herself? She shook her head, ridding images and inspirations.

She was thinking about the faces of her female crew, earlier, when Arlo had confessed his adolescent indiscretion of thievery. The way he had told it—well, you forgave him on his humbled tone alone. Those girls had seemed to hover between wanting to mother him or maybe wanting to run away for one *damn* afternoon and lie beside this Halsey fella—all but Laura, of course.

On that rock together, Lily had listened as he'd gone into even more detail. "She met him at a tent revival," he said about his parents. "She told me this when she told me the one and only story she knows about my daddy. The one and only story I've ever believed about my daddy."

Lily frowned, confused.

"I've heard other stories about him," he explained. "You know, the legends and rumors kind: *Heard your daddy got shot at over in Georgia, pocketing pennies outta the plate.* Or the one that goes, *There's another gal in Tennessee and one in Alabama left all alone and full of DorrieBee Halsey . . .* then they'd say, *He ain't no man of God,* and then they'd spit." Arlo grinned at his own telling.

"That's terrible," Lily said.

"Not really. I don't believe any of 'em, anyhow. Mamma's is the only *first-person* account that I have ever heard. It goes: *I met the only*

man who ever loved me on one silvery morning in September. Mamma's a
poet, sometimes. And hers is the only story about my daddy that I
truly believe."

Lily had watched a blush rise up his neck, splotching his cheeks. He
grinned and then said, "That night, after they were together, Mamma
said he preached like a lion for the Lord. Next day he was gone. Nine
months later to the day, I came into the world roaring, just like my
daddy. Mamma swears to this."

"Have you ever gotten close to finding him?"

"No." Arlo shrugged, playing with a small twig he'd caught drifting by. "Seems like he's always two steps ahead of me. But I ain't giving up. Sooner or later I'll find him, and in the meanwhile, all that
churchin' can't be hurtin'." He grinned at his own slanted rhyme.

Lily had swished her swollen hand under the cold water of the
stream and wondered if that little prick electrician had run to his boss
and told the whole story on her and if the girls were worrying about
where she was. She didn't care. There had been a cool breeze coming
off the creek; her hair, sweat-stuck to her neck, dried by it.

She had dared a look over at him. He stretched out his long body
and crossed his arms under his head. His eyes were closed, and Lily
had imagined that he probably really could fall asleep just that quick,
even on a hard rock, if he'd had a mind to. He had a scar on his upper
arm—a checkmark—nearly three inches long and knife-blade thin
and Lily had shivered with the possibility of that truth. And then she
questioned how she could think such a thing. And then realized she'd
thought a lot about Arlo Halsey these days. Something that both confused and intrigued her. She hadn't felt this interested in another person in a long time.

On the porch now, Lily lit a cigarette. Since Hannah had gone to
Amsterdam, she had refrained from smoking in the house. She didn't
want to get into a habit she'd be cranky about giving up when
Hannah came home, *if* Hannah came home, Lily thought, dejectedly.
Lately, in those e-mails, Hannah had begun referring to the apartment
she shared with the brilliant lesbian and the German-almost-duke as

home. This latest remembered e-mail caused Lily to clench her battered fist, sending pulsing throbs up her arm, reminding her of her bad day.

"Why'd you hit him?" Arlo had asked.

His words had startled her, she recalled, as his own half-lidded study of her had been going on all the while she'd been picking over him.

She frowned. "He needs to know who's the boss on this job."

Arlo shielded the sun from his eyes. "Seems like he'd know that, whether you'd hit him or not."

"Had to show him who has the power this time around."

"So you gave *him* the power—on purpose?" Arlo raised his brow, contemplatively. "I find that odd." He slid his body down into the pool, not removing his shorts.

"You gotta be missin' something," Lily said. "I didn't give him any power. I took it back."

Arlo looked at her. "No, you showed him *force*. Two different things."

This had stopped Lily. Confused, she decided on the extreme. She slid down into the pool and swam over to a grotto of rock that splashed a small waterfall from above. Arlo could about reach it by stretching out from the rock. He swung himself up and under the waterfall, then reached down and helped Lily up to where she could be showered by the stream as well.

"What do you mean two different things?" she finally asked, leaning back against the granite.

Arlo had let icy water splash over his upturned face. He then shook himself like a dog. "You're the boss on this job, right?" He didn't wait for an answer. "So, you already have power."

She nodded, following him.

"So, when you punched him, you used unnecessary force."

Her look told him that he was losing her.

"Like this," Arlo shifted. "A cop already has power 'cause he's got a badge, right? And if the crook is being compliant 'cause he knows the cop's the boss, then the cop doesn't need to club the guy, right?" He only paused for breath. "But if the cop clubs the crook anyway, they call it *unnecessary force,* and the crook's suddenly got the power. The cop's in trouble."

"Are you comparing me to a cop?" Lily asked.

"All I know is that a lot of bad guys get out of their crime because some muscle-headed cop used a boot instead of a badge."

"Maybe they're right."

"No, it happens 'cause no one trusts the system. Far as I can see, anyway."

"And how do you know so much about it?" She challenged him as if an ordinary citizen couldn't make the same claim, just from reading the papers.

He shrugged. "Look at all the cop and lawyer shows on TV. . . . Hell, just look at Rodney King. That guy's been in and out of jail for years. If those idiot cops had just relied on their own power, instead of using unnecessary force, they could have avoided a big old riot!"

"Probably so . . ." Lily mused. "But that's pretty old news."

Arlo ignored her. "You are going to have to answer for that," he said, pointing at her swelling hand. "It really didn't get you any more power, did it?"

She blew across her knuckles. "Maybe not." Then she grinned and looked at him. "But it felt good."

"Oh, yeah. That looks like it feels real good. We'll see if it was worth it."

In fact, it felt like hell, she thought.

"You gonna measure by your head or by your fist?" he asked.

She laughed, "OK, I'll stick to a tape."

"Look, you're the boss, no matter what." He made a swipe at a passing minnow.

Lily had jumped back in and swam to another sunny boulder and climbed up. "Not for much longer," she said as she watched him swim across.

The full length of him had reached her within two strokes. The muscles in his back mimicked the ripples of the water as if he, too, were something of a fish. He dove under. Natural, she decided, as she waited for him to rise for his breath. When he finally did break surface, she noticed that the sun had stirred up the dusting of freckles across the bridge of his nose. His angles, she saw, matched in his jaw and chin and the straightness of his spine. As he lifted himself out, the cut of his abs and dance of his pectorals sliced the water.

"Whatdya mean?" Arlo climbed up beside her. "Not for much longer?" he asked, distracting her from her admiring.

She stumbled, "Oh, my brother James is aimin' to shove me out of this job. Didn't you hear? I'm sure the rumor is all over the site."

"Why would he do that?"

Lily threw him a look. "He's a lawyer. Took over the money end of Cameron for Daddy, but he doesn't know anything about carpentry. I think he'd just as soon be rid of the whole thing. It's turning out to be a disaster for all of us. I think he feels obligated to our mamma. So, he'll never let it slip from his fingers. But, I'm sure he won't mind if it drops from mine."

After that, the pair sat side by side; every now and then their shoulders would tap, accidentally. Arlo seemed oblivious to these touches, she thought, but for her, each small contact zapped a tiny electrical shockwave under her skin.

Lily recalled this last bit, stuffing the end of her burning cigarette into the empty beer bottle and watching it smolder. A wasp nest was beginning in the corner of the porch ceiling, she noticed. At sundown she'd get out the hose and spray the buggers in the dark. *Get them before they get you,* she'd once told Hannah. Grabbing another beer from the fridge, she carried it and a towel of ice cubes back out to the porch and sat on the glider.

That afternoon, Arlo's concern had evidenced in the deepening creases around his eyes. He had made no gesture, no move, just sat with his knees pulled to his chest and his chin resting on his crossed arms. After a time, the sun had dried their skin and left their clothing cool and damp. They pulled their socks and boots back on and made their way through the woods.

"So, what are you going to do?" Arlo had asked, referring to the uncertainty of the business's future, as they had walked in line.

"I can't let my daddy down either," she'd explained. "But Mamma's got something up her sleeve, so I think I'll play along with her for awhile."

As they had rounded a bend, the path forked unexpectedly, veering left and depositing them in a small clearing surrounded on three sides by trees. The path through which they'd slipped had blended back into the forest behind the folds of foliage. Before them, a clifflike ledge jutted from a solid wall of granite, offering a natural shelter. A camouflage tarp stretched from the outcropping to the ground. The lean-to protected a sleeping bag resting on a raised bed of pine straw. This was an encampment. There was a fire pit whose coals, Lily noticed, were still smoldering.

To the side of the camp, in a thickly branched crab apple tree there hung, like a giant mobile, one large cooking pot, a saucepan, teakettle, spatula, knife, fork, spoon, ladle, a frying pan, and two tin cups, each twirling on twine tied to the tree. At the back of the dwelling, there was a mirror propped above a tin basin and a neat row of toiletries all encased in those plastic camp gear containers for toothbrushes, soap, and a razor. Beside this was a large Tupperware bin with a lid, which Arlo had flipped open and pulled out a vacuum-packed baggie with a white T-shirt sealed inside. He took out larger sacks, as if pulling meat out of a freezer, these two containing his blue jeans. Socks and underwear were in their own packages.

"Keeps everything clean and dry," he had explained.

There was one metal deck chair with green and white weave. A low stump in front of it served as its hassock. Arlo had offered the seat to Lily, who declined.

"You live here?"

"Home sweet home," Arlo grinned.

"How long?"

"A while. Till I get on my feet. You know."

Lily had nodded, making her way around the little space. There were canned goods along the wall, boxes of pasta, dried beef and fruit, and in another clear plastic container she saw a stack of books and magazines.

"I read a lot," Arlo said, noticing her taking note of his library. "And," he had jumped toward his makeshift bedroom, "check this out—my latest purchase." Triumphantly, he retrieved and held up a black, transistor radio. It was the kind, Lily recalled, that she'd saved up six whole allowances for when she was eight. She remembered stuffing its tiny earplug in, late at night, and falling asleep to the new AM station that played the first rock and roll she'd ever really heard.

"And of course," he had continued, and threw open another container full of double-A batteries. "Not bettin' on that pink bunny. . ." He smiled.

"What about your mamma? Does she know you're living like this?"

Arlo shrugged. "She's got enough of her own worries without adding me to 'em. I'm fine. Weather's good. By the time it starts getting cold, I'll have enough money to get a real place. Anyhow, I like being outside."

Lily had started to walk around the site when Arlo tapped her arm.

"We better get back," he said. "I, uh, just wanted you to know where you could find me if you had to." He turned and made for an opening in the trees. Before he slipped through, he said, "I'd rather no one else know about this . . ."

"No problem. Safe with me," Lily said. "I'd hate to hear that you'd been strangled in your sleep."

He laughed. "No kidding. I don't know what I've done to make Laura so mad at me . . ." He disappeared through a slip of bushes.

As she made to follow, Lily saw a piece of paper drop from Arlo's back pocket. Scooping it up quickly, she could just make out the scratchy handwriting:

To think is an act of choice.—Ayn Rand

She had put it in her own pocket. *Stealing*. She didn't know why.

Now, pulling the paper from her pocket and rereading it, Lily repeated the quote out loud. Rocking gently on the glider, she set the scrap of paper to the side and placed the towel of ice onto her bruised knuckles. She sipped her beer and thought about Arlo living out there in the woods all by himself. His camp was neat as a pin. Everything had its place. Even the packed earthen floor, she recalled, bore the hatch marks of a broom. She had to give him credit for that, for sure; but what about that family of women who raised him? Why was he living out in the woods when there was family?

Having come from her own big family, she couldn't imagine this being allowed. They'd find her, she figured. The aunts would come by with casseroles and her brothers would probably sneak in and hide money in the pots and pans for her to find.

She pictured Arlo now, by firelight, washing up the last of his dishes, tying the pots back up in the tree. Candles and the oil lamp glowing soft yellow, bouncing shadows off the back wall of the ledge. Maybe he was sitting in his lawn chair, sipping a cup of coffee and listening to his new transistor radio. What would he be tuned to? She wondered. A baseball game? Music? Jesus? Or maybe he'd already slid into the sleeve of his sleeping bag, his flashlight positioned on the page of whatever he was reading now.

She imagined the darkness of the forest pressing in on him, staved off only by the glow of his lamp. How long, she wondered, would he read like that? Until his lids would lift no more? Till his lamp wore itself out? Did he dare reach above and eliminate the only barrier between—she considered—himself and *them*? The night creatures and spirits that moved only by darkness, caught occasionally in the eerie shaft of moonlight. *Them.*

She didn't think Arlo would feel this way. Probably he would feel the exact opposite. She envisioned how, in the swallowing darkness, Arlo might even feel himself to be one with *them*. *Know thine enemy.* She could hear him actually thinking like this. He knows a lot of quotes, she thought. One minute he's paraphrasing Aunt Bea, from *The Andy Griffith Show*; next thing, he's quoting some famous philosopher. She picked up the small piece of paper and smoothed it between her fingers as she read it and read it again.

To think is an act of choice.—Ayn Rand

Hannah had read Ayn Rand. Lily recalled the author's name on the spine of a book on a shelf in her office. So had Cat. Not Lily. She only knew the name because the two women she loved most in the world read whole books that Ayn Rand wrote.

Nine

Lily awoke to the smell of coffee and bacon. For a moment, as she lay with her head near the foot of her bed and her sheets tangled around her waist, she felt disoriented. Not only was she not exactly sure of *where* she was, she wasn't sure of *when* it was, either. This feeling intensified as she opened her eyes, and from her awkward position, the vision of her mother loomed over her. Against the bedroom door jamb leaned Sophia, spatula in hand, hair pulled back in a braid. She was watching her daughter awaken. It was when Sophia actually spoke that Lily jumped, flipping herself upright and shaking her head to make the fog clear.

She pulled a sheet up around her naked shoulders. "Mamma, what are you doing here? How'd you get in?"

"You don't have to hide behind that sheet; I've washed that body with these very hands, remember." Sophia turned and headed back for the kitchen. "Hurry up and get dressed; we've got to *strategize.*"

That word again, Lily thought as she pulled on her jeans. What was up with her mother? Lately, she was like a one-woman CIA or FBI or something. *Strategize;* she guessed that Sophia probably just liked saying the word.

Lily sat down at the table where Sophia had set a place for her. There was a white envelope with her gynecologist's return address.

"What's this?" Lily picked it up.

"It's a notice from Dr. Cole's office. You missed your yearly physical. It came to my house, yesterday."

"Shit," Lily said, sliding the letter to her. "How long have I been living here? You'd think Shelley would know where I live by now. I've only been going there for the past ten years."

"Well, I think they got a new girl working in the office down there. Probably just a mix-up."

Lily turned the envelope over. "You opened it?!"

"Yes, I opened it." Sophia shoveled bacon, eggs, biscuits, and gravy onto her daughter's plate.

"Mamma, you can't just go opening my mail! I'm a grown woman. This is private!"

Sophia waved the spatula. "Nonsense. It's medical, and you're my daughter. That's not private." She scooped the rest of the breakfast onto her own plate and sat down.

"How do you do that? Justify like that?" Lily put her fork down. "You can't just go snoopin' into people's stuff. I mean what if this had said something terrible?" She flapped the envelope at Sophia. "Like I had cancer or something?"

"I'm your mother. I'm the first person who should know. I gave birth to you. For goodness sakes, if your own mother shouldn't be the first to know about your health, then who should?"

"You know what I mean, Mamma. This isn't about my health; this is about my privacy."

"Well, in this case one doesn't have anything to do with the other."

Lily sipped from her coffee cup and calmed herself. She wasn't going to win this one.

"Anyway, it's not a problem; I arranged for another appointment for you."

"What?!" Now Lily sputtered. "You can't just go making doctor's appointments for me. I'm an adult; I can take care of myself."

"Apparently not, because when I called over there and talked to Little Bertie . . . you know she's been made office manager now," Sophia added, mentioning her niece, "she told me this is the second appointment you've missed."

"I'm busy."

"Not too busy for this, missy. I set up a mammogram for you, too."

Lily got up and threw her napkin on the table. "That's it. Listen, Mamma, I am only thirty-five years old. They don't even recommend that you get that till you're over forty. It'll cost me a fortune and my insurance deductible hasn't been met yet."

"I've already paid for it."

"Geez . . . geez."

"Lily Nelda," Sophia sniffed, hurt. "I just lost your daddy; I am not going to lose my only daughter. We were just discussing this in my women's studies, *Zest for Life* class. Ninety percent of these tests come back negative, but wouldn't you rather be safe than sorry?"

"There's been no test! There is nothing to come back ninety percent negative. There's nothing wrong with my breasts for god sakes. I do the shower exam; I check them out when I'm lying on my back in bed. I'm fine. Do you hear me, old woman?"

"Watch it, or I'll go with you!" Sophia cleared her plate away.

It was all over at that point. Lily flopped back into the chair. She'd lost this argument the minute that envelope had landed at her mother's house. As Sophia opened her mouth to issue another round, Lily held up her hand. "Enough," she said. "Fine, I'll do it. Don't you say another word. I'll do the pap but I ain't havin' the blamdamnit mammogram—and Shelley will agree with me."

"All right, if Shelley says no mammogram then fine. But you better not miss this next appointment." Sophia ignored her protests on the second helping of breakfast, and it was then that Lily noticed her mother somehow seemed younger. "Now, let's get down to the real business here." Sophia scurried out of the kitchen and came directly back, this time carrying a gleaming black briefcase. New.

Lily frowned.

"If James gets to have one, so do I," Sophia said, springing open the locks with a couple of quick silver clicks.

Who is this strange woman? Lily had only been five years old when the first Cameron grandbaby had arrived. As far back as she could remember her mother had always been a grandmother. This generally made her seem older than she really was. Even Daddy affectionately referred to her as *granny,* something she didn't seem to mind. Sophia had baked cookies, knitted little booties, kept a collection of cloth books, Disney movies, and soft toys—all for the grandbabies.

Even as a kid, Lily had understood that all of these things were not for her, but for all the nieces and nephews who seemed to arrive annually, for a couple of decades. Cameron births had been petering out these past few years, as neither she nor her brother Kevin had made any of their own contributions. Kevin, she thought, would probably be something of a contributor to the family line, someday. In the beginning, when they were younger, she and Hannah had talked about adopting kids. It seemed like a long time ago when they were actually excited about it. Lately, though, Lily didn't believe that they'd be adding to Sophia's grandmotherly duties. How could they with Hannah gallivanting all over the globe, anyway? Somehow, this made her sad and this sadness surprised her.

Watching Sophia whip around the kitchen while her strong hands wielded the iron skillet, all this discussion of mammograms and pap smears made Sophia seem no longer like some old granny. Sophia was a woman with a mission and Lily had become her cause.

"So," Sophia began, sitting down across the table from Lily, a pair of reading glasses perched on the bridge of her nose, "because you hit the electrician and skipped out on the job for the afternoon, James is threatening to pull you off and sub the whole thing out. Got it?"

Lily nodded.

"What that means is that *we*," she raised a brow at Lily, "have to convince James that you're not the *violent offender* he believes you to be."

"*Violent offender—me?*"

"His words."

"Well, you just leave it to me; I'll set him straight. That little prick had it coming . . ."

"Lily, you've done enough right now. James is a lawyer. All he sees in that crack you landed on that fella is a lawsuit against Cameron. And in this instance, I'm afraid both he and the electrician have a case against you."

Lily dropped her head.

"So, what am I supposed to do? Apologize to everyone? Kiss ass? Promote the prick to head prick?"

Sophia ignored her daughter.

"We've got to make your action seem more . . . *immediate*," was the word Sophia chose. "As if it were a *reaction,* if you get my drift."

Lily did not, and her bafflement showed. She watched Sophia, somewhat exasperated, lift her glasses from her nose and sigh deeply.

"Do I have to spell this out for you?"

Lily just stared.

"If James thought that you hurt that fella because he had harmed you first, well, there's no way that James would take his side. Don't you see?"

"He did harm me first. Way back when in Greensboro . . ."

But Sophia interrupted. "I mean, if he harmed you more recently and more—physically . . ."

Her mother's discomfort was apparent in the bounce of her knee—a nervous tick her daughter had inherited.

Sudden dawning struck Lily. "Mamma, are you suggesting sexual harassment?"

At first Sophia was silent, but then she plunged ahead with her scheme. "You don't have to accuse him of it to his face or in front of anyone else. All you have to do is make James think it happened, and you're off the hook."

Lily could not believe the deviousness of her mother's plan. She wanted to explain that in this day and age, falsely accusing a man of taking that kind of advantage was just not done. It made everyone pissed—the cops, the judges, and most especially women. It was the ultimate wolf cry. Feminists everywhere would hunt her down and burn her at the stake; women who lied about this were as bad as the perpetrator himself. She began an attempt to explain this to her mother, who stopped her lecture with a raised hand.

"I'm not saying that we'll bring charges, or fire the guy, all I'm saying is that if *James* (and only James) believes you were defending yourself, well, it would solve a lot of problems."

"How do I convince James of this without him firing the guy himself? Or worse, taking him to court? I do know one thing about my brother, if he thinks Glock took that kind of unwelcome liberty with me, he'll have him jailed."

"Not if we do it right. James is going to be on the site this morning and you're going to convince him that it happened and then convince him to let it go."

Lily looked at her mother. She could not believe what the woman was proposing. "I can't go around accusing an innocent man of something like that."

Sophia looked at her daughter, "No man's innocent of that."

"Mamma! That's just not so."

"All men are either doing it or thinking about doing it or wishing they could do it. Why, even Jimmy Carter admitted to his own lustful thoughts way back in the seventies." Sometimes—often—Sophia was safely tucked in earlier decades like a history book whose pages got stuck together around 1982.

"Yeah, but Mamma, he didn't mean he wanted to go around groping women. He just meant that he had desires, like all normal men."

"So he said. It's semantics. Means the same thing."

"Mamma! It does not!" Lily could see by the look on Sophia's face that this portion of the argument was over and she was ready to get on with the plan.

"What about Arlo?"

"What about him?"

"He knows the truth."

"Well, then, keep him out of it," Sophia told her. And that was the end of it.

It was nine-thirty before Lily and her crew landed on the job. Lily had done everything just as exactly as her mother had laid it out. She made a stop at the lumberyard, taking her time, and when she'd finished there, she took more time than usual getting to the site.

There was James, just as Sophia had promised, pacing around in a big circle, his steps recorded by the dusty ring in the yard.

"All right, gang," Lily called over her shoulder. "My brother's here to *inspect* us, so do me a favor and move like friggin' marines."

The girls, a full crew since Micah's hangdog return, leaped out of the back like they were unloading from a plane, hitting the ground while strapping on their belts and making their way across the yard. Lily grinned as she watched each one tip her cap at James as she went by.

Lily herself jumped from the van with more gusto than she really felt and took long strides in her brother's direction. She was smiling and by the time she reached James, he seemed so perplexed by her grin that he allowed her to guide him away from the workers (the Prestige Electric guys, too) to where they couldn't be overheard.

"Glad you're here," she said.

"Where the hell have you been?" His face reddened and he loosened his collar.

"Lumber," she said, thumbing over her shoulder at the van, where two-by-fours were stacked and tied on the roof. She interrupted his beginning interrogation. "Listen, we gotta talk about what happened yesterday," she said.

"That's why I'm here."

"Good, good." Lily nodded. "Look, I'm willing to forget the whole thing and even keep the little pervert on." She jerked her head over her shoulder toward the group encircling Glock, who was staring in their direction. Lily noticed his fattened purple lip. "But if he tries it again, I'll yank his dick off."

The word *apoplexy* popped into her head as she watched her brother's face go from human to cartoon. His eyes bugged, his head shook, and he made that *yaddayaddayadda* noise. He was not intelligible. Something about her stupid temper.

Lily leaned in close, looked back over her shoulder toward the house. Arlo, she was relieved to see, was nowhere in sight. This was the part she wanted to be very careful about. Arlo, she was sure, would be disappointed in her cowardice. But it wasn't Arlo she had to answer to—it was Mamma.

Now, standing in the hot sun with part of the plan already under way, Lily put her hand on James' shoulder and stood on tiptoes so she could whisper in his ear. She didn't want to meet his gaze. She didn't want him to ask a lot of questions. She merely wanted to plant the seed and have it take root.

"You heard what happened, right? How that little electrician grabbed my . . . you know . . ." She let the suggestion dangle.

James looked startled and she could see his slow deflation, like someone uncorking a Macy's Parade balloon.

"I don't wanna make a big deal about this, James." Lily slung her arm over his shoulder. "I mean, I've been in this business a long time. I've been grabbed by the best of 'em."

"He molested you?"

"Oh, let's not call it that. Let's say he got a little too friendly, shall we?" Lily lit a cigarette. "But I ain't gonna just sit there and take it, now am I?" She looked at James who looked impaled by both mortification and disappointment. "I don't have six brothers for nothing. I mean, I *do* know how to defend myself. You taught me that!" She slapped his back.

As she watched her brother's capitulation, Lily's own conscience tugged at her. But she was only being her mother's instrument. And Sophia, who meant to champion her daughter's cause till its successful end, could be as protective as a lioness with her young. But Lily also knew that lionesses were often especially harsh on whichever cub was currently out of favor. She was glad she wasn't James.

As Lily had left the house that morning, Sophia had called out to her, *"All's fair in love and war. And this is war, Lily . . ."*

Bobby Dean and Jeremiah Glock were waiting by the work vans as Lily and James approached, James straightening his shoulders and tie with the same determined look Lily now recognized as their mother's. It was James who addressed the pair.

"We're going to let it go this time," he began.

The two men exchanged looks.

"We're even going to let you keep your job, Jeremiah." James turned to him. "Just don't let it happen again."

The little electrician's ears turned red and he sputtered at Lily, "What'd you tell him?"

She smiled. "We'll just let those *bygones be bygones*, now. I'm willin'." She stuck out her hand. "Even?"

Jeremiah snarled but Bobby Dean put a hand on his shoulder. "Come on now, Jeremiah, we all got off to a rocky start. Let's wipe the slate clean."

Lily knew Bobby Dean's job and familial ties were gnawing at his allegiances.

Jeremiah jerked out of his grip. "I didn't lay a hand on her . . ."

"That's enough now. We all gotta get along here. We got work to do." Bobby Dean turned to Lily. "We'll all mind our own business on this job, now." He tried to nudge a handshake from Glock, who ignored him, and so he extended his own hand to Lily.

"That's all I ever wanted anyway," Lily said, shaking it. Fine with her, she thought. The idea of touching the greasy palm of the little prick electrician made her skin crawl. But as she watched him rummaging around in the back of his van, she knew it wasn't over between them. Apparently this *was* war, just as her mother had said. This time around, Lily figured, she'd really better watch her back. A guy who makes a hobby out of picking on other people wasn't one to rest when the tables got turned.

She caught sight of Arlo rising from a corner of the porch and walking out to his jumping spot. He pulled the rope from his back pocket and began his routine. She wondered if he'd watched the whole scene, figuring what had happened. Lily felt her cheeks sting. He'd surely have little respect for her now—knowing that she lied to save her own skin.

She didn't think about it for too long, distracted as she was by Dolly starting to play her fiddle under the big shade tree in the side yard. Micah had also begun strumming her new lute and the two Jennies, their whistles.

"What the hell is going on?" James demanded.

At first Lily cringed, but then said, "It's ten o'clock, James."

He frowned.

"Got to give the employees a fifteen-minute break at ten o'clock," she said over her shoulder as she pulled a rope from the back of the van.

He harrumphed.

"Hey, it's the law. You should know." Lily walked him back over to his car. "You should take one for yourself," she said, and wrapped the rope around her hands. "I got my own jumping to do."

She could tell that she was irritating the fire out of James but he could hardly say anything. Then he appeared to think of something else, and turned on her. "Malcolm Galway called me . . ."

Lily interrupted him. "Taken care of. Ordered the tile myself—this morning."

James' mouth opened and closed quickly like a startled fish. Finally he didn't say another word, just left. Before his dust was gone, and with Celtic music and rope slapping in time behind her, Lily pulled her cell phone from the van and dialed her mother's number.

"Mission accomplished, MammaBear," she said.

"Good. Now, come over as soon as you're done with work. We need to make the next plan." The mastermind hung up.

It wasn't till later while they were all taking a small siesta (as Lily liked to call these after-lunch rest periods), that she had a chance to talk with Arlo alone. There was something unnerving about the distance that was between them today, and Lily didn't know if that was just her guilty mind or if Arlo had placed the space there for himself somehow. She wandered over to a shady spot on the porch where he was hunched over a book.

"What're you reading?" She felt awkward, aware of her intrusion.

Politely he held up the worn paperback, so she could read the title: *The Prince.*

"Fantasy?" She settled on a step and sat down a little distance from him.

Arlo smiled and shook his head. "Unfortunately all too real."

"What's it about?"

He cocked his head as he thought for a minute. "Basically, it's about how a ruler takes and keeps power over his people by means of devious political maneuverings."

"So what's new about that story?"

"Well, this guy . . ." he lifted the book, showing her its cover again. "He basically feels like when it comes to getting and keeping power, anything goes—and mostly that it's OK. You've heard the word, *Machiavellian,* right?"

She had, but she was damned if she knew what it meant.

"Like raping, pillaging, and murder can be justified?" she ventured.

"Maybe not so blatant." Arlo tapped his finger on the book. His green eyes looked thoughtful. "To me, it's more about head trips. Ego and cunning—like that."

"Fixing the odds?" Even she couldn't help but grin, sounding silly to her own ears.

Arlo didn't laugh. He said, "Kind of. See, the prince gets power through acts of bad faith, trickery, outright lies. You know what I mean."

Lily shifted uncomfortably. She knew where this was going. *But how could he know?* she thought. *He was too far off this morning to hear what was said, wasn't he?*

Now she felt like he was looking right through her. She turned away, trying to focus on the girls playing their music under the tree.

"There's a problem with the whole idea, though," Arlo said, persisting. "It's doomed for failure from the beginning."

"Why would that be?"

"That kind of conniving? It always comes back to bite you in the ass."

"How do you figure that?"

"'Cause every single person on this planet has the capacity for it. If it really worked, we'd live in chaos and kill each other off. Hell, we'd eat each other alive, if we thought we could make money on it. Who'd be left?"

Lily felt queasy. She swiped her damp forehead with her shirtsleeve and shuffled her feet, examining a crack in one of the porch steps.

"Course not every person has the stomach for it," Arlo said. "Just the capability. Mostly depends on character." He withdrew his finger from where it had been keeping his place, and stuffed the book into his pack. He shrugged. "At least, that's how I take it. In a nutshell."

"A nutshell, huh?" Lily said, almost under her breath.

That evening, instead of going home, Lily headed for her mother's house and from there the pair trekked up the side of the ridge. The footpath offered only a ribbon-narrow passage, meant for creatures who slid single file through mountain laurel and rhododendron. It was Sophia, not Lily who led both the way and the conversation.

Mamma was telling one of her favorite stories. Her words sometimes caught on sudden quick gusts blowing past Lily so she could only hear their sounds, but not catch their meaning. Not that it mattered. She'd heard the story before. Knew it by heart, and had even dragged Hannah up here so she could tell the story, herself. Unlike Sophia, though, Lily had never seen the ghost child.

Only Sophia had. According to her, it was a tiny ghost girl called Willow, who would trot along the path calling out to someone as she ran. Sophia had actually heard the child's voice, she said. Small and scared, trembling yet clear. Sometimes, though, the little figure would silently hurry along the ridge, as if trying to make it home before darkness settled. A mist always shrouded her, muting the outline of her small frame and somehow blending with the color of her smoke-colored nightgown.

Once, when she was young, Sophia had felt little hands brush her legs and had stepped aside, startled, letting the child pass and then disappear until the only sound left was of someone's feet rustling through leaves along the path ahead of her.

Now Mamma paused at a gap in the trees that opened the whole valley before them. She had stopped telling the story. Lily caught up to her, and they both looked down at the view. Lily could nearly see the top of her own chimney just a few ridgelines away. The red barn on Cat's farm was tiny but quite discernable. Most prominent was the steeple of the Union Calvary Church, the one that centered their little village. It was the point from which the whole settlement stemmed and spread in a circular expanse of mostly white houses, old fences, and fields on the outskirts edged by the bowl of the mountains.

"What are we doing up here?" Lily finally asked, huffing, her smoking habit evidencing itself.

"I was talking to Daddy . . ." Sophia began.

"Mamma!"

"Oh, now," Sophia patted her knee reassuringly, "what I meant was, Daddy's *spirit*." Sophia stopped her daughter's attempt to further protest. "Just listen to me for a minute."

Lily waited.

"Ever since I was a child, I've come up here to listen for that little lost Willow. Just seemed to make sense that I could come by to talk with your daddy, too. And, sure enough, it was his pipe smoke I smelled, right over there." Sophia pointed just yards away to the base of a big walnut. "You know how he would love to sneak away with his pipe and good book and rest under a big tree. Well, that's where his pipe smoke stopped me, right under that walnut!" Sophia's eyes were half-closed, a smile on her lips. "I actually laughed thinking how happy he must be to not have to sneak anymore."

Lily wasn't sure how worried she needed to be. Her mother had always been a little superstitious. Mostly it was harmless, and sometimes even seemed logical, like not stepping on cracks and planting potatoes in the moonlight to get the best yield. It was pretty much accepted in the family that Sophia and her own mother and grandmother before her had a small gift of Sight. Most mountain women had a bent toward it, Lily knew. Not Lily herself, though. She'd never even had so much as a goose bump. That said, it didn't really seem unusual that Sophia would have had an encounter with her dead husband, Lily's daddy.

Lily cautiously stepped over and eased down into the curve of the walnut, just as Jim might have. And just as his body must have, hers fit neatly into the hammock of its thick, exposed roots. Closing her eyes, Lily wished she could get one small whiff of her daddy's cherry tobacco. But there was nothing, no comfort even in knowing that he had probably been the last person to rest here. She couldn't sense any presence at all of her daddy, which saddened her. Quickly rising, Lily joined her mother back on the rock.

"So, what'd he say?"

"Said it was his shoelace untied."

"What?"

"The reason he fell off the ladder." Sophia looked at her daughter. "The old fool stepped on his own damn shoelace."

Now Lily saw the edge of tears tumbling in her mother's eyes.

"I asked what happened and he laughed. Said he felt silly admitting such a thing." Sophia was sobbing now.

Lily put her arm around her mother. "Ah, Mamma," she said. *"Rather go by my own foolish hand than by the wickedness of someone else's.* Remember what Granny used to say?"

Sophia straightened and gently shook Lily off. "Anyway, that's not why I brought you up here." She pulled a copy of Jim's will from her sweatshirt pocket and opened its blue cover. "I brought this," she said, smoothing the folds of the paper. "I haven't really been seeing it with a clear head. Until this morning."

Lily was somewhat uncomfortable having to view the document again. Especially up here on the side of a hill where the ghost of her father or some little lost girl might suddenly appear out of nowhere.

"Mamma, can't we go back down and do this in the kitchen?" She found herself shivering. Cat would have laughed at her for her silly superstitions. *I'm the Cat, but you're the Scairdy,* she would tease Lily when they were kids.

"Too much of a chance of one of the boys dropping by," Sophia was saying. "They come every day, one or another of them. Driving me batty."

Lily sighed and turned her attention to the flattened page. She read the passage and then read it again. Finally she looked at Sophia.

"I don't get it. If the business sells right now, we all split it evenly?"

"Well, you kids will split what's left after my share, which is half," Sophia underlined the sentences with her finger. "But, look, read here. *If under Lily Cameron's supervision, Cameron Construction thrives for five years henceforth, Lily Cameron will retain control of the full fifty shares not already owned by Sophia Wright Cameron."*

"So James would just as soon get rid of this responsibility and have his pittance now, rather than chance getting cut out down the road. Is that it?"

"Seems like it could be."

"Who decided that?"

Sophia shook her head. "I think your father saw it as a way for you to build security. Or to be fair in case you chose not to."

"But why did James make me keep it? Why not just convince me to sell now?"

"That's what I've been wondering. Which is why I sat down with all the paperwork today. There's something I didn't know about; a condition. Seems James agreed to run the business side of Cameron, to ensure its success. In five years, some kind of stock option investment plan goes into effect and whenever Cameron sells after that, James reaps big benefits."

"Depending on whether you and me decide to sell, right?"

"Yes, and of course, what its future worth would be." Sophia smiled. "In other words, if we get bigger and better, we'll be worth a lot and James would get a huge return on his investment, unless we chose to keep it . . . or . . ."

"Or . . ." Lily was having an *ah-ha!* moment, ". . . if we crash and burn, James could be out a bunch of money!" She felt half-triumphant, half-appalled at having figured out her brother. Almost. "But why the shift? How come he's been acting like he wants the business to fold?"

"I don't know that he does want it to fold."

"Says he thinks it's going to."

Sophia nodded and sighed. "But does he believe that? What if we sell our portions of Cameron now, with its good reputation, new equipment, and contracts, but James keeps his part—even maybe buys some of our stock. Then maybe puts the running of the company into some big moneymaker's hands."

"You mean he doesn't trust me," Lily said.

Sophia tried to put her arm around Lily's shoulder, but Lily was pacing now.

"How dare he not trust me! Next to my daddy, I'm the best fucking—sorry Mamma—carpenter in this whole county . . . maybe even the whole state!"

Sophia's eyes followed Lily as she strode back and forth, thumping her palm with her fist as she went.

"Do *I* doubt James' lawyerin'? Do *I* say, 'Hey James, let me come and poke around your business, make sure you're runnin' it right'? Hell no! *I* mind my own business. *I* got respect for my brother in his own field."

Sophia was nodding, patient, agreeable.

"Not that I respect much else about him. But that's beside the damn point." Lily waved her hands over her head. "Have I ever done anything to make anyone in this family doubt my abilities? Did I ever build a wall that fell down? A roof that collapsed? Doesn't Girls with Hammers have just as good a reputation as Cameron Construction? That little weasel lawyer, I oughta wring his goddamn neck!"

"Amen, sister!" Sophia said. "That's the spirit!"

"I'm not going to let James have his way with this one, Mamma. I'm just not. I'll give up Girls with Hammers if I have to . . ."

"No, Lily, I think there's a way that we might be able to have our cake and eat it, too. By hook or by crook, we'll just take control of this little old business. Don't forget, your mamma had a hand in building it, darlin'. You just stick with me."

Suddenly her mother sounded like a one-woman corporate takeover team. Like Arlo's Prince, she emanated a fierce confidence that Lily wasn't sure she liked.

"All right, Mamma," she soothed. "But we do this on the up-and-up from now on. I'm not gonna play James' lying games anymore. It wears me out trying to keep all the faces straight."

"Well, what do you propose? I already have some plans in mind."

"Gotta do it my way. I'll just do what I've always done, run the tightest, best crew I know how—in spite of my limited funds. First thing, I'm going to finish this Galway B-and-B. Because I know I can. We'll do a great job—and I'll show James. It's not work I like, but I am gonna make this a showplace."

"Now Lily, you don't have to prove anything to anyone."

In fact, Lily knew she had a lot of people that she had to prove a lot of things to. *Myself, mamma, she wanted to say. I gotta prove me to myself. To Daddy. Maybe even to Hannah. But she didn't say it to her mother, after all.*

The sun was beginning its slip behind the farthest ridgeline, bands of gold and crimson ribbon streaking layers across the sky. The two sat on the rock, leaning against each other for a little while, both lost in their own thoughts. It was Sophia who interrupted their contemplations.

"I think this might all work out for the good, Lily. It's kind of a mess right now, but things can be fixed. I've seen and been through much worse. We'll just take care of things as they come. And by the way, your doctor's appointment's coming up, don't forget. . . . One thing at a time, like you say."

Lily nodded, sighing. "Yeah, too much goes on and I just get all balled up. If I could get just one set of monkeys off my back, I'd be happy. Between James and Jeremiah Glock and Malcolm Galway, I'm chewing enough gristle to choke a bear."

"What's going on with Malcolm Galway?" Sophia asked.

"I told you about the busted tiles, Mamma. And then that *life-partner* of his, Patrick, he comes snoopin' around the site the other day."

"By himself?"

Lily frowned. She'd almost forgotten how annoying Patrick's visit had been. "Comes by himself with his little clipboard, which I wanted to shove up his ass after about two minutes." She glanced at her mother, "Sorry."

Sophia grinned, "I didn't spend half my life around tradesmen to be squeamish about a little cussin'."

"Right. Sorry." Now she was apologizing for *not* swearing. Sometimes you couldn't win around Sophia. "Anyway, that Patrick went around the place complaining about Malcolm being *too nice* about the *work in progress,* making little checkmarks and *tutting* noises, and calling me *Toots!*"

"Tutting noises?" Sophia echoed. "Toots?"

"It's a Yankee thing, you know, going *tut, tut, tut,* between his teeth and tongue every time he made a checkmark on his friggin' clipboard. Little pansy. Gay guys get on my nerves." Then, in spite of herself, Lily again said, "Sorry."

Sophia was looking at her with a small smile. "Lily, please stop apologizing to me. I am not some fragile flower who's about to wilt at an off-color remark!"

For the first time in her life, Lily was seeing a different mamma from the one she'd grown up with. This Sophia was more sophisticated than the plump little hen her children assumed. All those years Lily had spent at her daddy's knee, really never thinking much about

her mother. She was finding that Sophia was much more of a con-
tender—beyond the realms of domesticity—than her brothers or
even her father could possibly have known.

"Sorry. Guess I kinda forget myself sometimes. And you always
seem like such a *lady* to me. I mean—not that you ain't smart or anything—just delicate."

"It's all right, Lily." Sophia leaned into her daughter's shoulder. "I
know you've been your daddy's girl all your life. And me—well, after
having all those boys and suddenly getting me a girl, I was in heaven."
She was staring off—to the hills—to another time, maybe, Lily
thought. "I didn't have a chance with you," Sophia went on. "Your
brothers and most especially your daddy were so taken with a little
pink bundle around, why, I don't believe I fed you more than twice,
myself, once you were weaned. Those boys, one or three of them,
would jump the minute you fussed. They changed your diaper,
rocked you, carried you on their backs," she paused and folded her
arms across her chest.

Lily tried to imagine brothers acting all goofy over her. What she
actually remembered was quite different. They'd teased the fire out of
her, knuckle her thighs, or set off firecrackers in her dolls. Once,
Kevin had chopped off a braid while she slept.

Sophia said, "We didn't even know if you could actually walk by
yourself until the time when you were two and a half and we'd found
you alone, asleep in the barn. Your daddy swore you were just trying
to get away from all the attention."

"Guess James changed his feelings about me some since then," Lily
said darkly.

Her mother took on a sad look. Lily wondered if it bothered Sophia
to have her children battling like this.

"Well, dear, it does seem like those men have abandoned us—to
one degree or another. So, it's now time for the women of this family
to band together. That would be you and me."

Sophia stood and looked at Lily. "Let's not be thinking about what
your daddy would expect. Let's think about what you want for yourself, Lily. What's *your* dream?"

It stopped her to have her mother ask this question. All her life, she'd told her daddy that she wanted to be her own boss with her own carpentry company. Now she was being pulled in all sorts of directions. She was fighting James, taking on someone else's business dream, trying to align herself with her mother's ambitions for her. But she knew deep down that Girls with Hammers would always be what she really wanted, and she knew she would have to confess this to her mother.

"I just want everything to work out . . ." she said softly to Sophia. Her mother nodded. They turned to head back. As they passed by the old walnut tree, Lily paused to tighten a shoelace. The waft of cherry pipe tobacco circled her, engulfing her like a cloak, and there was no doubt as to its origin. She remained squatted, breathing, testing her senses and sensibilities at the same time. She thought to stop her mother, to call her back to verify—but then the scent was gone. Lily sped up, and fell in behind Sophia. They walked in silence, downhill. After a moment she said, "The truth is, Mamma, I just want Girls with Hammers back, same as always."

Ten

Over the next few weeks, the job began to tighten up. The remaining crew, including Dolly, the two Ahs, the Jennies, and Arlo, were beginning to find a nice rhythm together. Every morning at ten, Lily and Arlo would jump rope while the band turned the time into a practice session. Most of them had cut back on their cigarette smoking, with the exception of Laura, whose daily disdain for Arlo seemed to be calibrated by the number of cigarettes she smoked and by how hard she smoked 'em. Lily noticed that the closer she, Lily, became to Arlo, the more of a fiend Laura became.

Lily also noticed that in addition to matching Arlo's rope-jumping cadence, the pair had been developing a working rhythm. It reminded her of the way that she and Cat used to move together, like two lumberjacks on either end of a newly waxed crosscut saw, just a smooth push and pull with no jamming the blade. There'd been moments with Arlo when she'd reach for a hammer or drill and before her fingers could make the tool, it would land neatly in her palm, as if Arlo had read her mind or at the very least, anticipated her move. She tried to stay focused on this work relationship, but she'd had moments when she found herself staring at him, or when in the pass of that tool from his hands to hers, if by chance his fingers might linger upon or brush her own, heat would burn in her cheeks and she would look away, downward by preference.

As carpenters, the girls with their hammers were shaping up nicely, Lily thought as she made her way through the B & B. They were now into the finish work. She'd put Dolly to the final tasks in the barn building. "You've had enough experience," she told Dolly, who smiled with the praise. Lily felt that she could be trusted. Dolly was meticulous, detail oriented, and amazingly quick. No board could stand askew and no door would swing ajar after Dolly got done with them. The Jennies, it turned out, had a knack for cutting and coping crown and base molding—a skill you either had a gift for or not. Each morning, Lily noticed, the pair jumped from the van and fairly skipped to their work stations, smiling warmly at each other and teasing about how together they were the best finish-carpentry couple in the country. That very morning, from the back of the van, White Jennie had admitted, "We feel like we're falling in love all over again. Don't we, baby?" Black Jenny, with her head resting on her girlfriend's shoulder, said, "It's like when we first played the whistle together—we're simpatico and symbiotic. Not to mention syncopated. Pure symmetry."

Lily would have preferred to work with Arlo as a team, but the imbalance of the pairing made it impossible. Laura hated Arlo and Micah hated Laura. Doing the math put Micah happily by Arlo's side and left Lily reluctantly dragging Laura behind her. Mostly the angry little woman remained quiet. Lily would stick her on some job that she could do by herself, which seemed to content her. The few times that there had been a two-girl job, Lily found Laura to be a somewhat reluctant participant, although once, she helped Lily figure out a quick system for hanging shutters. In spite of this seeming easiness on the surface, there was something rumbling beneath Laura's cold exterior. As much as she tried, Lily just could not bring herself to trust the girl.

It really had little to do with the way Laura picked at Arlo. While Lily could have done without the daily poking and near accusations, Arlo seemed to take it all in stride and so she, Lily, tried to ignore it. And although it was really aggravating when Laura would quote from books or movies or drag out whole articles to prove her points, Lily couldn't help finding some of the information interesting. The last theory Laura had broached with the group came from a *Psychology for the New Age* magazine, which noted that there appeared to be a growing phenomenon of homeless adolescent males roaming the country and living in woods.

"A *symptom,* the article suggested . . ." Laura said, knowingly, ". . . found in boys raised by fathers who'd joined the *Iron John Men's Movement* of the early nineties."

And the last thing that Lily had to admit, regardless of how much anger seemed to be brewing beneath that red hair, Laura could play that guitar of hers. She got lost in it. With her eyes closed, she was riding riffs that hypnotized herself and everyone around her. It was similar to the way Lily got lost in carving a piece of wood, or Cat in writing down her stories. Lily felt that deep down there was a genuine love of peace inside Laura.

But today you wouldn't know it. When Laura had slammed into the back of the van that morning it was like a suffocating cloud of ugliness had been dragged in with her. Her mood and the matching expression on her face were foul. If she had been a cartoon, Lily thought as she peeked at her in the rearview mirror, there would be steam coming out of Laura's ears.

"What's the matter, Laura?" Dolly asked, turning around in her seat. "You look upset."

"Nothing," was what she said.

Something was definitely up, Lily thought. Let her sulk. She'll come around.

But by noon Laura had not only *not* come around, she had become downright ornery, snapping at Dolly for walking off with a hammer, kicking a pail of mud that had hardened up unexpectedly, even though it was she who'd left it open overnight. When Laura slinked to the back of the van to eat her lunch, rather than on the porch with the rest of them, they all began to speculate.

Dolly wondered if she'd been dumped.

"Who would be with her to begin with?" White Jennie rolled her eyes.

"Now, Jen," Black Jenny said. "You might be a little forgiving today. The girl is obviously in distress."

"Well, I pity the poor soul who got fooled into thinking there was a human being in there. Hard-core ice queen if you ask me."

"Maybe," Arlo ventured, "she's having her time of the month?"

"Hah! Typical male response," White Jennie accused. "If a woman is moody or upset it must be *female troubles*." She glared at him.

"Now, now, don't go getting your drawers in a knot." Arlo eased her down gesturing with his palms toward the ground. "That's not what I meant. I just meant that it's a fact; women go through these physical changes that affect emotions and their bodies and, and—all kinds of things. Am I right?" He looked around for support.

After a few moments, Lily burst out laughing. And the rest had their way with him:

"Did you see his face? So serious."

"He's gonna make some girl a sensitive husband."

"Raised by a pack of women, all right."

Arlo reddened.

"Neanderthal!"

He stood and they all snickered. Making to leave, he headed down the stairs. Before he made his way across the yard he turned and faced them.

"You know, you women are a bunch of hypocrites."

"What's that supposed to mean?" Dolly asked, stung. She was being the least hard on him.

"You want men to be *sensitive*—to *listen*. You want to be *heard*. And when we do, you act even worse than the men you accuse. Hell, I'm not afraid to talk about sexuality, or my feelings, or to listen to yours. I know all about *cycles* and *convergence* and *moon times* and *tides*. If you think I don't notice when you're all just a little edgier, poutier, crankier, and weepier, well you're wrong! I know exactly what's going on!" He spun on his heel and walked off down the road.

"Dang," Lily said, watching him stride off. "I think we hurt his feelings."

"Must have."

"Wonder if he'll come back," White Jennie murmured. Then she giggled.

"All right now," Lily warned. "No more laughing at poor Arlo. He was trying to be helpful." And then she laughed again, herself. She knew he'd be back, if only to prove how he—as a man—would not ignore his responsibilities. There was also a part of her that admired the guy for his candor, as sloppily sensitive as it appeared. Growing up with a bunch of insensitive older brothers made you appreciate these younger men with their feelings.

While Arlo's unexpected moodiness had been a small distraction, it still did not change the cloud around Laura. After lunch, while she was fastening down some closet flooring, Lily thought to broach her, but when she got near enough to ask what was going on, Laura growled and just kept banging nails. Lily decided Dolly had probably been right. Someone—lord knew who—had probably dumped Laura.

It was late in the afternoon when yelling brought all the girls running out to the courtyard. The Prestige Electric guys were cleaning up the last of their stuff, having nearly finished the wiring—all without another incident between Jeremiah and Lily, except for a couple of reciprocal snubs every now and again.

But the scene before her spurred Lily to the center of the courtyard. Arlo and Jeremiah had squared off. An expensive nail gun, belonging to the Cameron crew, was on the ground between them. From the back of his usually spiffy white T-shirt, Lily could tell that Arlo had, at least once, rolled, or been rolled, on the dusty ground. There was a small cut above Jeremiah's eye, from Arlo's knuckles, Lily reckoned. What was going on?

Bobby Dean was poised on the outskirts and Lily positioned herself on the opposite side, where she could jump him if he got into this. She noticed that it didn't look like Bobby was fixing to do much of anything except watch.

"Whoa! Whoa!" Lily yelled. It didn't stop them, so she threw a high-pitched whistle into the air using her two fingers, the way her brothers had taught her when she was a kid. Neither Arlo nor Jeremiah unlocked their grip. Their eyes held as they circled each other like tomcats in an alley.

"Hey now," Lily yelled again, this time getting closer to the pair. But Arlo hissed at her, "Get back!"

She stepped sideways just as Jeremiah's bare fist came swinging by her chin, swiping only a whisker's distance from Arlo's. Following his arching sweep, Jeremiah's body dove forward and Arlo cracked down on his neck with the back of his elbow, holding him pinned to the ground like that. Arlo looked at the group now circling him. A purpling bruise, Lily noticed, was egging on his temple.

"He was making off with the nail gun."

"Wasn't me," Jeremiah moaned from below Arlo's knee. "It was him. Lemme up an' I'll prove it."

"Let him up," Bobby Dean said.

Lily nodded.

Jeremiah got up, spitting dirt from his mouth, and wiped his eyes before he spoke. He glared at Arlo.

"I ain't the thief here. Ask him who's the thief, 'cause it ain't me. Yeah, y'all think he's so squeaky clean. I mighta been in the can on account of drunk and disorderly, but not 'cause I was no thief. Not like this guy." He thumbed toward Arlo. "He was there." Jeremiah was looking at them all, now. "Him and me was in jail together. Over in Marion, two years ago." His angry eyes swung back to Arlo. "Tell 'em," he said.

Everyone was staring at Arlo now, even Lily. But especially Laura. Arlo, on the other hand, was searching the ground. Then he looked up at Lily and said, "Sure, I was there all right. But you're wrong about my charge. I was in for vagrancy. Not robbing." He looked away again.

Even though she felt his shame, she didn't drop her eyes. "That true, Arlo?" she asked, her voice soft. "'Cause there ain't no shame in that."

"I didn't have a place to stay that winter." He shrugged. "Got picked up sleeping on a park bench and they threw me in jail for the weekend." He looked back at Jeremiah. "Truth is, I was thankful for a warm bed and a hot meal."

"You're a liar!" Jeremiah pointed his finger and then swung around and pointed at Lily. "And *you're* a liar. What you said about me!" he looked around at the others. "And the rest of you are working for liars. Be sure this'll all come back at you. Lying begets lying. It's in the Bible. It's *sin!*" Jerking away, he yelled at Bobby Dean, "I'm taking vacation. Call me when you get off this fucking nutcase job."

Not until the next morning, when she showed up solo on the job site, did Lily get a chance to talk with Arlo alone. She carried two cups of coffee to the porch where he waited.

"Where are the girls?" he asked, his eyes searching the van behind Lily.

"I gave them the day. I thought we all could use some time off."

"Yeah?"

"And I wanted to talk with you alone."

Side by side, they sat on the railing overlooking the low-lying wooded valley, whose middle was cleared and cut by a swath of dark green rolling terrain all the way to the creek bed beyond. Lily blew across the top of her coffee. She noticed the swelling on his forehead and resisted the urge to touch it with light fingers.

"So, yesterday," she began, "when that little prick had you on him, what set that off?"

He shrugged. "Don't know exactly. He was carrying off the nail gun case. I told him to drop it, but he wouldn't. Said I was accusing him of stealing. Brought up that he was thinking about how he and I were in jail that time, and did my boss know. Said I was the thief here. So I hit him."

Lily grinned. "He makes you want to, doesn't he?"

"Haven't wanted to do anything like that for a very long time," Arlo said. His voice was quiet, subdued. "Not to anyone."

"Yeah, well he deserved what he got. He's outta our hair now and that's all I care about."

"You sure?"

"What? That he's not out of our hair? That joker's a weenie. Always was, always will be. He's a loser, Arlo."

"I'm thinking it might be time for me to move along."

"Leave?!" Lily's heart sped and a dread began to fill her. "Why? Why leave now? Things are good, *between us* (she almost said). "I mean things are going good. We're getting done. I couldn't have done any of this without you," she said, shyly.

"I don't like causing scenes," he began.

She interrupted, "Yeah, well, I'd rather have the scene than eat the cost of a nail gun." She leaned back, sipping her coffee, wondering how she could get into it.

"That's why it's probably time for me to go. You can finish with the rest of the crew." He looked at her.

Their eyes held and now Lily did reach to his forehead and he let her. "That's quite a bump you've got there." Gently she caressed the bruise and brushed his hair from his eyes. And then she stopped. Quickly and suddenly exposed, she almost did not know where to place the wayward hand; as if of its own volition, dropping to her lap, she wrapped her fingers around her coffee cup. She looked to the woods—for some distance—trying to obliterate her self-created intimacy. "So," she said, changing the subject, "about you being in jail."

He looked at her. His eyes caught the sun but he didn't look away. "Everything I said was true, Lily." He raised his hand. "Scout's honor. I was a vagrant. Just like I am, now. Have been for a while."

"Why, though?" Lily had been wondering about this. He'd talked about his family and how much he loved them. Why wasn't he living with them?

"To tell the truth, my mamma's mad at me. Ever since I said I was going to find my daddy, Mamma won't speak to me."

"I thought she wanted to see him again."

"That's what I thought, too." Arlo shook his head, then sipped his coffee. "Guess she wants to let it rest. Leave him be. Let bygones be bygones, she says."

"Kind of hard when the bygone is your own daddy," Lily sympathized.

"That's the truth of it."

"So, you're living out in the woods 'cause . . .?" She hoped he would fill in the blanks, which he did.

" 'Cause, I'm trying to save enough money to find my daddy, and then go back to college."

"*Back* to college?" Lily asked.

"Yeah, I've already done two years."

"What'd you study?"

"Poetry, mainly. Some philosophy and a lot of literature. Useless to most, but I love the stuff."

"My friend Cat's a writer. Went to college for all that. Now she's in Scotland."

"Doing what?" Arlo asked, politely.

"Teaching little Scottish girls about American literature." Lily said this, and suddenly felt proud, somehow.

"Do you miss her?"

Lily grinned. "Like the devil."

He looked a little shy. "She like a *girlfriend* or something?"

Lily laughed outright. "Heck, no!"

He shrugged.

"I got Hannah for that," Lily said, quickly. "Me and Cat have just been best friends since we were six years old. She's a writer—has a book and everything. A collection of stories," she said. "Do you write stories?"

"No, some poetry, mostly. I like reading it, taking it apart. I do that with most every kind of writing. Fiction, plays, philosophy, even history. That's why I want to go back to college."

"So you can teach that stuff?" Lily asked, concerned.

He laughed. "Or are you asking what will become of me?"

"No, I mean, what do you want to be when you grow up?" she said, grinning.

Arlo hesitated, then reached behind him and pulled a thick three-ring binder from his backpack. He handed it to her and Lily thumbed through. The different colored tabs marked the well-worn pages. His handwriting in pencil or black ink had headed sections of the entries with titles like *Humanities 213* or *Literature 356*. Below these were what looked like lecture notes, homework assignments, and the like. Interspersed were penciled poems, erased and changed, some scratched out or with reminders. There was even a beginning of a story for what looked like a creative writing class.

"What is all this?" Lily finally asked.

"Well, after I had to drop out of college, I couldn't stand the thought of falling behind. I know enough about how classes work.

The first few days you can get away with being there, even if you're not signed in. Sometimes the professors don't know about it till the end, when they get their grading lists and discover that you're not even on it. This way, you can get the course syllabi, schedules, and book lists, and now with so many courses outlined on the Web, you can even get your nightly homework. It's easy to keep up."

"Keep up?" Lily was feeling rather astonished.

"Sometimes, when I can afford it, I buy the used books. I use the computers in the library any time with my library pass, which you can get even if you're not a student. Did you know that?"

Lily shook her head.

"Big lectures are easy to get into . . . no one even notices you. Most professors are happy to talk about their classes or ideas or if you pretend to be interviewing them . . . those guys love to talk about their stuff."

"And you do this to *keep up*?"

"Right." He smiled at her.

"But you're not getting any credit for it."

"Yeah, well, if I was doing it the legitimate way, it'd be called an audit, but that still costs money and you kind of have to stick to the schedule and arrange the workload with the professor. As soon as I save up enough money, I'll pay the tuition and get the credit. In the meantime, I'm keeping abreast of things."

"Then what?" Lily herself had never had much interest in a college degree. Not like Cat who'd spent over six years doing it, over in Greensboro, while Lily was working on her apprenticeship. The apartment they had shared had been consistently cluttered with mounds of papers and stacks of books and poor Cat pretty much buried under it all. It wasn't real, Lily remembered thinking once, as she listened to Cat's fretting about homework assignments. It wasn't real, all that worrying about where the comma's supposed to go. Real was making sure that beam you just raised wasn't going anywhere.

Arlo interrupted her thoughts. "After that, I want to go to England to study Blake. He was one crazy fella. But a great poet! Maybe I'll get a doctorate at Oxford and become a literature professor."

"Blake. You can get a doctorate in one particular guy?"

Arlo's laugh cut the air. "Pretty much. I'm guessing a bunch of others have already done that. I'll find something else. But I love Blake. He was a genius, both an artist and a writer. He had visions and was visited by ghosts his whole life. That'd make you nutty, wouldn't it?"

Lily nodded.

"Course he did get married. His wife helped him write down all his stuff. He did all these amazing illustrations—a lot of them had religious themes. But he pretty much died unknown."

"Sad," Lily managed.

"He wrote one poem that's my favorite. About seeing the world in a grain of sand, heaven in a wildflower. . . . Ever hear of it?"

"I might have read it on a greeting card, I think."

"Poor Blake, if he only knew his life's work had been condensed and reproduced onto some acid-free paper courtesy of Hallmark."

"Well, shouldn't poetry be for everyone?" Lily asked.

"I guess. I guess there's just a part of me that thinks it should be cherished, not exploited."

Lily let that sit between them. She didn't know enough about literature to be suddenly debating its worth. She looked over at him. At the determined way he carried himself and the almost always present half-smile that lingered on his lips. There was something so serious about Arlo—something substantial and real, she thought, and yet innocent. She wondered if he really did believe in himself—in his writing—the way Cat did. Or was he too modest and naive to be able to be successful? Finally she asked, "So, why a professor? Why not be like Blake and write your own stuff. Let somebody teach about *your* work?" She dusted her seat as she stood.

The question seemed to slow him as he rose with her. He pursed his lips and looked thoughtful. "I guess I've wanted to be a professor ever since I saw *Educating Rita*."

"Stop it." He was teasing her now. But he did it with such a straight face she almost believed him.

"OK then. I've wanted to be a professor ever since my mother said that finding my father and going to college were equally fruitless pursuits. How's that for an answer?"

"More like the truth," Lily said. "But I'm guessing that's only knee-jerk reasoning. Why really?"

They began their descent down the stairs into the yard.

Arlo thought for a while and then looked at her. "Because I love the stuff. Poetry, I mean. Literature. Because when I see the volumes and volumes lining library shelves, I get panicky thinking that I'll never have enough time to read them all in my lifetime. But if it were my job I might have a chance. And because I'm smart enough, and I love it enough, I know I'd be great at it."

Here was that confidence again—and all that passion. He did remind her of Cat, and in some ways he reminded Lily of herself, as well. She'd always known she could be a great carpenter, mainly because when you're smart enough and love something enough, it stands to reason that you'd be really good at it. Being a girl had never interfered with her dreams. Just like Arlo: being a vagrant didn't seem to be getting in the way of his ambitions. In fact, maybe it was exactly the opposite. This gypsy life seemed to have honed his imagination very well.

"Why don't you take some classes?" Lily suggested. "They can add up, you know."

"No, I want to be a real student, full-time, someday."

Lily climbed into the van and started it. Arlo had retrieved his backpack and slung it over his shoulder. She grinned at him. "So I don't have to worry about you being some kind of desperado bank robber or worse, now, do I?"

Arlo shook his head and laughed. "Just a lousy bum, ma'am. But I am willing to earn my keep."

Lily waved. "Well, have a nice weekend. Get some studying done."

But Arlo had already turned and was striding toward the clump of trees that bordered the back of the property. As Lily drove away, she tried to recall that quote from Blake again. *Grains of sands in heavens and wildflowers. . . .* She struggled to think of it. She wanted to remember it to tell Cat, but she was sure she had it wrong. Who remembers that kind of gunk? But, then she was glad that Arlo could remember stuff like that at the drop of a hat. Somebody had to.

When Lily got home, she'd read the e-mail from Hannah telling her about a trip to London, from which the group had just returned. The message went on about how amazing the city was and how they'd toured the Victoria and Albert Museum and how the clever German, Hoerst, had enchanted them with stories and legends surrounding the histories of all that they'd viewed. Hannah then confided that she loved the German, but the brilliant lesbian was a challenging presence. The pair had even taken to staying up late and arguing world politics, Hannah seemed to despair. But Lily thought she detected a hint of pleasure in these left-handed complaints about the passionately embattled debates, and it was this that was making Lily nervous.

Eleven

Once she had finished remodeling the living room, cleaning out closets and reorganizing the work van had taken up much of Lily's weekend. But, she'd also slept some and answered e-mails from Hannah and Cat, and she had made herself a gourmet meal. By the time Monday morning rolled around, she felt refreshed and alive and was only hoping that the rest of the gang was too. Mostly she was hoping that Laura had slipped from her melancholy state and was ready to at least be somewhat sociable.

What she encountered was not even close to what she'd been praying for. Sure, Laura had changed her tune—hell, she was nearly euphoric; grinning and handing out Hersheys Kisses the minute she climbed in the van. Humming a little Celtic tune and smiling at each of them, Laura might just have joined the Krishnas or spent her weekend getting laid; whichever it was, Lily was relieved by Laura's shifted attitude—no matter how she came by it. Whatever gets you through the night, Lily thought. She was just happy that everybody was happy. Unfortunately, all that happiness was short-lived. The scene that opened before them, as they approached the B & B, was a circus.

There was a mob (that's how Lily saw it) milling around a small swatch of earth, outside the big house, a bunch of men looking practically stitched together. They stood with disapproving matching furrowed brows and pursed lips all turning toward the van as she swung the truck into the driveway.

"What the fuck is going on?" she asked, confounded, startling the blissful bunch in the back. Dolly leaned forward, squinting, counting and then naming the figures before them.

"Your brother, James, Lil. Your mother, too." She glanced sideways at Lily as she also worriedly surveyed the scene. The collective breath of her crew was hot on her neck.

"Get back," she almost yelled, then surveying and running up her own tab on the gathered bystanders. There were the Galway boys, Malcolm and Patrick, Bobby Dean, a cop, and Jeremiah Glock. Glock?!

Lily rolled the van around the bunch, circling like a warrior around a wagon train. Only she didn't feel like the attacker, she felt like a lamb about to be slaughtered.

"Oh boy," she uttered. "This is not how I was plannin' to start my day."

"Where's Arlo?" Laura asked.

"He's probably laying low," Micah said defensively. "Knowing him, he's smart enough to hang back till the dust clears."

"Or at least till we got here," Dolly assured. "He'll show."

"All right now," Lily said as she cut the engine. "Everybody, just keep your mouths shut till we find out what's going on, OK?" She glanced back, for assenting nods. "Lord knows what this is all about."

Climbing from the van, she had no time to take more than a few steps before she was surrounded. Voices descended upon her, until she finally reached the cop and pulled him by the sleeve away from the rest.

"Why Jake McCann, I haven't seen you since high school," Lily said, relieved to know the face behind the badge. In this case, she could have been even a little too familiar. Lily smiled, thinking how funny it was that Little Galway's very own sheriff also had once been the boy who rode his motorcycle buck naked down the hallway and through the gymnasium of the Mountain Stretch High School. Course, that was back in the seventies when streaking had been the craze.

Jake grinned shyly. The crook of his front tooth the same as it was that day when, after his capture, he was led smiling and waving and wrapped in a quilt donated by the girls in Mrs. Schreck's Home Ec class, to a waiting sheriff's patrol car much like the one he now drove himself.

"Lily Cameron," he said, nodding. "Been a long time."

"Seems so, and then not," she said, with her own little grin.

"Sorry to hear about your daddy."

"Thanks. Hey, I heard you were a cop. Guess that run-in back in seventy-nine had some kind of effect." She smiled.

"It did. I had to stand buck naked before my own mamma and look her in the eye," Jake said. "That'll teach anybody a lesson, you reckon?"

"How is your mamma?" Lily remembered the feisty old widow who kept a cob pipe clamped between her teeth and a tall hickory pole by her side. It was said that she would beat any one of her eight sons with that stick if he got out of line. It was also said that she turned out one last kid at age fifty. To Lily, old lady McCann had looked like Methuselah's wife herself—shriveled to a tanned prune.

"She's still kickin'." Jake smiled. "Mellowed a little. Now she just carries a cane."

Lily laughed and then there was a small silence and they both looked to the ground.

Jake, shy all over again, asked, "You still keep up with Cat Hood?"

Lily then recalled the crush that Jake had had on Cat back then. He'd been adolescent awkward and only once had advanced an invitation to a movie to which Cat had diplomatically replied, "If I were ever going to like a boy, Jake McCann, it would be you. But you know that I like girls better."

Jake McCann had gotten the best kind of rejection a fella could have asked for, as far as Lily could see.

"I do keep up with Cat," Lily said. "She wrote that book, you know."

"My wife, Doreen Connelly—you remember her? She read it. Has it right on the coffee table with Cat's autograph inside."

Lily nodded. She was now growing impatient with all the catching up. It was part of the routine, this she knew; but she wanted to know what the hell was going on. She scanned the tree line behind the sheriff, hoping for a glimpse of Arlo, but he was scarce.

"So, Jake," she finally asked, "what on earth are we all doing out here this fine morning?" She was trying to sound as casual as if they were at Sunday services.

Jake straightened up, back to being to the professional law enforcement officer he'd become. If he called her ma'am, Lily thought, she'd have to hit him. But he didn't. He didn't even have his clipboard. He just nodded for her to follow him inside the house, where no words were needed for an explanation.

Lily could see that the place had been vandalized as she made her way around the interior. Tools, the ones she was accustomed to leaving on site, had been taken or trashed. Big holes had been kicked in the new drywall. Spray-painted scrawls of black, red, and green obscenities ran throughout the house: *Homos get out, queers fuck hammers,* and there were swastikas and other symbols of hate crudely drawn. The upstairs master bedroom sported the most vile stuff. Someone had urinated in the stone fireplace and above this scribbled, only just legibly, *Die, Faggots!*

Lily felt like she'd been kicked. A repressed choking sound was the only response she could manage. "Let's get out of here. It's makin' me sick."

On the landing before they went outside, Jake stopped her. "Any idea who might've done this?"

"Maybe. But it could have been kids."

"What about that Glock fella?" He gestured outside. "Heard ya'll had a run-in."

"Yeah, I don't know what he's doing here."

"Your brother James, at your mother's insistence, made Bobby Dean bring him by my office. Any chance of him being the culprit?"

"We did have that run-in," Lily said. "Two to be exact. But I can't see him being this stupid this soon afterward."

"Anyone else?"

Lily did not let her fleeting thought escape her mouth. She could hardly believe that her mind had run straight to James, her own brother, as a conspirator, and so she dispelled the notion with a shake of her head and stepped out into the sunlight alongside Jake.

The "mob" had moved to the shade of the porch, where they were huddled; her girls were standing a ways off smoking, and James was pacing while the Galway boys sniped back and forth about their suspicions of who had done it. In their panic, they resurrected hate crimes from Stonewall to Matthew Shepard, and were convinced that they were next on the KKK's extermination list. "Bad enough the Negroes have to contend with this—now us?" Patrick said, his nasal Alabama accent cutting through the neutrality he'd cultivated while living over in Charlotte. For a gay guy, Lily thought, you sure are a racist pecker. Meanwhile, Jeremiah was sitting on the porch with his back to a corner, shifting his eyes from one face to another. Only Bobby Dean and Sophia seemed relaxed. They were swapping old stories about cousins once and twice removed as Lily and Jake drew near.

"Well?" James jumped toward his sister expectantly.

"Well?" The Galway boys ran toward them and chimed in.

Everyone was looking at her. Only Laura did her the favor of not targeting her with questions. The redhead was busy, filing away on her purple nails.

"Well, it's a mess," Lily said to one and all. "It's a lot of work wrecked and a lot of work to fix." She looked around. "Anybody got a clue? I don't suppose you did this, Glock?" she asked, point blank.

"I *knew* that's why ya'll brought me here! I *knew* the minute I saw this mess ya'll would be blamin' it on me." He looked around to them. "Hit weren't no more me than hit were me stealin' tools the other day." He spat. "That's the dang truth."

Somehow, Lily believed him. Stupid as he was, she didn't think Jeremiah would do something so blatant after all that had gone down the week before.

"Anyway, where's your boy?" Jeremiah asked Lily. "I ain't seen him around. Bet it was him done it."

It was Arlo to whom Glock was obviously referring. It was a question that repeated itself with the turn of each head, as if Glock's query was a call for a search party.

Suddenly Laura seemed more interested in the situation. "Yeah, haven't seen much of him since that altercation last week." She looked over at Jake McCann. "Mr. Glock here and Arlo Halsey, our co-worker, served time in prison together, you know. They had an argument that ended pretty ugly. Mr. Halsey hasn't been seen since."

"That's ridiculous," Lily said. "Arlo went right back to work and you know it, Laura."

"What was the argument about?" the sheriff asked, now taking out his notepad and pen.

"It doesn't matter, Jake," Lily argued. "This hasn't got one thing to do with the other. Personally, I don't think Jeremiah here had the balls to do this. And Arlo wouldn't have a reason to do it. It's vandalism and we've got to set to fixin' it. OK, girls?"

But James was shaking his head. "Need a police report," he insisted. "For insurance purposes."

Now the Galway boys jumped in, demanding justice against this *heinous hate crime,* as they called it. James reverted to his own brand of lawyerly calming, but to no avail. The Galways knew a frontal attack on their freedom to be gay when they saw one, they said. There'd be no calming them, Lily knew. Hell, she really couldn't blame them. She'd watched swishy boys get beat up every day all through middle school, before their parents could send them off to military school to try to turn them into *real* men. It never worked and in most cases just made it worse. If they didn't quit or get tossed out, a lot of them tried to kill themselves. No wonder the poor buggers were nervous.

Sheriff Jake finally raised his hands in the air and backed off, saying he was calling for reinforcements. He sat in his patrol car with the radio till his deputy arrived. The day was blown, Lily knew, as everyone took turns reciting anything they could remember over the past few days. Even Mamma and Jeremiah had their chances to speculate.

Lily left them all and went to sit in the cab of the van. Let 'em all talk themselves out, she decided. In here, in spite of the heat, she could breathe a little easier. No one else was around to suck her air away. Through the windshield, Lily caught a glimpse of Laura searching the tree line. She's hunting for Arlo too, Lily figured, only for different reasons. She felt queasy now. She wasn't sure if it was because of some fear she was feeling for him, or from a fear *of* him. Did she really know this Arlo fella? What if he had made up a pack of lies?

But then she remembered how he'd looked at her that day on the porch. How her fingers had brushed his bruised forehead; how his eyes hid beneath thick lashes, shadowed, intriguing her stare; she'd wanted in there. Because in there was something real, something raw and sexy igniting the same in her. And this is why she knew Arlo couldn't have done the vandalism. He felt it too, and this she could tell by the heat of his breath, when she got that close.

Her mother's voice coaxed her from her mind's wanderlust. The day had been wasted and Lily, once again, would be shelling out money to people who didn't work for a minute. Sophia had joined her in the cab, forcing Dolly behind with the rest of the crew. Instead of leaving with James, Sophia said, "Just drive."

Hours later, on matching stools at the bar in OzGirlz, Lily and Sophia sat shoulder to shoulder, sucking back margaritas. Lily'd pulled Ruthie aside and made her promise to load the drinks with ice. They'd ordered a giant plate of layered nachos and cheese and beans and, *"whatever else you can think to heap on there,"* Sophia had told the little hippie chick with the dangling blue dreadlocks. Their nachos arrived and Sophia looked over at Lily. "Helluva day, huh?"

"Damn, Mamma." Lily chewed the stem of a cherry she'd snagged from the bar. "Things are so screwy. I don't know what to believe or what's even going on. None of this makes sense and all of it is making me crazy."

"Who do you think did it?" Sophia lifted her glass and held it to her forehead.

Lily sighed. "Seems like it shouldn't be any one of them. Then I can just as easily reason out how it could be nearly all of them." She laughed. "Hell, I could reason out how it could even be me!"

"Oh, Lily."

"I mean, anybody's motives could be enough, Mamma."

"What do you mean?" Now, Sophia seemed to be encouraging a most taboo exploration.

"Like . . . I did wonder if it could've been James. I mean, now I'm thinking he wants rid of me. I know he's your kid, too, so I don't expect you to agree with me."

"Of course I don't agree with you, Lily Nelda Cameron! We're hardly one of those Shakespearian families—falling on intrigue and power, toppling monarchies and each other."

"Shakespearian families? Mamma, what are you talking about?"

"Oh, you know all those plays. My book group has just finished reading them. I never did pay much attention in high school. That

King Lear—he was a harried old coot—all those daughters fighting over him. Whew! What a lot of dysfunction going on in those families."

"Book group?"

"Didn't I tell you? You remember Georgia Stetson? She was at your daddy's funeral. Anyway, she told me about this reading group that was just getting started. Said it was a real good thing to get into reading—for a widow, an all."

"Mamma, you don't like to read."

Sophia looked at her daughter. "What do you know about what I like?"

Good question. What did she know about what her mother liked? Lily wondered. Sitting before her was a woman who was uncannily familiar and then not, like running into a skinny friend who suddenly got fat.

"There are times when I don't know myself what I like," Sophia said quietly. "Now that Daddy's gone I'm even more unsure, or surprised, or even shocked by what I find I like. I do like reading. I like going down to Galway to the art museum, and to that little coffee shop with all those beautiful European girls and pastries behind the counter. I like going to the Indy Theatre and watching French films with subtitles."

Lily watched as Sophia twisted her napkin. A small smile made a feeble push against the trembling around her mouth, then a single tear spilled and splashed. Lily reached across the table and covered the wetness on the back of her mother's hand. "Oh, Mamma . . ."

Sophia raised her head and looked over Lily's shoulder, across the room, maybe even past the brick of the wall. "I miss being touched," she said, and then brought her eyes to meet her daughter's.

Lily felt the heat of the intimation burn in her cheeks, but she did not, as badly as she wanted to, break the hold of her mother's gaze.

"Me and your daddy . . ." Sophia's words came haltingly. "We'd always fall asleep wrapped around each other. Like a couple of spoons in a drawer. Till now, I didn't know how much I liked that."

The image of her mamma and daddy snuggling each other in the darkness of their bed made Lily embarrassed and happy and sad all at once. It sparked her own longing for what she liked and missed with Hannah. But unlike Sophia, Hannah would be (hopefully) returning to the scoop of Lily's body, the space now filled by Hannah's pillow and the lingering faint scent of her. Lily wondered if Mamma had left Daddy's pillowcase unlaundered, so she too could drift off with the last faint scent of him filling her breath.

Sophia slid her hand from Lily's and brought her napkin to her face, dabbing her eyes and then blowing her nose. She took a deep breath as if to revive herself and then tapped Lily's hands away saying, "Whew! I better ease up on these drinks. Look at me; I'm a mess. Let's get back to the business at hand."

Lily felt somewhat spent by the exchange. But pleased. Pleased that her mother had held her hand, pleased to have imagined her parents asleep in each other's arms. And most especially, she was pleased to know that the love she shared with Hannah closely resembled the love shared between her mamma and daddy. They were alike, she and her mother, Lily thought as she watched Sophia straighten her composure with a quick loosening of her hunched shoulders.

"Besides, people can change, you know," Sophia now said, matter of factly. "Maybe I just never had any time to read or go to movies, running around after you young'uns all those years." Every now and then, her mother would play this guilt card.

And every now and then, Lily would play right into it. But Hannah's words now came to her: *"It's just a story, honey. You don't have to engage in it."*

"So, you obviously don't think it was James?" Lily asked, returning the conversation to its previous topic.

Sophia seemed relieved to be back on less intimate ground. "As mad as you might be at your brother," she agreed, "I hardly think that he was behind that destruction over there. Whatever little plan he's got going on, James wouldn't do *that!* He doesn't hold those horrible feelings," Sophia said, defending her son. "He wasn't raised up that way."

"No, but his wife does," Lily argued. "Rebecca told me herself that she was praying hard for my salvation."

"Oh, that Rebecca; I just try to ignore her." Sophia wrinkled her nose. "Except last week she called up all upset because she found a love note between her Emily and Delores and Matthew's little Stephen."

"Upset? They're kids. Can't be more than ten?!"

"I know, honey. But that Rebecca went on about how the South was going to hell, with race mixing, whites marrying blacks and Mexicans, and sinfulness, boys marrying boys and girls marrying girls. Asked me wouldn't I be upset if Emily married a black man."

"She did?" Lily was now leaning back in her chair, amazed by this conversation that had taken place. "What'd you say?"

"I told that girl I didn't care what color the man was. I told her, with my kids, I didn't care about color or sex, I only cared that they didn't bring home an asshole."

"Mamma!" Lily sputtered.

"And, I told her that up until that conversation, I thought I was batting a thousand."

Lily howled at this, laughing and being glad all at once that this strange woman was her mamma. "Good for you, Mamma."

They both filled the quiet with a small giggle. Then Sophia brought them back to the subject at hand. "So, who else might have done the vandalism? What about that electrician?"

Lily downed a last swallow of margarita. "Probably not. I don't think Jeremiah did it. He's a mean little prick, but he's not stupid. OK, well, not completely. But he's got a good job. I can't see him risking it for some piece of revenge, at least not on that scale."

"What about this Arlo fella?" Sophia ventured. "I mean, Lily who is he, anyway? Your daddy had only just hired him when he died. And where was he today?"

"It wasn't Arlo, Mamma. I just know it!"

"All right. Don't get upset. It's a legitimate question. But you don't really know this fella."

"I do know him. He wouldn't do it." But even to herself, it sounded hollow. She did *not* know him.

"OK, then," Sophia said, organizing herself now. "How about those girls?"

Lily thought about this for a minute. The vision of Laura bent over her nail filing flitted through her mind, and of Dolly measuring a two-by-four three times before making her cut. She said, "Nah. There's a couple of moody ones, but none that scary. I think that it was some bored teenagers with too much time on their hands."

"I hope you're right." Sophia set down her empty margarita and smiled happily as a new one appeared before her.

"That'll be the last one, Ruthie," Lily scolded. "I don't need to be carryin' my own mother outta here."

"So, I talked to Desmond Faulk," Sophia said making Faulk sound like folk. "He's the lawyer in town that your Uncle Gifford told me about. New fella."

Uncle Gifford was Sophia's older brother. He was proud of his lawyer nephew, James, but he'd always thought it unwise to do business with family. He'd been encouraging Sophia for a long time to hire someone other than James.

"Looks like there might be a way that Cameron Construction could be sold," Sophia said. "You and me could do some of our own investing in the company. Making even more'n if we held onto the whole thing ourselves. Turn it into a corp'ration." Sophia was having a bad time with pronunciation now. "Even if we just break even. It'd cut James out, though."

"So, when do we do it?" Lily's glee was not one bit concealed. She wanted to get this ball rolling. She wanted out of this Cameron Construction mess and back to her own safe little haven of Girls with Hammers. She had this feeling that she'd better do it quick, too; she didn't think her crew was going to be together much longer.

Laura and Arlo had both mentioned wanting to go back to school. The Jennies were considering moving to California to get away from the last slinky temptation that had sidled up to Black Jenny after a performance. Her defenses were down most of all, she claimed, in this town where the pickens were slim and the girls were a plenty. The minute the groupies caught sight of her muscular biceps, smooth skin, and big brown eyes, they came panting like puppies, White Jennie had confided in Lily. Black Jenny *was* beautiful, but mostly just full of herself, Lily had decided. White Jennie had also confided that she believed once away from these dogged fans, she and Black Jenny could begin anew.

This would leave Dolly and maybe Micah, who, although she was nice and sometimes a hard worker, was also delicate and without much stamina for the job. Maybe, Lily considered, it'd go back to the way it was before—Lily and Dolly and Girls with Hammers. That'd be better than this, she thought, but she was not much comforted by the idea. The jobs would be unmanageable without an adequate crew.

Then she allowed herself one tiny wishful hope: maybe it could go back to being just Lily and Cat and Girls with Hammers. She dared imagine them laughing in the van together—soaking their feet in the Scots Bourne with their overalls rolled to the knee, her and Cat stopping by The Pocket after work for a game of pool and a beer. Damn. Lily let the wish float away. It was only a spiteful tease, anyway. Nothing would ever go back to being that simple. This was something she was coming to accept. Her mother was trying to explain the selling and then reinvesting process, but she had been defeated by the last margarita. Weak drinks, or not, Sophia was drunk.

Later, long after she'd dropped her mother off (again) at home, Lily lay on her back in bed, so many thoughts running frantic through her mind. Another day had passed and no word from Hannah. Lily comforted herself with thinking that Hannah's new important position was probably consuming her days, forcing her to drop, like a sack of flour, into her bed each night. But fear took over as she recalled the e-mails that had preceded this new silence. Those messages were full of tales that always managed to include mention of the brilliant lesbian roommate. And this thought forced Lily to her side, scrunching herself into a tight ball. What was going on over there? Was Hannah getting involved with another woman? And then a voice—Cat's—*What about you, Lil? Who are you getting involved with? A man?* She wanted to shout Cat from her head; instead she hummed, but not enough to keep the thought of Arlo from rising.

Where had he been today? She wondered, missing his presence. Something told her that he hadn't been far off. Not at his campsite, but closer, in the woods, just beyond the B & B—or maybe even closer. There had been one moment of strangeness, while she and Jake McCann had investigated the upstairs master bedroom. She thought about it—how she'd somehow felt another presence, a kind of energy, urging her to get Jake out of the room. She'd half-ignored it then and had only begun thinking about it now, as she was focusing on Arlo's disappearing act. Now, that queasiness in her middle made her think that Arlo Halsey may very well have been right there in that room the whole time watching her and Jake. The tingling she'd felt earlier was now replaced with goose bumps, and not the fun kind either.

Twelve

Sex! It was on her mind. It was in her dreams. Its reminders of what she was missing were everywhere: television, magazines, billboards, and the Internet. Each morning she'd open her e-mail to dozens of invitations to watch young hotties in a variety of outfits and situations all promising views of positions never before posed. If Hannah didn't get home quick, Lily might be forced to download a contortion that could, if practiced, bow her up for life.

She stared up at her ceiling, waiting for the room to brighten with the morning sun. Last night, she'd watched one of those TV news programs, the kind determined by a ticking second hand around a stopwatch face, called something like *72 Hours, 365 Days,* whatever. This particular episode was about a bunch of teens who decided to pledge celibacy till marriage. They were encouraged to *please themselves in the privacy of their own rooms.* Before the hour-long segment was over, more than half had done the dirty with each other. Those kids weren't stupid, Lily thought. Solo sex never does more than take the edge off.

Mostly, Lily thought, as the sky turned pink outside her window, what she wanted was Hannah's hands on her. She could nearly feel them now, just as she might any morning as Hannah would often reach across the span of mattress, sliding soft sweet talking fingers into warm places, coaxing Lily to a dreamlike awakening nearly always accompanied by an intense pulsing between her legs. Hannah would dip below the sheets and cover Lily's naked belly with butterfly kisses. She imagined those deft hands caressing and stroking hot spots, from the torturous teaser at the base of Lily's spine, to the fiery scorcher that lighted the tips of her toes. Now, as she rolled onto her side with these thoughts reminding her of her deprivation, she gripped Hannah's pillow tightly—sure she would go mad in her imagining.

Finally, she flung herself out of the bed. "Arrgghh . . ." she roared as she turned on the cold water in the shower and forced herself to stand beneath it. She found a sudden empathy with teenage adolescent males. The cold water did the trick—this she found interestingly and disappointingly true. She stayed under the icy spray just long enough to lather and rinse her hair. The cold shower was plenty long enough for her to think straight again.

And what she was thinking straight about was calling Hannah and really having a conversation, not just an e-mail exchange. Maybe they could talk about Lily coming over for a visit. They'd mentioned that at one point in some earlier e-mail, before Hannah seemed to be so busy. Lily'd never been out of the country, well, except that one time, when she accidentally made a wrong turn and she and Cat had wound up in Tijuana, but they just turned around and came back. Maybe, she thought excitedly, she and Hannah could have a second honeymoon. Make it romantic, spend time getting reacquainted, rekindling their first love. It'd also give her a chance to get away from all that Cameron Construction mess as well.

These were her thoughts as she fumbled through her address book for Hannah's phone number. It was a million digits long and in her nervousness, Lily had to hang up and try again twice. She shifted from foot to foot, a habit from childhood, but then the shifts were more like hops and her daddy called her a little jumping bean.

Through whistles and clicks and then some staticky grumblings, the phone at the other end of the connection began its foreign-sounding ringing. On the third trill, the receiver was lifted (by Hannah, Lily imagined) and a female voice came thinly over the wire, the greeting nearly indistinguishable over the loud music and laughter coming from the background.

"Han?" Lily shouted.

The female voice yelled back, "Who? Who are you trying to reach?"

"Hannah. Hannah Burns?" Lily stuck her fingers in her own free ear, to no avail, realizing that it only works if you're in the same room with the noise. She heard the sound of the receiver being cupped by a discreet palm. When it released its covering, the music blared again and then Lily thought she heard some not-so-discreet whispering. The unfamiliar voice returned.

"May I tell Dr. Burns who is ringing?" The voice carried a slight British accent.

"It's me, Lily," she yelled, feeling somewhat childish. What she wanted to say was, *Who the hell are you?* But she waited.

Lily could hear the hand-off of the phone and the background music diminishing. Soon there was a click of a door being opened and another as it closed, muffling both the bothersome music and the even more bothersome laughter.

"Lil?"

"Hey, Han. It's me."

"Is there something wrong?" Hannah's voice was distant and sounded distant and it was the second that made Lily's heart ache.

"Wrong? Heck no. Does something need to be wrong for me to call my girl?"

Hannah fumbled on the other end. Lily wondered if she were as disheveled as she sounded.

"No, of course not." Hannah composed herself. "I'm just surprised. I know how you hate dialing all those numbers and how much more you hate talking on the phone. That's all."

"Well, I hadn't heard from you in awhile and so, I thought I'd take a chance and catch you home. So . . . there you are . . . home."

The door behind Hannah must have pushed open, because the music came blaring over the phone. Another voice, male this time, said something and Hannah asked Lily to hang on . . . when she came back she apologized.

"I'm sorry, Lil. We're kind of in the middle of a dinner party, here. We're celebrating an award we received today. We got notice this afternoon. It will mean more money for us. I'm sorry I can't talk right now."

"No, hey, it's OK. I know I called unexpected. Just wanted to make sure you're doing all right, is all."

"Can I call you back?" Hannah asked. "Later? When all these people leave?"

Lily sat back—dejected. Her fantasy of a trip to Amsterdam flew right out of her. Even if Hannah did want her to come, she guessed that she probably wouldn't fit in too well with all those new award-winning friends of Hannah's.

"Sure," Lily said, but didn't mean it. "Call me later. But remember, it's morning here and I might be on a job."

"Well, if I don't get you, I will send you a really long e-mail, OK? Promise."

"No problem. Have fun at your party."

The receiver left her ear and seemingly returned itself to its cradle. She sat staring at it. It was James climbing up her back stairs that scared the dickens out of her. He was dressed in his business suit and carrying a briefcase. Lily met him at the door and invited him up for coffee. She did not like the look on his face or his unannounced appearance, but she wouldn't let him see it. After she offered him some of her breakfast, which he declined, she encouraged him to talk, since she had a schedule to keep.

He cleared his throat. "There was a lot of damage done yesterday."

She nodded. "The insurance will cover it. Right?"

"Um, yes, but . . ."

"Up until now we've been on schedule, yes?"

"Uh, right . . ."

"And aside from having to clean and fix up this mess . . . there's no other worries, true?"

He seemed to brighten at the prospect of bringing in a surprise concern. "No, there is, actually, a problem . . ."

Lily waited, frowning, her gut tightening.

"Malcolm Galway and his partner are going to pursue the investigation," he started.

"What investigation?"

"The hate crime . . ."

"Oh for God's sakes. No one was hurt. The place can be fixed. It's ridiculous; it was probably kids. What does this have to do with us, anyhow?"

"Well, you can't go back to the site to work till all the evidence has been gathered, for one thing."

"Christ." Lily threw her hands up.

James sat back against the chair. Folding his glasses into his lap, he rubbed at his temple and began his recitation. He talked about saving face, of recouping losses and cashing in on investments. He talked about his kids' braces, his wife's new Lexus, his concern for Sophia, his law firm, and on and on.

Lily watched him. She saw the new lines of worry around his mouth and eyes, and the way his fingers smoothed and smoothed against the stem of his glasses. The gray at his temples had, since the funeral, begun to pepper all of his hair. An even shock of it mopped boyishly above his brow. He named his adversaries and adversities as if he were recounting football scores.

After his breath and interest were winded, Lily set aside her plate and leaned forward.

"How many women you got working for you, James?"

He thought and answered seven.

"And how many men?"

"Two, just me and Walter." He named his partner.

Lily nodded. "What would happen if all those women quit because you and Walter were men?"

He looked confused and then wary, as if he were sniffing a trap.

She didn't wait. "Would that be fair? What would you do? Give up?"

He smiled and said, "C'mon, Lil. What's your point?"

"James, did you ever work for Cameron Construction?"

He nodded. "The worst summer of my life. I was sixteen and Mamma—she was pregnant with you, I believe—had me go work with Daddy to get me out of her hair. The other brothers were too young to be sent off. Hell, Kevin was only a year old. I guess one less kid around was better than nothing."

Lily smiled. She could just picture Mr. Clean here, on a work site.

"It was hot and dirty. I had to fetch and haul and stand and hold. Mindless stuff. Those guys," he frowned remembering. "Talk about rough. Bad language, disgusting pranks. I suffered plenty, being the boss's son. All those stupid jokes about farting and females. God, it was awful."

Lily sipped her coffee.

Finally, he looked at her. "How do you stand it?"

Quietly, she began, "First off, they're not all like that. Daddy wasn't; Pappy isn't."

He nodded.

"It's my business, James. You think I don't know what you're talking about? Try being a girl on the job. Try being the boss's *daughter*. You know that little prick electrician? Glock? He once piled cow shit in a mud bucket I was using. Poured white paint on top of it. . . . I scooped it up and smeared it right across the brand new drywall."

James wrinkled his nose.

"I've been teased, groped, once pinned against a truck by some drunken plumber who was sure I wanted to check out his pipes."

The look on James' face registered a mix of amusement and alarm.

"I've been in this business a long time. I understand it."

"So, what are you saying, Lily?"

"I'm saying that you gotta have some faith in me. You gotta realize that I know how to run this kind of business. I mean, I know that you are some kind of hotshot lawyer—and I'm proud of you and for you about that. But you just got done telling me that the one and only time you tried your hand at carpentry—well, you were something of a failure."

"Hey now . . ."

"Look James, you can't run something you don't know anything about. You can't apply what you know about the lawyering business to something like construction. It just ain't gonna work."

"What do you propose?" He looked annoyed but Lily suspected he might also be feeling some kind of relief.

"Ya gotta get outta my way," she told him.

"I'm not in your way . . . I'm just telling you what I know."

"That's the problem, you are always telling me what you know, even if it's got nothing to do with what we're talking about in the first place."

"That's not fair."

"James, since Daddy died, have we ever just sat down and talked about the business? Like maybe over a beer? Instead, you summon me for appointments or show up at my back door with your briefcase in hand."

He lowered his head.

"Have you ever asked me what *I* know about this kind of work? Ever thought I might have an idea or two, since it's *my* business? No, you just *tell* me what *you* know all the time."

"OK. So I guess I'm just used to *fixing* things."

"Right. But, this thing ain't broke, James. Not totally. Not *yet*."

He made a face that said he wasn't so sure about that.

"Look, if everyone—you, me, Mamma, everyone involved—runs around envisioning the fall of Cameron Construction, well, it will surely fall."

"All right, so I get out of your way. Then what?"

"You give the accounts back to Mamma."

"Lily, Mamma doesn't need to be worrying about that kind of thing."

"Open your eyes, James! Don't you see that Mamma is just plain miserable not having her job? She joined a book club!"

"That's what she should be doing."

"Well, maybe that's what she should be doing with her spare time, now that she's without Daddy. But she shouldn't be forced to vacation when she wants to work. She should be allowed to work if she wants to work."

"Fine," James said. He slouched back against the chair as if he were about ready to give it all over. "I have things on my mind, Lil—not just Cameron Construction. Rebecca's got all these plans for the house, and then there's Jeff's tuition. It's a damn lot right now."

He sounded defeated, and Lily wondered if he were in worse straits than she'd imagined. "James, are you all right?" she asked cautiously, after he fell silent. She wanted to reach a hand to his shoulder but didn't.

Shaking his head, he straightened his back and tie at the same time waving off her notions. "Oh, it's fine," he said, clearly recovering from his weak moment. "I . . . Rebecca . . . well she doesn't know about things. . . . I just don't want to have to disappoint her, you know?"

Lily found herself remembering a younger, more genuine version of James. He'd been the brother who came home most frequently from college—the one who, though he could be pretty pompous, would ruffle her hair and bring her presents. And, she recalled how when she was about seven, James had brought Rebecca Wesleigh home for the first time. The Wesleighs were a "good" family, and Rebecca was a beauty. She'd even made a debut; they were from that kind of old Southern aristocracy. Rebecca's father was a doctor, a third generation doctor, Lily's grandmother liked to brag. *Old money, old ties,* Granny Cameron had cackled hearing the news about the girl her grandson had gotten to marry him.

But Rebecca had always been something of a stranger to Lily. From what she had seen over the years, it seemed James spent a lot of time keeping her and their kids happy. Skiing trips and Disney World were standard vacation fare. There was a yearly membership at the country club, a bigger house every few years, a bigger swimming pool with each one. These were just some of the ways that James' money was spent. But somewhere along the way, it seemed to Lily that James had confused all this materialism with success instead of seeing the real truth—that it was really only family that mattered.

The two had been quiet for a few minutes before James said, "It'd just be better if we didn't lose anything in this investment deal. That's my concern right now."

Now Lily did reach out, resting her hand on her brother's shoulder. "After we get done with this Galway job, we'll reassess the situation. How about that?"

He nodded.

"There's got to be another way, James. A way in which we all win."

He stood up. Buttoning his suit jacket and then leaning to snap shut his briefcase, her brother looked at her. "Well, if you think of something, let me know. I'd love to find an easy way out of all of this."

It had taken a whole week for the police and everybody to finish the investigation, not that it went anywhere. They knew no more about who did it on day five than they had on that first morning. But Lily was glad to be getting back to work and with a full crew on board.

On the third day back on the job, after the crime scene tapes had come down and after the crew had cleaned up, Lily was rounding a corner near the entrance to the outside barn when she just about ran over Arlo and Laura. They were standing close together. So close that Lily was embarrassed for a moment. And then she was shocked. Laura was the last one she'd expect to be standing that close to Arlo. She noticed the look they exchanged, and how they fumbled out of each other's space, actually adjusting their clothes. Lily could hardly believe she'd apparently interrupted an intimate moment.

"Sorry, sorry." Lily tripped around them then turned around as if to confirm that she'd seen what she'd seen. They were studiously avoiding looking at each other, or at her. Lily was feeling a blend of righteous indignation laced with pure unadulterated jealousy, she was not happy to admit, even to herself.

"I, uh, was just helpin' Laura here get this bit outta the drill," Arlo said, holding up the tool. He handed it over to Laura, and then quickly withdrew into the barn, mumbling something about getting back to work.

"Everything all right?" Lily asked Laura.

"Sure." She held up the drill. "Just couldn't get this thing out."

"You and Arlo?"

"Oh, we're great pals," she said, rolling her eyes. She looked at Lily. "Your boy there—you ought to be careful, Lily. Not everyone here is who they appear to be."

What the hell did that mean? Lily wondered this only to herself. She didn't want to indulge this odd little woman's leanings toward the ominous.

"Not you either, Laura?" Lily said, half teasing.

"Hey, I've got nothing to hide." She took out a cigarette and lit it. "I almost wish I did. But I'm not much of a doer."

"A doer?"

"Meaning I'm not one to instigate anything; not much of a follower, either."

Lily had no idea what she was talking about.

"Playing guitar, well, that's about as much doing as I do." The tiny redhead patted her tool belt. "This is the first job I've ever had where I'm actually not sitting down."

"So, what do you think of it?"

Laura stared at her for a moment and then Lily could swear her whole expression changed. She brushed past Lily as if she had suddenly lost patience with her. "I think I aspire to greater things," she said, stomping away.

Lily wanted to follow her, to ask her what she meant by that. Then she wanted to sock the little twit right in her stuck up little nose. What kind of remark was that anyway? *What are you doing in your life now that's so great?* Lily wanted to shout after her, but she didn't. The truth was that Laura seemed a little pathetic, suddenly. She was a good guitarist, but unable to really share her talent with the band in the ways that would have improved them. She was a cold human being, and hardly anyone's friend. And what did she think she could become that was better than being a carpenter? Everyone was different, Lily knew; but as far as she was concerned, aspiring to be a carpenter was a pretty damn good thing. And she was giving Laura the chance to improve her lot in life by becoming one. *It's never too late to be what you might have been.* Lily was having a hard time getting that quote out of her head.

Thirteen

After dropping all the girls off at their respective homes, Lily decided to stop in at The Pocket for a beer. It had been a long time since she'd been to any bar other than OzGirlz. Not since Cat had left, for sure. One night, not long after Cat had taken off for Scotland, as Lily and Hannah drove by the seedy little joint, Hannah had offered, *"Want to go in and shoot a round?"*

Maybe had Hannah just asked, *"Wanna play a game?"* she might have taken her up on it. As it was, she had declined, knowing just racking up the balls would have made her long for Cat, whom she was missing pretty badly. But tonight Lily thought she could use a little company—even if it was of strangers—and somehow OzGirlz seemed out of the question.

There were only three other people in the place, not counting Dave the bartender. Two of them were sisters, twins, Lily remembered, older than she. They'd probably gone to high school with her brother Ben or maybe Kevin. Lily knew them because she'd done some repair work at their tanning salon on the old Galway Highway.

They were identical, both brown as butter beans, with long golden honey-colored hair, matching white Keds, short shorts, and striped tube tops. They turned from their corner table to stare at Lily as she came in. Their mutual interest dissipated the moment her gender was noted, Lily was sure. At the far end of the bar, at his usual place, was a guy named Monkey. Lily had thought it was horrible, calling someone monkey, but the guy himself insisted on it. He wasn't young, but he wasn't very old, either. He always wore the same jeans, boots, and black T-shirt. What did change were his ball caps, a different one every time she saw him. Sometimes it seemed that he had one for every day of the week—maybe even of the month. Monkey didn't say much, just stared at the TV above Dave's head and drank his beer.

But, if you asked him one question about his cap du jour—well forget about it, you'd be trapped for the next hour. Monkey'd tell you everything there was to know about the cap.

Apparently there was a lot to know. Where a cap was made, what the material was, how the brim was configured to curl or not to curl. How the particular logo emblazoned on the front impacted the hat's history or its fate. But to Monkey, the most important thing seemed to be the nature of the cap's *acquisition*. Because Monkey only ever *stole* ball caps—and mostly he stole them right off the very heads on which they had initially sat.

So, anyone who ever asked Monkey, "Where'd you get your cap?" was in for a long beer to accompany the story. Lily decided not to get involved, and made her way toward Dave at the opposite end of the bar. From there, she could just make out the bright orange tiger paw on the front of Monkey's cap.

Dave noticed her looking over at his currently silent customer and said, "You either got to *have* nuts or *be* nuts to rip the hat off a Clemson fan, don'tcha think?"

She grinned.

"Usual, Lil?"

"Same as always."

"Haven't seen you in here in awhile. Sorry about your daddy."

"Yeah, me too."

Dave set the Newcastle down in front of her. "On the house."

"Thanks."

"Hear from Cat?" Dave put an ashtray down for her, reminding her that she was in fact, missing her cigarettes. If you were quitting, this wasn't a great place to come.

She said, "Every day. I miss her, but she's doin' great. Hey, how's that new baby of yours?"

"Not so new anymore. She's toddling around, got some teeth, says Da-Da—but my wife says that's just a sound and has got nothing to do with me."

Lily laughed. "You like being a daddy?"

Dave smiled. "I'm a mess about her."

Another three customers came through the door. With a nod, Dave excused himself.

Lily sipped her beer and let her mind wander back to the conversation she'd had with her mother that morning, while getting coffee at a downtown café. She'd run into Sophia, who was standing in line with two other older women at the new hip Café Shack—where guys and girls with slick dyed hair and polyester shirts scurried back and forth behind the counter, clicking quick questions off studded tongues; things like, *"Did you want a power boost of echinacea or maybe ginseng added to your mocha latte?"*

Nothing like here, where the clientele might be rough and moody, but at least they were real.

Lily had been so startled to bump into her mother at the Shack, that she hadn't even recognized Georgia Stetson standing beside Sophia. Within two seconds, her mother was introducing Lily to another woman, Genevieve Trueblood, who, Sophia prattled on, owned a *beautiful* house on the golf course.

"Mamma, what are you doing downtown this time of day?" Lily managed, once Genevieve had also been allowed some attention. Then the two women turned to study a menu.

"Oh, we're having a girls' day out. I've joined the Herb League, at Gen-eh-veeeve's invitation . . ."

"Why do you say it like that?" Lily frowned. *"Gen-eh-veeeve."*

"That's her *name,* dear." Sophia bubbled. "It's French. Anyway, we're going to the Fourth Annual Aromatherapy and Flower Essences Forum at the Civic Center."

"You're kidding me, right?" Lily pulled on her mother's elbow when she whispered this in her ear.

"Oh, Lily, stop. You know I've always been interested in herbal medicine. Remember how when you were a little girl and I'd make that poultice out of lamb's ear and camphor for your cuts and scrapes?" She turned away, not waiting for an answer and ordered herself a coffee and bagel. Lily remembered no such thing.

After she'd paid, Sophia turned to find her friends. "Oh, Georgia and Genevieve have found a table, I'm afraid I'll have to leave you, dear."

"But, Mamma, I need to tell you some good news." Lily stopped her.

"Yes, then, go on," Sophia said, looking past Lily's shoulder and waving her index finger toward the ladies at the corner booth.

"I got your job back—at Cameron!" Lily was triumphant.

"You did?" Sophia asked distractedly. "How did that come up?"

"I had a long talk with James, but I'll tell you about that later. The good news is you can start back tomorrow!"

"Tomorrow?" Sophia frowned. "Well, I can't tomorrow. I've signed up for the Senior Citizen's Second Semester courses at the college. My class starts tomorrow."

Lily turned to see the women waving Sophia to join them. "Class? What class?"

"I'm taking the Ancient Celts of Scotland. It's being taught by a true Scottish professor!" And on that note, Sophia had excused herself from her daughter and joined her new friends.

"Ancient Celts of Scotland," Lily now muttered out loud sipping her beer, and swiveling around on her bar stool. "Book clubs, herb clubs, aromatherapy . . . and, and Gen-eh-veeeve . . ."

Interrupting her thoughts was the ringing of the bell above The Pocket's door. Lily looked up to see the hunched figure of Arlo Halsey coming through. He scanned the dimly lit bar, squinted past her, as if he didn't see her, and began to make his way to the back. Her heart danced a double time and her cheeks flushed. But she did have the nerve to call to him as he went by.

"Hey, Arlo."

At first, his brow contorted in different directions, confusion and surprise. Then he smiled, recognizing her.

"Lily. Hey, I didn't see you there," he said, pausing at her seat.

She gestured to the empty bar stool. "Join me?"

Hesitating at first, he ran one more scan across the room and then moved to sit beside her. "I'm meeting somebody, but they're not here, yet. So, sure. For a minute."

"What can I buy you?" she offered.

Dave returned with a Budweiser even before Arlo had a chance to answer.

"Come here often, I see," she said, and lit a cigarette.

"Nah, but when I do, I usually go for a Bud. Guy's got a memory like an elephant," Arlo said. "What about you? You come here often?"

Lily smiled. "Oh, me and The Pocket, we go way back. I was fourteen the first time I snuck in here. My friend Cat and me. We'd tag after her brother, Will. He was this big biker guy. Nobody'd mess with Will Hood, and so nobody messed with us, not even to card us."

"Things are different now. They check for everything."

"True. Back then, a ten-year-old could go right up and buy a pack of cigarettes out of a machine. I think that's why I started smokin'."

He smiled "'Cause you could?"

"Something like that, probably. After me and Cat got our own motorcycles, we'd come down here about every night, it seems like now." Then she laughed out loud. "God, those were wicked times. I don't think I could play that hard anymore. Gettin' old."

"Nah." Arlo waved away the notion. "Not you, Lil," he said, and eyed her in a way that caused her to shift in her seat, leaning away from him. "Hell," he continued. "I can barely keep up with you. And none of those girls with hammers can hold a candle to you. You're in great shape—for whatever age. You're perfect, Lil." This last made him lower his eyes to his beer and lift the bottle to his lips.

His admiration embarrassed the fire out of her. Her foot was shaking a mile a minute and her fingers twirled strands of hair around and around. She also had to admit that she was also feeling a great pleasure in his words.

She changed the subject back to its origin. "Toward the end of those wicked times, these last few years, Cat and me would stop in to play a game, drink a couple of beers, but only on Tuesday night. We got tamer." She drained her glass. "Well, 'cept for that one time when we about killed each other in here. If it hadn't been for Dave, I might not be settin' here braggin' this tale," she said in her best Uncle Remus storytelling voice.

"What happened?" Arlo asked. But his eyes were now darting toward the door every few seconds, Lily noticed.

"Oh, we had one of the biggest arguments in our career of being friends; one thing led to another . . ."

"You mean one swing led to another?"

She laughed. "Dave here, finally pulled us apart and kicked us out."

"How long ago was that?"

She confessed. "Last summer."

It was clearly unexpected. The swig Arlo had just gulped came spewing out his nostrils. When he began coughing, Lily pounded his back. The cough was complicated by his laughter. "Couple matronly ladies fightin' it out," he sputtered. "What a sight that must have been."

Thrusting a napkin in his face, Lily motioned Dave for a glass of water. As Arlo's choking subsided his laughter increased, and when he looked up at her, tears in his eyes, she grinned and began her own gale. Finally, they were leaning against each other, exhausted and trying to stifle more fits of giggles (over nothing) when the door to the bar swung wide. A big bear of a man entered and moved slowly toward them. Lily figured he must be over six feet five—and built like a proverbial brick shit house.

Her eyes landed on his belt buckle, in what looked like the shape of a large round silver (dinner) plate. She looked from it up the length of his massive frame. Will Hood was a giant, she thought, but this guy made him look like a toy. The hulk didn't smile and he didn't even glance at her. He just stood. Waiting? She wondered.

Arlo abruptly shifted; both his demeanor as well as his body seemed to slide right off the bar stool. In his sudden seriousness, he slapped a five down on the counter.

"Later," he said to her, and Lily watched him follow the behemoth to a dark corner booth, where they settled in, and their attitudes saying they'd forgotten all about her.

Slowly, Lily turned back in her stool.

Dave, who was also watching the scene, leaned forward. "How do you know that young fella?" He meant Arlo.

She looked up. "Works for me. Why?"

"Been in here a few times. Meets that one sometimes and another seedy lookin' guy other times."

"What do you know about him?"

Dave shrugged. "Not much. Always a lot of whispering going on, and once I thought I saw money go between," he paused, narrowing his eyes at her. "I try my best to forget about seeing that kind of stuff in here."

Lily finished off her brew, wondering if she might have another.

"That boy of yours is a scrappy one, I'll say that for him," Dave said. "He had that big guy up against the wall one night. I don't know what went down, but suddenly he grabs him by the shirt and pushes him like he's a rag doll. I was glad they settled it themselves, 'cause I was not relishing going over the rail to break that one up."

"I hear ya," Lily said and added another five to Arlo's, still on the bar. "Gotta be goin'."

"Good seeing you, Lil."

"Dave," she said, and saluted.

Before she went out into the dark, the bartender called her name. "Watch yourself with these fellas," he warned. "Bad company."

She wondered if Arlo and his giant date had heard.

At first their conversation was strained. Hannah had called telling Lily that since the roommates had decided to catch a movie, she had all the time in the world to talk. At first Lily wasn't sure this was as comforting as it was probably meant to be. She could hear their mutual uneasiness, and something else, when Hannah talked about her life. Her voice dipped and rose in her enthusiasm and Lily tried keeping track of when those peaks and valleys happened and if in fact they were connected to Heather, the brilliant lesbian. In the end, though, even more disconcerting, Heather hadn't even been mentioned at all.

Lily decided not to bring up a possible visit. The whole idea now, after listening to all the busy-ness of Hannah's life, felt like she would be more of an inconvenient intrusion than a welcome distraction. On the surface, things seemed smooth, but beneath all that pleasant catching up, there was discontent and it seemed that they had each chosen to avoid its potential, here on the phone. Their discussion found its comfort zone and each had accepted her place in it.

"It's getting creepier and creepier," Lily said to Hannah. "I mean, before the big guy got there, I was all set to ask Arlo about him and Laura, but now—well now there's a *goon* on the scene."

"Baby, don't go getting yourself mixed up with any dangerous types. I don't like this vandalism business."

"You think I do? It's downright—scary. I'll be glad when the damn Galway B-and-B is done and I can get back to normal life."

"Speaking of which," Hannah said from far away in Amsterdam. "Just how back to normal do you want to get?"

"What do you mean?" Lily listened fascinated by the silent beats it took for words to scoot back and forth across the world. She waited for Hannah to receive and send a return.

"Well, we're getting our work done pretty quickly here. We tried for a third grant, but the institution turned us down. So, it looks like we'll be finishing up here soon and we'll all be going our separate ways."

Lily didn't hear the same joy in Hannah's voice that she felt rising within her. "Does this mean you'll be coming home? I mean to our home, not to your sister's?"

"Of course I'll be coming to our home. I thought we'd decided that?"

"We did." Lily faltered, not wanting to get into anything difficult now, here on the cusp of her life returning to her. "I was just worrying that maybe . . ."

"What, Lil?" Hannah sounded a little short.

"Just that, well, we've been so disconnected, I wasn't sure how connected we still are . . . at least how connected you still are . . ."

"Oh, Lil. It's been hard, I admit. And, I've done a lot of thinking." She stopped and in that silence, so too did Lily's heart. "There is something I want to talk with you about when I get back, but it will have to wait for us to be together, face to face."

"Is it bad?" Lily couldn't help from blurting.

"It's not bad. I don't want you to worry. Just know that I'll be coming home sooner than expected."

Aside from the usual, less than heartfelt, salutations, this is how the conversation was ended and whether Hannah had wanted her to worry or not—she was, big time.

Fourteen

Saturdays are good for getting out splinters and thinking, Lily recalled her daddy saying these words as she worked the latest sliver with her pocketknife. As the wood worked its way out of her thumb, she wondered how many feet of loose pine shards were swimming around in her body. She'd been pulling splinters every Saturday since that first time she'd sat on the back porch with her daddy.

"If you're gonna be a carpenter, you'd just better know that Saturday is the day for gettin' out splinters," Jim Cameron had said as he gently eased a slender shim from his daughter's palm. Tears tried to make their way down her little cheeks but she bit her bottom lip to stop them. She wasn't more than five.

"How come Saturdays?" she had questioned, trying not to look at the gouged skin around the wound.

"Well, heck, carpenters don't have time to be stopping and picking at every little teeny splinter that gets 'em in a day. We'd never get our work done. So, we get 'em all at the same time, on Saturday mornings, so we can go out dancing with our girls on Saturday nights."

Even at the age of five, Lily remembered, she'd been comforted by the idea that if she grew up to be a carpenter, even if she did have to go through this painful extraction once a week, at least at the end of the day there'd be dancing with girls.

She missed her daddy, she thought, and tears, this time, did spring and run over her cheeks in spite of all her lip chewing. She wished she could talk to him, to ask what she should do about all this mess that he, inadvertently, had created when he took that fatal step off the ladder.

It had been like moving through water these past few weeks. Everything pushing her in ways she'd never been pushed before. She reached between her feet and picked a small stick off the porch floor. With her pocketknife, she peeled back its bark. Funny how you could stay in the same place doing the same thing for your whole life and then suddenly, it all changes, and you did nothing but wake up that morning, same as always.

At times she was no surer of the people she'd known forever than she was of all the strangers who'd infiltrated her life. Everyone, from her mother to her most recent elusive hireling, felt like a foreigner. And those she loved and needed most were among strangers in other lands.

"There better be a big lesson in this for me," she said to no one, the tears wetting her whole face now. "I ain't goin' through all this shit for nothin'."

Along the newly skinned stick, the knife blade cut notches, one for every change. *Daddy, Hannah, Cat, the jobs, those silly girls with hammers, Arlo.* She stopped her carving. "Jesus," she said out loud, "Why are you torturing yourself like this, girl?"

Tossing the knife and stick to the ground, she swiped at her face with both hands to brush off the last evidence of tears. Standing and reaching high toward the rafters of the porch, she took a deep breath, shook out her shoulders, and jumped down onto the soft ground in the yard.

"Enough feeling sorry for yourself, Lily Cameron." She hadn't thought she'd ever talk to herself like this in her life. Hell, she'd never been alone long enough to have the need to start that conversation. Altogether, including Mamma and Daddy, there'd been nine of them at home while she was growing up, then Hannah for the past fifteen years, and always Cat everywhere else.

Through her back orchard, across pastures and tobacco fields, and over a couple of creeks, ran a footpath that nearly joined Lily's house to Cat's farm. It was a good hike and a great cross-country ski trail that they'd used often in winter. Lily decided to take a walk.

The sky wasn't called Carolina blue for nothing, she decided, as she squinted up into it. The sun was high and the breeze that was having its way with the day made for a comfortable hike through the woods.

It was a busy place; early morning was market day for the birds and rabbits and squirrels. They were jibber-jabbering at one another from their storied nests above to their tunneled dwellings, below. The carpet of leaves rustled busily to expose those who scurried undercover. Lily herself made deliberate racket as she walked along, signaling any dozing rattlers of her oncoming presence.

She looked ahead toward the crossroads. It was there that the path ended, dissected by the paved road that allowed cars, tractors, and trucks to get in and out of the cove. The road crossed the creek that halved the valley into its northern and southern ranges. As Lily approached, she saw that there was something large in the intersection. How large, she couldn't really detect from this distance.

The thing looked lumpy and long as if it were humped from the pavement, or perhaps it was a thick fallen branch. But then she thought she saw it move. She wondered if her eyes were playing tricks on her, as shadows moved around it like fat black crows pecking away, not *at* the thing in the road, but just pecking as they *became* the thing in the road. Then she couldn't see them at all: the object itself appeared to have vanished. *Mirage,* like they have in the desert, Lily told herself.

She glanced over her shoulder, down into the dip of a tobacco field and up its far and rising bank, to the Lambert's farmstead, a neat stone house with surrounding outbuildings, all tidy with white chickens scattered across the yard and geese squawking her arrival. She could pick out fence rails and even the pump at the porch—the small rocks edging the cornfield were clearly identifiable; but when she looked back toward the road, she saw the long object and she still couldn't make out what it was.

Somehow it seemed as if the distance between herself and the thing did not narrow, and the object continued to shape-shift. She began to imagine man-made items: a plastic garbage bag, bumped from the back of a pickup on its way to the dump; a tricycle missing its front wheel; a busted lawn chair. Then her mind returned to natural objects and the thing became a possum, and a giant turtle on its back. It wasn't any of these things, she knew. It was something terrible. This last push of morbid curiosity swept her onward until she was now only a few feet away—and then upon it. *It* being the gruesomely skinned torso of a headless deer. At least she was pretty sure it was a deer.

Somehow, Lily managed to scrutinize the hollowed rib cage of the animal. The flesh, now drying, stretched and wrapped, like packaging around the bone, as if dressed out in holiday Saran Wrap. She scanned the remains in silence until off to her left a snap of something in the darkening woods startled her. Gooseflesh rose and for a moment she felt like a woman in a Stephen King novel. She thought to kick the carcass from the path of oncoming traffic, but then she didn't want to touch it—not even with her sneaker tip. Instead of continuing on her journey toward Cat's, she turned and ran back down the path to her own place.

Minutes later she was flopping, winded, onto the lush bank of the creek that cut her orchard in two. Panting, feeling sticky with heat and fear, Lily pulled her boots and socks off, and plunged her burning feet into the cool rushing water. She lit a cigarette and leaned back on her elbows, trying to shake the image of the dead deer. But it would not be shaken. Her earlier obsession with it had burned the mutilated visage into her brain.

It had literally pulled her toward it. Every bit as if it had snatched her by the neck. Maybe there really was some kind of seduction in the grotesque. Cat had once lent her a collection of stories by Flannery O'Connor. She'd told Lily at the time, "You won't be able to put it down. Southern grotesque is captivating." Unlike now though, Lily had not been enticed by those macabre tales. After she tried out the first one about a family getting massacred by a gang of escaped convicts, Lily had given the book back to her friend and said, "Sometimes I really worry about your sensibilities, Cat."

But now, she worried about her own sensibilities. Before even reaching the deer she'd known that it would be an awful sight. Still, she had gone toward it, lured by its distorted limbs, by not knowing what it was.

Hannah would say it was a *sign*. "Nature provides signs for us. If—that is—we're paying attention." Hannah was a big believer that animals were always paying attention, always leaving signs for one another, like calling cards. "*Communication,* Lil. They do it better than we do, that's for damn sure!" Lily imagined the sort of sign a deer would leave. *I passed this way; here, this is my patch of fur on this briar bush.* But no furry animal would skin another and take its head. What kind of fucked-up sign, Lily wondered, was this deer carcass supposed to be?

The creek water bubbled around her feet and she sighed, leaning back farther and shading her eyes against the sun. Suddenly a large buck strode ghostlike and regal out of the brush on the opposite side of the stream. Lily counted; the magnificent animal carried at least an eight-point rack. He stood silent, white chest puffing, as if his stature alone was enough to warrant such bursting pride. Somewhere far off, a shot rang out and Lily watched the stag spring, virtually in that same split second, back into the cover of forest. She thought about the other deer—the thing lying in the middle of the road. It had no chest to puff out again. It was only a sticky vestige of itself—a sign of what happens when you don't pay attention to signs, when you don't get out of the way fast enough.

She'd been nearly startled to see only Micah, with the no-longer pink but brown hair, standing beside Dolly that morning as she pulled the work van to the curb.

"Where are the Jennies?" Lily asked, looking around as if they might suddenly appear from behind a bush.

Dolly explained, "They left town on Saturday."

"You're kidding me?"

"No, Jennie called and said they scored a room at a friend's apartment."

"Gone for good?" Lily stared, incredulous.

"Seems so." Dolly continued, "Jenny's gay father got her a job in the Castro district, doing what I can't remember. . . . So, yeah—they're gone." Dolly had that slightly shamed look she sometimes got when she thought she was disappointing you.

"Just like that?" Lily threw the van into reverse, frustrated. What was she going to do with two more workers dropping out?

"Just like that," Dolly said, handing over a piece of paper.

"What's this?"

"Their new address. So you can send their last checks."

"Shit," Lily said darkly. She one-handed the note into her shirt pocket.

After they picked up Laura, Lily's cell phone rang. She cringed when she read James' number, but answered it since they were supposed to be on better terms.

She listened perfunctorily to her brother's droning voice, then realized he was telling her something important. "What are you saying, James? Is this a joke?" For the second time in less than a few minutes she was accusing someone of stupid comedy routines. But James wasn't being funny.

"You better get down here, Lily," he said. "Right now!"

Lily slowed the van on its path to the lumberyard and reeled it around in the parking lot of the Hot Shot Café, sending the girls behind her sliding into each other. They headed toward the ramp leading to the highway going south and Lily pressed the gas, switching into the fast lane.

"Geez," Dolly said, hanging on to the seat back. "Where's the fire?"

"The Galway Bed-and-Breakfast!" Lily growled, pressing the accelerator hard to the floor.

Orange flames engulfed the second story of the old part of the house. There was little hope of saving any of that, Lily could see right away. The firemen had just gotten it under control, James told her.

"Christ, what happened?" She pulled her collar up and over her nose and mouth. The black smoke was sooty and thick.

"Arson. Smell it? Gas, according to the fire chief."

"God damn it." Like everyone else, Lily could only just stand back and watch as water from the hoses soaked the roof and blasted windows. She backed away from the rest of the spectators. She felt like she needed both air and space that wasn't shared by the group. After a moment, enough for her to gulp some cooler nontoxic breaths, Arlo came and stood behind her.

"When did you get here?" she asked him.

"'Bout an hour ago. It was already going. I ran to the road, toward the little store at the highway when one of those Prestige Electric trucks came by. They called nine-one-one from their cell phone."

"Prestige, huh? Glock?"

"Glock and Bobby Dean."

"What were they doing out here?"

Arlo shrugged. "Hoses got here about five minutes after the call. Been at it ever since."

Malcolm Galway, pacing around in a big circle with his phone at his ear, finally snapped it shut, but not until he had barked bitchy suggestions to the party on the other end. He targeted Lily and made a line for her. She watched as James joined him and the two got to her at the same time. So much for any alone time.

"Can you believe this?" the nervous little man asked.

Lily shook her head. "It's a crime. Really. A lot of work up in flames."

"I know." Malcolm rocked from foot to foot, breathing hard. "We had such plans."

Lily looked around and noticed that Galway's life partner was missing from the scene.

"Where's—ah—Patrick?" she asked.

"Well . . ." Now Malcolm was beginning to tear up. "I don't know. We've had an argument. He's been gone two days. I don't know where."

Lily and James exchanged looks.

Jake McCann—*Sheriff* Jake McCann—pulled up in his squad car and eased himself out. He tucked his shirt back down into his pants and straightened his tie before he approached. This time, he was carrying a clipboard.

"Hey, Lily. Haven't seen you in nearly twenty years and now suddenly it's twice in weeks."

"Not exactly how I want to catch up with old friends, Jake."

Jake nodded. "What do we have going on here?"

The fire chief approached. "Jake, we're sure it's arson. Whoever did it wasn't too concerned with cleaning up behind himself."

At this point the group had formed a semicircle around the two civil servants. Only Malcolm Galway stood a little to the side. He appeared overcome with emotion as he dabbed his eyes with an already wadded tissue. The last licks of flame had subsided and the firefighters were now just wetting down the rest of it. Only the battered and charred upper story and some clearing gray smoke hinted of the earlier blaze.

The chief led them to one of the trucks where a blackened can of gasoline and some burned rags had been salvaged from the wreckage.

"Found these, right in the corner of the living room. Like the guy went in and started the fire upstairs and then left the stuff right out in the open for us to find."

"Anybody mad at you, Lily?" Jake asked.

"What's a businessperson with no enemies, Jake?" she said, and then half-grinned before noticing that James did not find this amusing.

"Most recent?" the chief asked.

"Not really . . ."

"What about that electrician?" James asked.

"Glock?" Lily shook her head. "He's an asshole, but I don't think he'd do that." Then again, she did recall that Glock had been around that very morning, had even called the fire department. If Bobby Dean hadn't been with him, like Arlo had said, she might have offered up that information; but as it stood, she thought it best left in her head.

Suddenly though, there was an eruption, a crescendo of voices in heated speculative debate. Laura and Micah were yammering on, and Arlo Halsey's name was at the heart of the discussion. The two girls had yanked their hammers from their waists and were circling each other. Lily jumped in between the shouting and the threatening swings of steel. Right behind her, Arlo bound into the fray, grappling to hold Micah's arms behind her back to pull her away. Lily grabbed Laura around the waist and wrestled the hammer from her grip. The girl was kicking and yelling.

"Arlo . . . arson . . . prison . . . ask him! I swear!" Laura's jumbled words quieted as she was eased onto the grass by Lily and Dolly. Arlo had subdued Micah and made her sit a good distance away. The group calmed as though orchestrated by the fire chief's two outstretched arms that motioned them all *down.* He looked over at Laura, whose eyes still looked righteously fierce.

"It happened in Georgia," she said. "That's why it took me so long to find out about it." She glowered over at Arlo, who had reddened. He stepped backward and folded his long arms across his chest. Lily watched the quickening rise and fall of his breath, and thought she saw that same look in his eye as she'd seen in the eye of the big eight-point buck just before he fled into the protective cloak of the woods.

They were all staring at Arlo now.

Laura sputtered, "I mean, it was easy to find out about the stealing in Hickory and the vandalism in Greenville. But I had to really hunt state by state to find out the real reason he'd been in prison for over three years."

"And you know this for a fact?" the sheriff asked.

"Sure. Just go on the computer. You guys must have databases, right?" Her mouth drew into a purse of contempt.

Jake McCann and his deputy exchanged embarrassed glances.

"So look him up, if you don't believe me. Don't you guys have records on these criminals?" She grabbed a clipboard out of the sheriff's hands and scrawled down the Web site address. "Or, just ask him. He's standing right there." She pointed.

Arlo put his hands up and stepped sideways. He ducked his head. "People make—mistakes," he said. "I paid my debt. I did the time. That's not my life anymore."

Jake asked, "If I look this up," he waved the address Laura had passed on, "am I gonna find she's telling the truth?"

Arlo waited. He looked at each of them, pausing especially long on Laura's defiant face, and finally resting on Lily's crestfallen one. She couldn't look at him. All that she feared seemed to be coming true. She heard him say, "I suppose you will."

There was another pause.

"Don't you leave town," Jake warned him finally.

Lily loaded her crew into the van and they rolled out of the valley in silence. Arlo would go to his camp, she suspected. She didn't think he'd run off, but the whole thing was a nightmare. For a change, she dropped Dolly and Micah off first, pulling up to Laura's house last. Standing on the porch, Lily noticed, was a short young man with the same red puffy hair as the woman beside her. Laura followed Lily's gaze.

"That's my brother, Mark," she said.

Lily looked back to her passenger and ignored the proffered information. Before the little woman could slide back the side door, Lily reached out to stop her.

"You're fired," she said quietly.

"What are you talking about?"

"You're not welcome on my job anymore." Lily settled back into her seat, lit a cigarette, and fixed her eyes on the woman in the rear-view mirror.

"And why is that?" The fire in Laura's eyes matched the bright sun reflecting off her orange hair.

Lily could see it flare. She took a drag and exhaled slowly. "You're a mean little girl. You know that?"

"I'm fired 'cause I'm mean? That's your reason?"

"That's my reason," Lily said. She waited for the girl to exit the vehicle.

"You fire *me* for being *mean?!* What about your pyromaniac boy? Why not fire him for torching your job?"

"He didn't do it," Lily said, trying to sound more sure than she was.

"Oh my God. Are you *fucking* him?" Laura was now standing outside the open side of the truck. "You *are* fucking him!"

To this Lily shook her head and floored the gas pedal, squealing the tires. A few feet ahead she slammed on the brakes and the side door slid shut. The rusty cloud of dust kicked up by the tires matched the puffs of frizz poking from Laura's ball cap. Lily headed for home.

Fifteen

That night, the air had chilled and a brisk wind carried leaves and debris on its back across the valley and over the crests of pasture, up into the rises of the mountains surrounding her house. It was the first night for a fire in her fireplace in a long time. As Lily hunkered down on the couch and lit a bowl, another first for her in a long time, a knock on the back door startled and scared her. She packed away the pipe and then grabbed the shotgun that stood in the corner of her closet. People rarely dropped by, and never at this time of night. The day had made her skittish. She went to the back door, rifle in hand. The tapping had repeated.

"Who is it?"

"Arlo." But it didn't exactly sound like Arlo. It could have been someone else. She wasn't sure.

The steel of the barrel sweated, weighty in her palm. Lily did not shift its heft. Instead, her thumb pressed against the safety latch, easing it free of caution. Fear calmed as the double barrel rose slightly. Accuracy was not essential. Her daddy had counseled, *"Remember, you don't have to aim—just point. With all that shot blasting, you're bound to hit something."*

The lock on the knob, Lily noticed, was not twisted in place. Moving closer, sliding her foot beneath the door like a jamb, she leaned her full weight from thigh to shoulder, against its thick panel. She imagined him—if it was him—out there in the cold, bare hands stuffed into pockets, his thin jeans jacket doing nothing to protect him from the chilly wind swirling his hair into funneled spikes, his cowlick at attention. She wondered how he'd arrived. Not since the afternoon had she heard tires rolling on the road beside her house, she was pretty sure. Had there been a vehicle approaching at this hour, she would have noticed it for certain. And how, she worried, had he known where to find her? He'd not been to her house before.

Which meant she'd been followed. Lily didn't know when or how, but at some point she felt in her gut, that this was not Arlo's first visit here. A whip of wind whistled, slipping a small breeze through the crack, skimming her lips.

"Arlo, what are you doing here?"

"Would you let me in? I . . . we . . . need to talk."

There was an odd vibration in his voice. *Fear or cold,* she wondered. Would she let him in? Should she? After a second she released her hold on the gun in exchange for the doorknob. The click liberated the latch just as a gust of wind caught and pushed back both the door and Lily. Her immediate response came based on the notion that it was Arlo's hand and not the wind forcing her backward. She brought the shotgun even with Arlo's face as he made to step inside. His hands raised and he slowly stepped to the porch.

"Lil?"

He was not, as she had imagined, standing windblown and shivering in thin jeans. Instead, he wore a dark hooded fleece jacket, a woolen cap and gloves, and beside him, resting against the outside wall was a large frame backpack, apparently burdened with everything he owned.

"Lily, come on. I wouldn't hurt you." His hands were still raised. "Look, I'm leaving, see?" he said, not taking his eyes from her but reaching down for his pack.

She lowered the rifle. His look made her think of what a snake must register when it is threatened for merely being a snake. *Was* he a snake? She rested the gun barrel on the floor.

"How'd you know where to find me?"

Arlo paused, half down the porch steps. "I, uh, was passing by here, a few weeks ago. I noticed your truck."

"Passing by?" Lily interrupted. "Nobody ever just *passes by* here."

"Yeah, well, I was hiking. Up along the Parkway. I cut through a holler along some gorge. Can't remember which one."

"Hillary's Gap," Lily said. If you came down the switchback at Hillary's Gap it would spit you right out onto the road about a hundred yards above her house.

"Yeah, that was it," he said, grinning. "It started pouring rain. I came flying down that trail." While he didn't move one way or another, his hand loosened its grip on his pack frame. "So, I noticed the van and then I saw Cameron on the mailbox." He thumbed over his shoulder.

"How'd you get here?" She stood planted in front of the entry now. She rested the rifle between them.

"Walked. Hitched a ride. Walked some more."

They stared, each obviously deciding. Finally Lily gestured, inviting him inside.

"You gonna put that away?" Arlo asked about the shotgun. "I'll be on my way if you're not."

What would it matter? What if she refused and he turned around and disappeared forever? He was watching her intently as she was making up her mind. She felt a heat rise. He looked at her in that same way he'd looked at her when he was walking across the job site on that very first day. Eager and innocent—yet not really knowable, all wrapped into one.

"Wait here a minute," she said and closed the door behind her. After putting away the gun, she went into the bathroom and splashed cold water on her face. Though she'd been standing in the cold open doorway, she was drenched in sweat. Before opening the door again, Lily threw another log into the fireplace, sending sparks up the flu.

When she did open it, Arlo stepped gingerly across the threshold. He moved to the warmth of the fire, ungloved his hands, and held them to the heat. Without a word, Lily went into the kitchen and brought back a couple of glasses of water with sliced lemons perched on their rims.

She offered him both a seat and a drink and Arlo eased down into the leather chair across from her. Lily watched as he carefully steadied the glass to his lips. With a swipe of his big hand, he pushed his hood away and folded his cap into his pocket. Leaning forward, he rested his forearms on his knees and looked at her.

"I didn't set the fire," he started. "I admit I've been in jail for arson." Arlo stared at his fingernails.

"You're not admittin' anything; you just got caught at somethin'." Bitterness caught in Lily's throat. *Everybody makes mistakes,* she told herself. *But fire kills.*

"You're right. I didn't go around sharing the information." He looked up at her, his dark eyes catching hers, holding. "What would you have done?"

Lily wasn't sure. She guessed she wouldn't exactly have been bragging about it either. But she wouldn't have set a fire in the first place, no matter what. And that really was the issue here.

Arlo went on. "Stuff was going on at home. Don't get me wrong— I wasn't one of those kids *fascinated* by fire. I wasn't acting out or anything either. A guy hired me. I needed the money, so I torched a Laundromat. At night, after it closed."

She didn't know whether to be impressed or appalled by his candor. She chose neither and waited.

"No one got hurt," he said. "I made sure no one was in there."

"Jesus." Lily said. She shook her head. "How much money does a guy make for setting a fire?"

Arlo ran a hand through his already disheveled hair. "Fifty bucks. I was a dumb-ass kid. Fifty bucks got me three years."

"How old are you now?" Lily asked, thinking, *a lot of crap in a little life.*

"Twenty-five."

She had thought he was younger, but how could he have jammed such a history into his youth? "So Laura was right all along?"

He stared down, between his knees, to where his hands dangled. His hair now loosened from his cap wielded spiky barbs, soft and fine. She could have reached out and smoothed the bristles back, taming them with one stroke. He was a boy. His hands, she noticed, trembled slightly as he examined them for scratches and hurts. Taking a deep breath, he pressed his palms to his face, then exhaled and lowered them to look at her.

"Laura has some kind of agenda," he said.

Lily waited. It was not like at the beginning of their acquaintance, when Arlo could give just bits and pieces and no more, making her wonder, making her impatient. She had missed something in those confessionals. There had been something good in listening to his words and not having to endure these long pauses that followed them. It was clear to her now that if she had listened more intently to what

Arlo had left unsaid, to be imagined, she might not be sitting here right now, waiting for the web to unweave further.

Arlo cleared his throat. "Remember when you put me and Laura together on that upstairs closet?"

Lily thought and recalled that it had been during that first week. She nodded.

A nervous ripple seemed to shift through his body. Clearing his throat, he said, "Well, close spaces do funny things to girls." He kept his eyes now to his searching hands. And then he did let the silence speak the volumes of his story.

Her brows rose in understanding. "She put the make on you?"

He still did not look at her, but nodded. "I tried to be nice about it." He glanced up quickly. "I tried to explain that I wasn't in a space for a relationship." His cheeks burned a near crimson. "That I had a lot on my plate."

"How'd she take that?"

Arlo just shook his head. "You saw. You heard. That's how she took it. And kept taking it. Who was it who said something about a woman scorned? *Heaven has no rage like love to hatred turned, nor hell fury like a woman scorned.*"

"You're always quotin' something," Lily said, a small grin pulling at her lips. "What about the other day, though?" She was recalling the image of Arlo and Laura scrambling apart when she had happened upon them.

He shuffled his limbs again and in one great acquiescing sigh, he slouched back against the seat and began.

"Laura found out about the charges against me, the vagrancy, the stealing, and one for vandalism. I know it might be hard to believe, but of the twenty-five total felonies I've had against me, twenty of them happened in one night. I was fifteen years old."

Lily waited.

"It wasn't me who did this fire or the vandalism." He paused as if chewing something over in his mind. His decision appeared in the smoothing of his brow. "But it was Laura who did the vandalism at the job site," Arlo said quietly.

Now Lily was confused and her expression must have shown it.

Arlo looked as if he were struggling for the right words to explain. "I ran into this fella one night downtown. He was drunk and talking big about how he and this little redheaded chick and her brother had gone out and done damage to a house belonging to a couple of faggots. The guy was happy to oblige, he told me. Pissed in their fireplace, he bragged. Hated queers." Arlo looked apologetically at Lily and then continued.

"Laura was trying to frame you," she said.

Arlo grinned. "Something like that. What you thought you saw that day was the aftermath of me telling Laura that I knew about her doing the vandalism and her taking a couple of swings at me when I threatened to tell you."

"So why not just come out and tell me?"

"Male pride, maybe. Ego—chivalry. I don't know, Lil. I figured I'd just handle it. Not stir up a hornet's nest for any of us, if you know what I mean. Whatever. I just didn't. But I did negotiate future good behavior for the keeping of her secret. That's what you saw going down between us."

"Do you think she started the fire?" Lily asked.

"I don't think so. I think she's mean enough to mess things up a little. But fire? Doesn't fit."

"You're right. Besides, she's got an alibi," Lily said. "Me, no less. But what about an accomplice?" *I could be a private eye,* she thought.

"I just don't know, Lil. What I do know is that if they don't find the culprit soon, they'll be coming after me."

"But you said you didn't do it."

"You don't get it. Cops have to solve cases. That's their job. Even if they can't do it *factually,* they still got to do it *actually.* In other words, *anyone* behind bars for this would ease the public concern and make the cops look effective."

"But, Arlo. *You* were the one who called it in! Right?" She was making sure.

He nodded. His shoulders slumped. "Think about it. How'd I call it in? Glock, right? Glock hates me. You think by the time all the asking around gets done that anyone is going to believe I *didn't* do it? Haven't you even wondered, yourself?" He stared at her. "You can't deny it. You wouldn't have been holding that shotgun to my head a little while ago, if it hadn't crossed your mind."

Quietly she admitted that she had, that she had tried to convince herself that she *hadn't* suspected him—but she had. But maybe she still did wonder about it. Could she believe him? Maybe if she asked, she'd only hear a lie. How would she know?

Lily had known some ex-cons before. She'd worked with a bunch of them on a commercial job, back when she was an apprentice: tar roofers. It was the hottest, toughest, sweatiest job in all of construction. The profession was dominated by ex-cons. But a kind of breed of ex-con. Not like Arlo. Not so refined. With a smoke or a chew wad clamped in their cheeks, their muscular arms pushed hard against broom handles as they spread thick hot black goo across the flat of a roof like steaming icing on a cake, only not too smooth. Their shoulders, forearms, and hands were covered with blue-veined homemade tattoos, like graffiti, pierced into skin by the tip of a tiny staple or sharpened paper clip dipped into the snapped end of a Bic pen. They never said much and everybody else left them alone.

Lily was reminded of the night she had run into Arlo at The Pocket and of the goon who'd showed up to meet him. *Bad company,* Dave the bartender had warned her. That guy could have been a tar roofer, Lily thought; no doubt about it.

She risked asking. "That guy down at The Pocket—the one who came to meet you. Who was he?"

Arlo heaved another deep sigh. "That's Herbie."

"Herbie?"

"My stepfather." Arlo grinned and nodded. "I know, doesn't fit." And then he shook his head. "None of this fits. You remember what I told you about my daddy—my real daddy, DorrieBee Halsey? About him and my mamma falling in love for one day and getting me?" He didn't wait for her reply. "Well, that was the story my mamma told me when I was a kid, before she . . . went off."

Lily frowned. "Went off? Like left? Or went off, like the deep end?"

"Deep end. I was around six when she really plunged, but she'd been working up to it since the day I was conceived. I guess that's the real truth. What finally set her off, Herbie says, was having my daddy show up on the porch one day."

He continued his story quickly now, as if eager to get it all out. "I remember a lot of it. The man in the suit and tie, though, he's a little fuzzy. I was on that porch when he arrived. I remember squinting way up to see the whole of him, long and lanky. I guess like me. I remember him smiling and me smiling back, but then he touched my head and there was such a hotness about his hand and a pressure that felt really heavy, as if he were pressing down on me, that I remember feeling afraid." He stopped for a moment to take a breath and then went on. "The rest is mostly unclear after that, except Mamma standing behind the dirty screen door, watching, like a mother deer watching a wolf going after her fawn. Then Herbie flew out from behind her, onto the porch, somehow tossing me off to the side with one hand and grabbing a fistful of my daddy's hair with the other.

"Anyway, when the dust settled my daddy must have crawled off. I just remember pushing through the screen door, back into the dark living room. Herbie, poor guy, was kneeling by Mamma, who was staring straight ahead of her. From then on, I never heard my mother say another word."

Arlo stood and walked back over to the fireplace. He stretched his arms above his head, as Lily had seen him do many times. His long torso and legs showed well-defined muscle even through his clothes. He was like one of those Italian sculptures, like pictures of the ones she'd seen of *The David,* only taller. Then she blushed, recalling the statue's exposure. Arlo seemed oblivious to her scrutiny, still lost in his remembrances.

"Yeah, I learned the truth on my fifteenth birthday," he said. "Herb took me to a bar, to celebrate."

"On your fifteenth birthday?"

Arlo shrugged. "He was doing the best he could. Trying to keep everything together. Hell, he stayed with my mamma that whole time, her not barely moving from that chair, never talking to anyone. Herb raised me; he didn't have to do that. He could've left us both and taken off, but he didn't. Still hasn't. I got respect for him for that."

Lily understood. "So what happened at the bar?"

"Fancy Markham, good friend of Herb's, got drunk and got me to the side. Told me everything about my daddy, DorrieBee, and how he'd raped my mamma and left her full of me. How he'd come that day, maybe just to plague her—maybe to take me away with him. No one really knew why he came back. But when my mamma saw him petting my head, it was all over."

"Jesus," was all Lily could manage, once again. "So why all the mystery? Meeting up with Herb, living out in the woods. . . . I mean, Arlo, you make such a case against yourself!"

"I suppose it must look like that from the outside, but it's really not so ominous. Herb wrecked his back and is on disability. Mamma needs someone to come in and look after her. I live in the woods so I can save money to help them out."

"And DorrieBee Halsey?"

"I'll find him."

"You mean you really are looking for him? But why would you want to find him now that you know the truth?"

Silently the tall young man straightened and stared down into the flames dancing in the fireplace. His hands eased slowly into his pockets; Lily could see them tighten to fists inside.

"What are you going to do? Beat him up again? Seems like Herb already took care of that." She said this, and then felt a cold chill as his head turned away from the fire and his eyes met hers. They were black and dull and he was not smiling.

"I'm going to kill him," he told her quietly.

"You can't . . ." she started, but her words died in the look in his eye.

"You're thinking I'll get caught. But I won't. I'll be gone." He pulled his cap from his pocket and covered his head. "Which brings me to tonight; I'm leaving. I wanted you to know all of this before I left. I can't go back to jail, Lily. I can't find DorrieBee from jail, and in my experience, circumstantial evidence in the hands of an eager county sheriff means I don't have a chance for a fair anything."

"Now, wait a minute," she said. "I'll call James, first thing in the morning. We'll all go down to the station, together. We'll explain the whole thing to Jake McCann and clear this mess right up." She didn't want to even begin to address the fact that by becoming a murderer he was fixing to send himself to prison for life—or worse.

He waved her off. "No one's going to buy it, Lil. I'm outta here."

Her mind raced. Outside the wind chased itself around the house, howling its presence. "All right, look. Stay here the night. It's cold outside. It's late. You can get a good night's sleep and something in your stomach. If you change your mind, we'll call James first thing. If you don't, I'll drive you to the state line in any direction you want to go."

They were quiet for a while, and then Arlo agreed that he would stay, but only for the night. Lily scurried to the linen closet and brought clean sheets and blankets and two pillows. She began to make up the couch. Nervously she fumbled the bedsheet, nearly tangling herself within it. Arlo finally came to rescue her. Carefully he took the two straggling ends and snapped the folds free.

As they stood back to admire their combined efforts, Lily felt their shoulders touch. Unlike other similar times, neither pulled away. The heat of Arlo's breath touched her neck, sending fire to her toes. Heavy lidded, she leaned against him, his hands reaching around her, easing her to him. She rested her head against his chest, now rising and falling quickly, and listened to his heartbeat. Closing her eyes, she knew she could be swept away in this moment—this one last moment.

His knuckle caught her chin and raised her mouth to his—slowly, in slow motion, he leaned down to her lips, brushing them slightly, and then his tongue began a tentative probe and her lips parted, inviting him inside. She reached up and placed her palm against his cheek and kissed back, first soft and then with a kind of passion she had not felt in too long. Too long had she not felt this with Hannah—Hannah.

And it was this name repeating in her mind that stopped her. Lily pulled away from Arlo and he, as if awakening as well, stumbled from her.

"I'm sorry," he started. "I don't know what happened . . ."

Lily raised her palm to him. "Stop," she warned. "No sorry. No nothing." She watched him swipe the back of his hand across his mouth as if wiping away evidence.

"Don't say anything," Lily said. "Let's just let this be what it is. No more. No less."

He nodded. A small grin played around his mouth, but Lily did not encourage it. Her actions were mortifying to herself. She wanted away from this man, this boy, with whom she'd gone too far. "Think about talking to James in the morning. It would be the best thing to do. And if you won't, the ride out of here is still on the table."

As she lay on her back, in her bed, arms crossed beneath the pillow, Lily listened as Arlo moved around in the room across from hers, hearing his boots clunk one at a time to the floor. She tossed onto her stomach and pulled the pillow over her head. What had she done? What had that been? Was she a cheater? An adulterer?

No, Lil. It was just a moment. Cat's comforting voice sounded in her head. *Means only that you're lonely. That you felt something for someone. That's it. Let it go. No harm done.*

Lily fell asleep, trying hard to believe her friend.

The next morning, she walked out to the empty living room. The covers on the couch were folded and stacked neatly on top of the pillow. A white sheet of paper rested on top of them. Her heart skipped and she felt a little sick. Running to the back door, she yanked it open. The backpack that had rested against the wall last night was gone. There was no sign of anyone anywhere, no matter how long she scanned the horizon. She walked back into the house and read the note Arlo had left on the pillow.

Lily,

My mamma knows all about you. I called her two days ago, and when I told her, I could tell she was listening. I could feel her smile. I think she was glad to know that someone else has faith in me, too.
Be well,
Arlo
PS . . . I will never forget last night.

Sixteen

That first day, after the fire and Arlo leaving, Lily thought she'd go mad just waiting for some news from somewhere about something. There would be no work for a while, she knew. The fire at the B & B had sent more than just that house up in flames. It had handcuffed everything: Cameron Construction was at a standstill; Girls with Hammers was suddenly down to girl with hammer. Dolly had phoned that morning, saying she couldn't afford to be unemployed. She had a chance to score a gig with a band on its way to Ireland.

Micah had arrived unexpectedly, pulling into Lily's driveway in an old Volkswagen bus with hand-painted *Flower Power* symbols all over it—a bad Bob Mackie imitation. Micah had actually cried on Lily's shoulder when she heard that Arlo had left. Then she announced her own departure, saying that her *fascist pig* parents had threatened to cut off her trust fund if she didn't come back home immediately! "Such blatant misuse of power, don't you think?" She sniffed, wiping a tear and clicking her tongue ring against her front teeth.

With nothing else to do, Lily climbed in the MG and headed for the Galway Bed-and-Breakfast. She saw the cop cars and fire chief's truck as she approached the entrance and kept on going, not wanting to get involved unless she was asked. Instead, about forty yards past the driveway, she pulled over onto the edge of the road. There was an old logging trail and she edged the little car along its narrow, overgrown passageway, till she came to a chain across the trail. She got out and looked down the road from which she'd come. The MG was completely hidden in the woods. She locked it and headed down the path on foot.

Once she'd come to the river that she and Arlo had cooled off together, she thought she could make it to his campsite easily, but autumn's early arrival had begun changing the leaves already, and it masked everything. If she didn't know any better, she could have felt totally lost. But then something caught her eye, a scrap of bright purple. She glimpsed it ahead, a surprising flash among the turning yellows and greens. Hanging from a branch was a strip of material like some scrap torn from a T-shirt, maybe purposely tied, not caught. Lily yanked it free and stuffed it in her pocket. She parted the fan of leaves under which it had hung, and stepped through onto the slightly worn path. This was the way to Arlo's, she remembered.

The site was nearly unidentifiable, abandoned for sure but left nearly as if no one had ever lived there. There was the fire pit, of course, and he'd swept clean the hard-packed floor over which his tent had been set, but the only true telltale sign of habitation was what Lily found not out in the open but after a slight search of the overhanging rock, under which Arlo had made his bed. It was there covered with pine branches, a plastic container, about the size of a small footlocker. Lily pulled it out into the open near the fire pit, and sat down on the old stump. The box was pretty heavy. Carefully, she opened the lid. There were books, mostly paperbacks, ten—maybe twenty of them: *Of Mice and Men, Tacitus, To Kill a Mockingbird, The Collected Poems of Seamus Heaney,* a slew of others, most that she didn't recognize. Cat would have known them, Lily thought. Cat would have liked Arlo plenty.

Beneath the books were six notebooks. Each was labeled by years, not calendar years, but apparently Arlo's own, she suspected. One read *15 Years Old,* others noted, *16–17, 19* and so on. At the bottom she saw they stopped at *23.* She imagined that *24–present* was with him right now. She didn't dare open them. It was none of her business. Before she closed the lid, she noticed a folded piece of paper clinging to the inside of the box. Sliding it out, her cheeks flamed as she read her own name on the front. How could he have known she'd be nosy enough to hunt around his campsite? This was a little embarrassing. She wondered if there'd be any more notes waiting for her, in other places.

Please hang onto these for me. I'm going to try to come back for
them.

Arlo.

She tucked the note back into the box, snapped the lid and hefted it
to her shoulder. She carried it out of the woods and back to the MG,
wondering all the way just how she would ever keep herself from opening the notebooks. This was surely some kind of test, she thought. Or
some damn *sign.*

There was nothing to do with herself (except to spend some time
down at The Pocket). Maybe she'd even run into Arlo sneaking into
town from wherever he was now. Or maybe she'd meet up with
Herbie.

But it wasn't until her third evening at The Pocket when she was
knocking some balls around a pool table, that Lily felt a presence at
her side. She glanced up to find Jeremiah Glock practically breathing
down her neck. She gripped her cue tighter, and moved away from
him. Leaning over the table, she set a stripe in the corner. She'd ignore
the little prick, who was now draining his glass of beer. With her back
to the bar, she stepped around the corner of the table. Still, she clearly
heard Glock suddenly bang his beer down on the bar and she saw him
step in the way of her shot.

"Ain't on *your* job site, are we?" His chin jutted at her like some
beaky little bantam's chest.

"Outta my way," she said, moving around him.

"Can't make me do shit." He looked around. "Where's your boy,
huh? No one to protect you now, is there?" He pushed up against her.
"Heard he torched that job and left town. I told the sheriff everything.
Told him I knew Halsey from jail. He ain't gonna get far."

Again, Lily made to move around him, trying to ignore his idiot
presence as she knew she should. But sometimes you're not called to
ignore, she told herself. She tossed a prayer up that this might be understood. This little prick didn't know when to leave well enough
alone. He needed to get out of her way. She couldn't be responsible.

Leaning over her shoulder he bleated into her ear, "Heard you fucked him."

Lily swung around, the cue first above her head and then cruising down toward Glock's chest. It stopped midslam, caught by the big hand of Will Hood, who'd stepped up and, in one synchronized movement, grabbed Glock in a choke hold with his left arm and Lily's pool stick with his right hand.

Dave the bartender had been watching the scene as well and he jumped the rail, grabbing Lily from behind to pull her away from her target. Will pushed Glock onto the floor and pressed his face into the beer-stained carpet.

"Listen, you little pussy, I catch you pissing around my friend again, I'll personally come and yank your dick off." Rising, big Will picked up the electrician by the back of his belt and dragged him over and tossed him out the door. A drizzle of blood from Glock's nose marked the trail of his exit.

Dave straightened Lily and brushed her off. "You all right?"

She nodded and made toward the bar.

"Newcastles on me," the bartender offered. "Hood, you in?"

Cat's older brother nodded and pulled out the stool next to Lily. His grin showed a gold front tooth, a remnant from childhood, when a game of night war with real BB guns had pinged his tooth right out of his head. Will was still a giant, she thought, looking over at him. Since he'd married Marce, though, and settled down into parenthood, Will had tamed some. His once-bushy red beard had been trimmed close. Shoulder-length curls of auburn that had vied with his wild behavior for infamy had been shorn, still curly, but darker, with a peppering of gray.

"Seems like the last time I ran into you here I was pulling another joker outta the way of your swingin' stick."

"Eddie Thoms," Lily said nostalgically. "Yeah, I smashed his glasses against his face with the butt end of my cue before you caught me. But, man, I still don't regret it. I had just seen that Mary Donnelly, the one he'd got pregnant and married, with a black eye and a swollen lip. He deserved it."

Will grinned and lifted his beer in salute. "To the rescuing of Mary Donnelly!" he said.

They toasted.

"So, what's up with that little prick, anyway?"

Lily shrugged. She knew she had to explain something, but she didn't really want to get into it. "OK, so it's me you rescued, Batman. Thanks." She patted his shoulder. "Guy worked for me. I caught him stealing a tool. Nail gun. You know, pricey. I fired him." She sipped long from her glass.

"Asshole."

"Times two."

"I hear things aren't going so good over at Cameron." Will's voice was quiet now. "Heard about the fire and all."

"Unreal, no? I'm not sure what's going on. You know, I'm hoping that in the scheme of things—in that *everything happens for a reason* kind of way, that I'm gonna wake up tomorrow and all of this is gonna make sense."

"Do they know who did it?"

"Not really. They suspect a bunch of different people. But, this other guy who was working for me, it doesn't look good for him. He didn't do it. I know that for a fact, but, he has a record and he skipped town."

"Bad news."

"He didn't do it, Will."

"That would hardly matter, would it? *In the scheme of things.*"

Lily had to agree with that, and it was as much as Arlo had said. They were quiet for a while and then Lily looked over at the giant. "Shouldn't you be home with the wife and kids?"

He smiled and shook his head. "Nope. Part of the deal. Tuesday nights, I get to play pool."

Lily burst out laughing. "Damn—me and Cat used to play Tuesday nights. Did you know that? God, I miss her!" She looked around for his potential partner. "Can I get in a game with you tonight?"

"You can be the game with me tonight." Will picked up his beer and nodded over her to the table. They laid down a row of quarters, reserving the table for the next six games. Will chalked, and on a flip of a coin, he broke. Lily watched him squint, his whole face cracking, the same way Cat's would, eyes disappearing to slits. Lily remembered having had a crush on Will Hood when she was about eleven. He'd taken her on the back of his first dirt bike and she recalled feeling her arms around his muscular waist. He had smelled of baby powder. But Will had never seen her as anything but his kid sister's best friend. Now she was glad of that, but back then it made her mad.

"How's Marce and those babies, anyway?" she asked and watched him grin so wide, she thought his face really would crack.

"You know Lily, I've never been so happy in my life. Those babies. Twins. Oh my God, they're brilliant!"

She laughed and took her shot, knocking a solid into the side and another into place.

"Stryker," Will was expounding. "He's already walking everywhere. Running and falling all the time. But Mary Kate, she takes her time. She's always thinking it out first. They both call me Pa."

"Pa?"

He laughed. "Just like that, too. *Pa,* like I'm Dan'l Boone or something. Don't know where they got it, but Mary Kate says it first and then Stryker says it two minutes later."

It was funny—here she was at The Pocket, with big old wild Will Hood, talking about his twin babies. She erupted in laughter again. She couldn't help it.

He missed his shot and looked at her like a puppy. "I'm loony about 'em. Ain't I?"

"Pretty much. Cat won't recognize you. You've turned into a mush."

She knocked a couple more balls around the table, not landing anything. "Man, I'll say one thing, in spite of all this crap going on, at least there's some good things to look forward to."

"Like what?" Will eyed his shot.

"Well, in just a few weeks, Hannah is coming back from Amsterdam. Amen and hallelujah." Lily made the sign of the cross. "And then Cat'll be back."

Will made his shot and was looking for another. "Didn't you hear?" he asked.

"Hear what?"

"They asked Cat to stay on." He shot and missed.

"Stay on?" Lily felt a sinking and didn't even move toward the table. "For how long?"

"Sounded like indefinitely. Like forever."

"Forever? She can't stay on forever! What about her house and Melissa and her books and coming back to work with me and, and . . ." Lily had winded herself. She realized she'd been sounding like a pissed off, whiney brat, and felt a little embarrassed.

Will just shrugged and leaned in to set up a shot. "I don't know. All I know is that we got an e-mail saying that they offered her this full-time gig and it was a really good deal and she was thinking about it."

"How come she didn't tell me?"

He scratched on the next shot. "Fuck!" He put his stick down and went to the bar for another beer. "Maybe she hasn't completely made up her mind for sure. Yet. I don't know. All I know is that it took the pressure off of us for getting outta the cabin. The house isn't gonna be ready for at least another month, turns out."

He said some more stuff, but Lily had tuned him out. What if Cat stayed away forever? The only thing worse would be Hannah leaving forever, but that part wasn't happening. Hannah, thank God, was for sure coming back. She had called last night. "I'll be home soon, sweetheart," she had said. It had evoked a guilty flash in Lily then. But today, it was the one bright ray of light in Lily's whole miserable world.

Everything, she supposed, *happened for a reason.* If she started ticking off a list of all the crap that had happened in the past few months, well, she'd probably just want to shoot herself. But everything *wasn't* happening for a reason. Too many things were just plain falling apart. Cat not coming back? What kind of reason could that have behind it? Lily lined up her shot, slammed the eight ball into the corner and scratched it with the cue. "Fuck me, man," she said, and got herself another beer.

Seventeen

A sharp rapping at her back door roused Lily from her deep sleep. The sun was already high and she had to squint against its glare as she made her way through the house. Her head was pounding. She began to recall the large amount of alcohol that she had consumed the night before, after Will had broken the news about Cat not coming back. They'd played up their quarters, and then some, and for each round, Lily downed another Newcastle. Will, on the other hand, had stayed sober, another symptom of fatherhood. He had driven her home; of this, she was pretty sure. But she had no recollection after crossing the threshold. Somehow she had managed to change (at least she hoped it had been her, alone) into a T-shirt and gym shorts, although she noticed that she was wearing only one sock.

The rapping came again, and with one hand shading her eyes, she called out, "Hold your horses, will ya?" In her hurry, her socked foot slid and the other caught the edge of the rug. She stumbled, nearly landing in the fireplace. One knee slammed painfully into the stone hearth. *"Fuck!"* she howled.

Her palm pressed the rising egg on her knee. Just below the swelling, a deep gash was beginning to bleed. "Fuck!" she yelled again. The rapping came faster.

"Lily? You OK?"

It was Sophia. Lily hobbled to the door and unlocked it, spinning around and just managing to fall back into the big leather chair. Her mother flew into the house.

"What happened?" She pulled Lily's fingers from the kneecap and tried to stanch the ribbon of red that sprang freely from the gouge. But now it was flowing down Lily's calf and dripping onto the floor. "Oh, boy." Sophia jumped up, as if she were seven years old instead of nearly seventy. She was back in a minute with a wet kitchen towel. "Here, hold this on it. You might need stitches."

Lily dared a peek under the towel, and then closed her eyes. Her head was still throbbing. "Mamma, I think there's some butterfly bandages and a first aid kit under the sink in the bathroom."

She tried to bend her leg, wincing against the shooting pain that produced. *How bad could it get?* she thought. Her wonderment evoked a flash of her childhood.

She couldn't have been more than four years old:

"Hold it back here, Lily," Jim Cameron had instructed, gently sliding his daughter's little hand down the wooden grip of a hammer nearer the butt. "Now, steady that nail." He stepped away. "OK, now. Hit the head!" And with that, the heavy steel hammer swung down, catching and pounding her small thumb instead.

"Yow!" she had howled, throwing down the hammer and reflexively sticking her thumb into her mouth.

"That's it, Lil," her daddy had encouraged. "Suck the fire right outta there; that's what real carpenters do."

She did and it worked and she'd been doing it ever since; now almost every time she injured herself, she thought of her father. What would he say about a bashed-up knee brought on by a cranky hangover?

She began to breathe more slowly and thought to herself, *How bad can it get?* She took a deep breath and exhaled. For a moment she was a little dizzy but steadied herself by staring at the brass knob on the back door. It could really only get just so bad and then it'd have to quit, she reasoned. Her mother dabbed at the blood with the towel, murmuring gently as if Lily were still a child. Lily exhaled slowly, puffing cheeks like a woman in labor (she imagined). The fire in her knee was only getting hotter; she closed her eyes, again. Eventually, the pain began to steady, and dulled. She'd be OK, she thought; she wouldn't need stitches.

She leaned forward and took the towel from Sophia. "It's all right, Mamma," she said. "I'll be fine." Sophia was looking up at her, the concern in her eyes ebbing and being replaced by something else. She was smiling. "You *will* be fine, sugar. I see that now. You really will."

She'd been breathing through it all. Lily found herself giving back a smile, albeit a wincing one. She shook her head, letting the realizations in: she could handle this—all of this crap, from her daddy's dying to Hannah and Cat's leaving, to the job catastrophes from Arlo to the fire. Everything. *I'm still standing,* Lily decided. *How bad can it get?* she already knew. *Bring it on,* she dared, *I'll just suck the fire out of it.*

Sophia had soaped clean and spread antiseptic across the open wound on Lily's knee. The bleeding had eased and the butterfly bandages were enough to pull the skin together. No sewing up, thank God.

"Sure you don't want stitches? You'll have a nasty scar from this."

"I ain't trying out for Miss America any time soon," Lily said, breathing hard as the medicine worked its way in. She watched her mamma's tough hands work quickly, dressing the wound as if she'd been a Red Cross volunteer her whole life. It was a familiar sight, Lily thought. Taking her back to her childhood and other accidents that had set her mother in that very position, kneeling in front of her: a fall from a bike; a snag on a barbed wire fence; once, after viewing back-to-back runs of *Mary Poppins,* she'd attempted a leap from a roof, open umbrella waving as she hoped for a gust of a Poppins easterly wind. All by herself, Lily would have kept her mother in the bandaging business, but with a carpenter husband and six other kids, boys no less, she already had a thriving bandaging franchise.

"There," Sophia said, admiring her own job. "I think you'll live."

Lily grunted and attempted to stand. She unbent the knee, then rested her weight on it and decided she could walk. "It works! Thanks."

"Well, of course it does." Sophia pulled herself up and stood. "You're back in business." Then her eyes rested on the still-blinking numbers' display on Lily's answering machine. "I see you didn't pick up your messages last night."

"No. I did not. I, uh, got in kind of late."

Sophia raised a brow.

Lily felt a stinging rise in her cheeks. *How* did mothers do that? she wondered. Make you feel guilty, even without saying anything—even twenty years after you moved out of their house?

Sophia apparently had decided to let it slide. "They caught the arsonist," she said, taking the folded section of the newspaper from her bag and handing it to Lily. Centered on the front page was a large color photo of two men, being led away in handcuffs by police officers. The first was a tall skinny bald guy with a thin little mustache. The second man was shorter, pudgier. Then Lily recognized that he was disturbingly familiar, with his orange hair slicked back. She read his name below his photo: Mark Davis. Like Laura Davis. It was her brother. The same guy Lily saw on the porch the day she'd fired the mean little woman. Arlo had been telling the truth after all, Lily decided.

Lily skimmed the report as her mother talked over her reading, recounting the information twice. There had been a tip, the report said, an anonymous phone call to the sheriff's office. They'd found a Cameron Construction power drill and the pawn tickets for a number of other pilfered tools at the apartment that Mr. Davis shared with his sister. It was not his first run-in with the law, the article revealed. Lily shook her head. "Oh, brother," she said, and finished reading the smaller details. "Fool me once, shame on you, fool me twice, shame on me," she attempted.

Sophia looked surprised.

"Something Arlo said. I don't remember it exactly."

"Where is Arlo?" Sophia now looked at her, seriously.

Lily shrugged. "I don't know. He came by here—packed to go. He told me a bunch of stuff. I knew he didn't do the vandalism. But, considering his past, well, I could see why he took off." Then she tapped the paper. "This is good news for him. I don't think he did the fire, either. Puts him in the clear, at least for me."

"Well, let's hope he doesn't come back," Sophia said.

"Why?"

"He's an ex-con, and he knows we know that now. That's *bad company* we don't want to keep."

"Mamma! You don't know anything about this guy. He's had a lot of stuff happen in his life."

Sophia shook the newspaper, which she had taken back into her possession. She had raised seven law-abiding citizens through both good and bad stuff, and was having none of this lame excuse for not living right. "I have no patience to help out a healthy grown man who can't even help himself." She was firm about this.

"Mamma, you're being rather harsh," Lily said.

Her mouth was set in that steely way of hers that Lily recognized from childhood. *No means no and I mean it,* Sophia's words had always preceded the drawn tightness of her lips.

"Not that we Camerons aren't charitable, mind you. But sympathy only works when it's rightly placed." Sophia herself had been a Meals on Wheels volunteer for nearly a decade. Not to mention a veritable icon of the local Red Cross. "It's not about hard times," she said. "That boy can't possibly have seen hard times."

Lily stood quietly, waiting. Apparently Sophia had been thinking some about this Arlo fella. Something about him must have been worrying her. Lily, herself, guessed it would be better for everyone if Arlo stayed away.

"You remember Grampa Adams?" Sophia started after a pause. She was obviously talking to Lily, but her eyes looked away, as if she were half-hesitant about revealing too much of herself.

"Your daddy? Sure. I was ten when he died. He always carried two buckeyes in his pocket and he'd always give me one."

"Well, he wasn't my daddy."

"Mamma!"

"It's true. He was my step-daddy. He married my mamma when I was eight years old. My real daddy ran off with a gal from Bryson City the day after I was born and we never saw him again." Sophia put her bag down, and went to sit in a chair. With her hands together in her lap, she glanced over at her daughter. There was no self-righteousness about her now. Her mouth quivered some in a sad kind of way and she heaved a deep sigh.

"During those years that we were alone, me and Mamma—times were hard. If it hadn't been for the kindness of family, well, I don't know what would have happened to us. Mamma worked hard, had a lot of jobs. It was when she was working at the mill that she met Grampa Adams." Sophia allowed a smile to begin on her lips, a bit less awkward than she'd been. "See, Lily, people can get down on their luck, but if they don't try to make it better they're just gonna stay down. Grampa Adams was a reward of sorts for Mamma and me. 'Cause Mamma never stopped trying to help herself. She got training as a nurse and after she and Grampa got married, they saved hard and bought their house together, but it took a long time. So don't you go thinking that I'm begrudging anyone who's down on his luck. But, this boy, he doesn't live an orderly life—just seems to keep *choosing* this way outside the law for himself." She swiped at the air as if dismissing the whole fact of Arlo. " *'Good riddance to bad rubbish,'* as my granny used to say."

Lily was shaking her head. "I can't believe you never told me about Grampa before. Do the boys know?"

"They know. I just never could bring myself to tell you. And your brothers knew better than to let it come out. They knew how fond Grampa was of you. Once he'd died, it seemed pointless." Then suddenly Sophia was all business again. "I am here for another reason. If you hadn't been a *dirty stay-out* last night, you would have known that we have an appointment with James this morning." She looked at her watch. "In exactly thirty minutes. Hit the shower and scrub that fermented barley from your pores, child; you smell like a brewery."

The hot coffee and sausage biscuit her mother had managed to whip up while she showered felt good going down. Lily ate in the car as Sophia drove. Chewing, Lily settled back adjusting her sunglasses on her nose. She had a cranking hangover. James wasn't first on the list of people she would like to see this morning. She groaned.

"What's this all about?" she asked Sophia. It occurred to her that James was being his usual arrogant self, getting his mother to drag Lily out of the house without so much as a concern as to whether this was convenient for her.

"I don't know," Sophia admitted. "It's something of a mystery. When I asked him, he just said he'd explain when we got there."

Exasperated, Lily muttered a not-so-nice expletive that described her brother exactly.

"Now," said Sophia, not addressing her daughter's bad language. "Let's not talk about James. Let's talk about my spinning class. I started this week."

"I thought you hated knitting?" Lily said glumly.

Sophia laughed, "Not that kind of *spinning,* dear. No, this is at the Y. We ride stationary bikes to music."

Lily stared at her. "Mamma, do you think you should be exerting yourself that way?"

"You mean I'm an old lady and might have a heart attack."

"Well. . . . Does your doctor know about this?"

"Dr. Mallory not only recommended it, but he spins himself."

"Old Doc Mallory?! What is this? Some old people's class or something?" With a hangover, she decided, it was not called for to expect tact from a person.

"I'll have you know that it's a program called Fit for Seniors, and spinning is just one of the classes. I'm also taking swimming, aerobics, and golf. By the looks of you today, little missy, I could take you down in every one of those categories—*senior* or no *senior.*"

Lily shut her mouth. Sophia was probably right. She stared out the window for the rest of the ride as her mother reeled off her latest personal statistics; weekly weight loss, muscle gain, bone hardening. *Pliancy,* Lily pictured rubber bands for tendons. Sophia rattled off laps around the pool, lowered blood pressure readings and steady heart rates. "It's helping my golf game. I'm the third best in our league!" She looked particularly gleeful at the wheel, back in her own good graces, beaming like a third grader who toppled the last bully from the slide.

Lily's temples throbbed. She gulped coffee from her travel mug and wished it were whiskey.

In James' office they were greeted not only by James, but by Pappy and his two eldest sons, Adam and Bryson. All of Pappy's children were named in alphabetical order. Caleb came next and after that, Lily always lost track except for one named Ilene, who had been a couple years behind her at school. Pappy's grandchildren were now filling up the rest of the alphabet. The tradition had set like cement.

After the niceties, they all sat and James slid his glasses back up the bridge of his nose and began.

"Mamma, Lily . . . Pappy and the boys here have a proposal for us about Cameron Construction and I thought it'd be good for us to hear them out together."

Lily and Sophia exchanged glances, and then sat back. What was this?

Pappy cleared his throat. "Now, Sophia," he said, as if he were expecting an argument from her before she knew anything, "I know Cameron Construction's been—well—on the *downside* some lately."

One of his boys—Lily thought maybe it was Bryson—tittered nervously in his chair behind Pappy's. She tossed him a dark look, and then opened her mouth to respond to Pappy's statement about Cameron's woes.

"Lil, hear him out," James said.

She turned her scowl on him instead, but held her tongue.

"Yeah, well, see, Lily, me an' my boys been thinkin' that—seein' as how there's been a fire and all, what with a lot of the equipment and materials pretty destroyed—why, maybe you'd consider sellin' out if we kept to the price it would have been *before* the fire." Pappy was getting all balled up in his own words now.

Lily shuffled her limbs in her seat. She was waiting for the impact of the proposal to affect her.

"We'd be happy to keep you on, Lily, if you're looking for work," Pappy offered and smiled, knowing she had her own business to attend to. "And, Sophia, we'd love for you to stay and keep our books."

It was her mother who was first to answer. "Oh my word, Pappy, no. You have no idea what a relief this is. I am so busy with school and the herb club, not to mention my fitness program. Lately, I just don't have any time at all. I am going to retire, right here and now."

Lily looked at her mother. Sophia was dressed in a pair of light blue Gap jeans; a brown belt with a silver buckle threaded its loops. Topping this, a hunter green turtleneck, and below, a pair of extra white running shoes. Lily in her hung-over condition had failed to notice that the long braid her mother usually wore down her back was loose, and trimmed to her shoulders. Lily squinted. Was that lipstick? Sophia looked like a new woman. Retire? Then Lily saw something in her mother; at this offer, the last vestige of burdening stress had lifted from Sophia's brow. She glowed—much in the way she had when tell-·ing Lily about her new workout regimen at the Y. Now she looked positively euphoric.

Sophia *wanted* this, Lily realized.

More machinations and possibilities flew around the room, and in the end the six of them shook hands. They'd work out the details later. The price was right.

For the first time in months, Lily began to feel that proverbial weight lifting from her own shoulders. There was a kind of an easing in her mind, at the back of her neck where it met her spine. The pressure seemed to assuage its tension for the first time in a long time. She would be able to turn her full attention to Girls with Hammers.

"Girls with Hammers stays in business, though," she warned Pappy.

He put an arm around her in a rare gesture. "That's fine, Lil. Maybe I can even get you to sub-out some of my contracts."

Headed back, in the truck, Sophia turned down the radio. Lily noticed that she was now listening to National Public Radio instead of WKT Country. She turned to Lily, apparently noticing that what had minutes before been a shared excitement had somehow waned for her daughter staring out the window.

"What's wrong, dear?"

Lily looked away. She did feel relieved. Still, she didn't want to rain on Sophia's parade, but some kind of sadness seemed to be overtaking her. Maybe the hangover, she thought. But somehow tears were stinging her eyes and she couldn't quite stop them from spilling, one or two, over onto her cheeks.

"Honey," Sophia said, putting her hand on Lily's arm. "What's the matter?"

Lily brushed at her cheeks. "I don't know, Mamma. Everything is changed. Nothing's the same as it used to be. Daddy's gone and even though Hannah's coming back, well, she's gonna be different and what if she doesn't like me anymore?" Was she really discussing *love* with her mother? She felt suddenly as if she could run away—even from herself—if she weren't in a moving vehicle right now.

"I hardly think Hannah's that kind of fickle," Sophia said after a moment. "She's loved you for a long time. That's not going to change just 'cause she spent a few months away."

"Maybe. And, and, now that Cameron's going to Pappy and the boys, well, to be honest, Mamma, I don't really know about Girls with Hammers. I don't have a crew. All my contracts are dried up, and my reputation's been slashed. I'm not even sure if being a carpenter is what I'm meant to be doing anymore. I feel like the world is coming undone and on top of all this," and on this she sniffed loudly, "the worst is that Cat's stayin' in Scotland."

Sophia looked surprised. "I thought she was due back next month?"

"She was, but now Will says she got offered a permanent position. It sounds like she's staying."

"Did you hear from Cat herself?"

"No. Sometimes I think she just doesn't know what to say."

"Cat Hood *always* knows what to say, Lily. Now you listen to me and give her a call. She's your best friend; she'll tell you the truth. People call long distance all the time, emergency or no, and this one could register as either. You tell her you want her to come back to her old job. Tell her what's going on."

Lily shook her head. "I don't want Cat coming back here to rescue me. She's got her own new life and her own new job and I ain't gonna get in the way of that. I'll just wait till she tells me for sure. Then I'll decide what to do." And on this note, she buried her head in her hands and really started crying.

"Oh, Lily, sweetie. You need a break. A rest. Why don't you just take the next few weeks for yourself? Get ready for Hannah's return. Throw her a surprise party. I'll help. It'll take your mind off of all this, and when you can think more clearly, it'll all make better sense. And, don't forget you've got your doctor's appointment coming up next week."

Lily heaved herself up the back steps of the house, turning once to wave to Sophia as she pulled onto the road. She felt as if she were the one who was seventy, not her mother. Thinking about Cat hadn't helped her mood much. And all that drinking she'd done last night . . . it was just contributing to her general depression. Maybe Sophia was right. Maybe some quiet time, alone, before Hannah came home would just do the trick. There would be no way of talking her mother out of the surprise party for Hannah. She'd gone on and on about it. She'd be working on the details as soon as she got home, she said. Just as well. Let Sophia do the arranging. She, Lily, was not exactly in a party-planning mood.

She clicked on the TV and then clicked it off again and wandered around the house from room to room. The computer in Hannah's office hummed softly in its dimly lit corner, perennially on. Lily touched its space bar and the floating constellations magically disappeared. After signing on, she waited for the *You've Got Mail* signal to sound. The first two messages promised to enlarge her penis. Another offered a free sample of Viagra.

"To try out on my new big penis," she mumbled. The mental image made her giggle—an odd sound in the silence of Hannah's office. She clicked on the first of two real messages. It was from Hannah. The other one was from Cat, and Lily felt afraid to read that one just yet. Hannah's began, *I am missing you so much, not just because it is damn cold in Amsterdam, which it is, even in summer, but because I keep thinking how much I love you* . . . Lily read the rest and then sat back in the chair. She was smiling. She felt warm all over, and even happy. Happy enough, she thought, to dare herself to open Cat's e-mail, and read that. She clicked on it. "Bring it on, Hood," she said, also aloud.

    Hey Buddy,
    Hope you're doing well . . .

Lily skimmed at first, racing to the truth against her own will. Cat was rambling on about Scotland, something poetic but not very meaningful to Lily, who was feeling as she had when she'd been pulled toward the mirage thing in the middle of the road. She knew she wasn't going to like what Cat had to say, but she was drawn into reading it anyway.

The second paragraph began, as if Cat had had to warm up to it herself.

> And so, I like this place and they really like the work I'm doing with the girls. They actually want me to stay on indefinitely. I am learning a lot about my grandmother from her family here. The sisters are giving me so much good information for the new book, Lil. I think the Universe is providing me this opportunity.
>
> I'm guessing by now you're not too happy with me. Neither is Melissa. I think that we are working our way toward an end. I don't know why all this is happening this way, but it seems right.

She went on to say some more about how *right* it all seemed, as if she, Cat, were trying to convince them both. But Lily could read no more. Tears had begun to stream again, as in the truck, earlier. Her life was upside down and she just didn't have the energy to flip it back over, or maybe, there was no flipping over. Maybe she'd have to maneuver the next part standing on her head.

She attempted a response,

> Wow, Buddy, sounds like your life is going really well . . .

The rest of what she wrote was just a bunch of encouraging bullshit about, *events happening for reasons* and *hard decisions,* and how good everything was going here, none of which was true, all of which made her stomach tighten against itself until she resorted to pulling into a semifetal position. She hiked her knees to her chin. Once the lie was all in print on the screen, she pressed the *send* button. She even whispered, "Good Luck, Cat," as if she meant it. As if having Cat decide to stay thousands of miles away didn't make Lily feel the least bit miserable.

Three days later Lily found herself (at Sophia's persistent nagging) sitting half naked on crinkling white paper, wrapped in a freaking paper towel, waiting for Dr. Cole to examine her. She was in no mood for this and would have bailed out on the appointment once again, had Sophia not called and sweetly threatened to come and chauffeur her there in person.

"We can go to the new sushi bar afterward," Sophia had warbled. Rather than be faced with raw fish and her new perky mother, Lily had sworn on the cross itself that she would keep the appointment.

She'd growled at the young nursing assistant who made her get on the scale and told her she'd lost six pounds, and had moaned at the woman whose job it was to listen as the cold stethoscope pressed her chest. But when a big bossy RN with meaty fists handed her the little plastic cup, pointed to the bathroom and ordered, "Fill it," she had merely whimpered.

Lily reached behind, trying to close the gap in the gown that was sending a draft up her ass, when the door finally opened.

Sarah Cole and Lily had been friends for over ten years. Lily had been one of the young doc's first patients when she combined her practice with old Mallory's. The partnership had prospered; now that the old man had gone into semiretirement, and Sarah was expanding the operation by bringing in other women doctors and practitioners. "The most extensive all-women Ob-Gyn care in the county," the slogan said under the partnership's name. Old Mallory didn't care. "Time women docs start looking after their own," he would say when anyone asked him. But Sophia Cameron was one of the diehards that only wanted Doc Mallory looking after her. "Delivered all seven of my babies without a hitch," she'd stated.

"You look happy to be here," Sarah said, and Lily rolled her eyes. "Your mother called and said if you didn't show up, she'd come drag me up to your place for a house call."

"I oughta sue you. Sending my mail to my mother's house. I got some privacy issues with that, you know."

"It was a mistake," Sarah said. She had pale hair and deep blue eyes that twinkled a lot, and she was tall and thin.

"Mistake my ass," Lily told her.

"Relax and breathe normally."

Lily sat very still, imagining her own lungs under the doctor's stethoscope. Did they struggle to expand and contract, filled with the sticky nicotine and black Camel smoke?

"Any complaints?"

"Yeah, this thing is too cold. You need to get one that heats up."

"I mean healthwise, jerk. Lay back." She pulled the gown up around Lily's neck and checked her left breast.

"Jeezuz, Sarah, your fingers are freezing!"

"It's morning. My blood doesn't get circulating till afternoon. Sorry." She continued the exam on the other breast. "How's business?"

"I'm assuming you don't mean the breast business?" Lily made a face as Sarah pinched her slightly in admonishment. "Ouch! Business sucks. There's not even any business to talk about. I'm thinking of getting out of carpentry."

"Really?" Icy fingers paused over Lily's right breast and retraced their previous circles. "What would you do instead?"

"I don't know." Lily looked up at her, into the blue eyes that were looking thoughtful now, not twinkly. "Did you ever wonder whether you were meant to be a doctor? Or you're doing it 'cause your daddy did it?" Sarah Coles's father had been a surgeon. Anyone who'd ever seen the two of them together knew the daughter was cut from the same cloth as her father.

Sarah paused, shook her head. "No, I'm sure this is what I was meant to do. Daddy being a doctor was just a bonus. Aren't you sure about carpentry?"

"I thought I was . . ." Lily felt fingers center again and press . . . she winced. "Till this last year. Now I'm wondering whether this really is what I was meant to be my whole life. And if it ain't, well hell, I better come up with something else, pretty quick." Sarah's fingers pressed again just under her nipple. Then there was silence. She watched as Sarah pulled back and looked at her.

"You've got a lump, Lil."

"God damn it, Sarah!!" Lily sat up. "I knew this was fucking going to happen. I don't have time for this crap!"

"Lily, calm down. These things are ninety-five percent benign."

"Right, right. God damn it, Sarah, have you been consulting with my mother? I've got a million other things going on right now."

"Well, now you've got a million and one. Let's finish the Pap."

"No fucking way. Forget the Pap. I'm outta here, before you wreck my day anymore."

"Now, Lil. A Pap isn't going to make it any worse. And no matter what, you're going to need a mammogram. This lump is probably nothing."

"Nothing?!" Lily struggled into her sweatshirt, muttering beneath the tent of cotton. "It ain't nothin', I'm telling you. The worst—You wanna know the worst?!" Her head popped through the neck hole. "Mamma. That's the worst. Now I'm gonna hafta hear, *I told you so . . .*"

Sarah ignored her. "A mammogram will just clear everything up—you wait and see. Hang on a minute." And with that, the doctor slipped out.

Lily dressed and then leaned back against the examining table. She let her feet dangle, the paper crunching beneath her, then tentatively reached a hand up under her shirt and bra and dared to feel . . . nothing. How could you even feel anything in there? She wondered as she circled her nipple with her own cold fingers, rubbing, then squishing, then finally stopping in self-defense. There was so much lumpy junk in there, she had no chance of finding it on her own, no matter how many ways she squeezed or prodded. Anyway, she had no maneuverability with her bra on. Maybe at home . . .

Suddenly she noticed the pamphlets and diagrams that dotted the counters and covered the walls: *Self-Examination and the Healthy Breast; Breast Cancer and You; Broccoli and Breasts.* There were sketches of breasts with arrows pointing the directions of the spirals your fingers should make in searching out the pesky little lumps. Lily squeezed her eyes tight. *I just don't have room in my head to think about this right now,* she thought. *How long would she have to wait for answers?*

"Good news," Sarah said as she popped her head back in. "They can squeeze in both the mammogram *and* the ultrasound, right now."

"Squeeze? Isn't that a bad choice of words for a mammogram appointment?"

"I already told Maggie the mammography nurse that you have an attitude."

"I'm a carpenter. I'm supposed to have an attitude. What'd you expect me to have—a fucking party?"

"All right now," Maggie said. "Stand here, place as much of your breast as far onto the surface as you can." She pushed Lily closer to the machine. "Good, now grab this bar and, yep, that's it . . . steady."

"You're kidding me, right? A man invented this goddamn thing, right?"

Maggie ignored her. "Just relax while I crank this slide down. You'll feel a bit of discomfort as the plates flatten your breast."

Lily waited, and then howled as the machine flattened. "This is the work of some sadistic bastard who hated his mother."

"I'd have to agree," Maggie admitted.

"If guys had to have their johnsons flattened between Plexiglas, I gardamntee one of 'em would have come up with something way different than this . . . or a gun."

"Take a breath and hold it."

She did. The sooner it'd be over.

"That's it. Now let's get the other one."

"They'd make a contraption where the damn bone gets cradled in a heated fur-lined bun, with soft lights, music playing in the background, and a case of Bud. Don't try to tell me any woman had anything to do with inventing this thing."

Maggie let loose a good laugh. "I always thought the same thing myself."

"This is embarrassing," Lily muttered, slapping her other breast up on the slab. "I feel like I'm doing calisthenics in a Playboy Club."

"Are you comfortable?" Maggie asked before she took the next set of pictures.

"No, I'm not comfortable. Are you? I mean are you really comfortable doing this to women? You got some mother issues, too?"

The technician ignored her again and told her to hold her breath, and she dutifully complied.

"Already," Lily said, "I could come up with a better contraption than this muther."

"Oh?"

"Suction. A tubelike thing. Walk right up to it, stick your breast in. A little gentle compression and, badda bing! Picture snapped—humiliation minimal, the end."

Maggie handed her a gown and her X rays. "Maybe so," she said. "Radiology's down the hall. That's where they'll do your ultrasound." Neither Lily nor the radiologist could see or feel the so-called lump. Later, the news came back that the bugger had also failed to show up on Lily's mammogram.

This did not alleviate Sarah's worry and she wanted to get a second opinion. So she made Lily wait for Dr. Josephine Holliday to come back from lunch to do a second manual examination. "Just to be sure it really is nothing," Sarah said.

"It *is* nothing," Lily complained, hours later. "I've been saying it all along."

"I'm thinking that too, but there is a slight variation in the symmetry between the breasts. I want to be sure." Now Sarah was sitting beside her as they waited for the second opinion to arrive. It wasn't common for most doctors to sit with their patients in this manner. But since Lily had seemed especially disturbed, Sarah told her, she'd skipped lunch.

"Yeah, so you can be here for my death sentence," Lily said darkly.

"Cut it out. At your age and the history of this in your family, your odds are pretty good that it's nothing," Sarah said.

"Whatdya mean *history of this in my family*?"

"Well, you know. Sophia and her sisters have all had fibroid cysts. They are nearly always benign and many women who have them do not have a history of cancer. That's a good thing."

"Since when has my mother had them?"

Sarah shrugged. "Oh, gosh, years. Didn't you know?"

Lily shook her head. "She never mentioned it. Jesus."

Sarah patted her hand and stepped outside for a moment. "I'll be back."

Sophia, Lily wondered, why didn't you ever tell me? Did you tell anyone? A house full of men and an only daughter, but you never said a thing about any of it. Lily tried to recall that time—those days when she was a kid—a teenager, all involved with her own petty little world. She imagined her mother at the sink in the kitchen, or on her knees in the garden, or with clothespins clamped between her teeth, snapping sheets to the line. She thought of her brothers—older than she, moving in and out of the house, going to school, into the military, getting married, moving away. They'd been secure in Sophia's presence, but indifferent to her *being.* They were a troop in constant need of food and care. She was their provider. Lily remembered that most of the house went unoccupied while the Cameron kitchen had been teeming with teenaged boys and young men, their own and others. Sophia fed them all. And harbored her secrets. Told the boys about her father—once they were grown—but had never told Lily. Through all of this, Lily now wondered, did you harbor this secret? Did you tell Daddy even? Or did you suck it up all to yourself?

Those nights when Lily would sometimes creep down the stairs for a drink or a late night snack, everyone else soundly sleeping, there would be Sophia, long lost in her own deepness, hunched in the warm yellow light over the table, resting on elbows, a mug warming her cupped palms. *What were you thinking about Mamma? Worrying about?*

Lily wondered if Jim had been able to comfort his wife. And then, somehow, she knew that he had not been allowed. *Maybe that's how it was with Daddy,* Lily thought. *Maybe Sophia always knew, without his saying anything, that Daddy understood she was going through something bad. . . .* That while Jim would have been compassionate and loving, Sophia would never have let him know the truth. She wouldn't have wanted to burden him. And somehow, Lily could understand that.

Again, she pressed her hand against her shirt. This is nothing, Lily assured herself. Her heart thudded beneath her hand. *Damn, Mamma, you must have been scared shitless.* No wonder she'd wanted Lily to have a mammogram.

Sarah came back and said that the doctor would be coming any minute. "You OK?" she asked Lily.

"You ever see that poster of that woman with a mastectomy?"

The doctor shook her head.

"It's in black and white. You see her from the waist up, naked, arms flung wide, face up to the sky. She's got this vine tattooed along her scar. I always figured—if it happened to me . . . I'd do the same thing."

"You're not going to have to worry about that, Lily," Sarah said seriously.

"And then, I'd go to the beach and walk along with my shirt off and dare anyone to tell me to put it back on."

"You'd be that angry," Sarah said. Lily looked away. She wished Hannah were here. Hannah would have her hand on Lily's thigh as they sat here, and her head resting on Lily's shoulder. They probably wouldn't even need to speak.

Dr. Holliday approached, a long tall drink of woman, Lily decided. With her dark hair and her even darker eyes, she reminded Lily a little of Lurch from *The Addams Family,* although she'd never say such a thing to anyone. Lily found herself growing cold and she shivered involuntarily. Before panic could set in, though, Dr. Holliday winked at her and nodded. "I think we're all in the clear," she said.

It wasn't till she was halfway home, driving slowly along the river, when full relief hit her. She pulled over into one of the picnic area parking lots, got out of the van, and walked down to the water's edge. She stood with her hands jamming her pockets, staring down at the swiftly moving river. She'd made Sarah promise not to tell Sophia about the scare. There was no lump, the doctor had said. A clean bill of health was hers now; but she hadn't wanted her mother to worry. Let her feel good that she got me to the doc's and I'm clear for another year, Lily had decided.

She took a deep breath and squatted, fishing a long piece of grass in a shallow pool. For one lousy morning she had thought she might die. OK, maybe not die right away, maybe not totally croak, but worse images had come to her than the dying part. It was a familiarity with words like *chemotherapy,* nicknamed *chemo,* like it's your friend: and losing your hair; an operation; a missing breast, and the time taken out of a life to save a life. These thoughts came first and before the idea that she might die. And that last one was the least frightening of all. She reached for a blue stone resting on the sandy river bottom.

Nearby, a white egret hop-scotched across some rocks. *It's never too late to be what you might have been,* echoed inside her. Something icy shivered down her spine. What if they had found a lump? What if it had not been benign like 90 percent of them? It wasn't the dying or the balding or even the losing of a breast that had terrorized her. It was the consideration of being too weak to lift a hammer, to go on being who she was; that was her greatest fear. Another notion passed through her mind: *It's never too late to believe in what you have already become.*

Eighteen

Lily's heart was pounding hard against the inside of her chest. So hard that she covered it with the large bouquet of roses she held, the first she'd ever bought for Hannah. She hoped that the thickly layered petals would mute the hammering that was loud in her ears. Looking around at the other people who were also waiting for arriving passengers, it didn't appear that any were disturbed or even noticed the booming reverberating inside her. She couldn't figure out why she was so nervous. It wasn't the first time that she'd ever had to pick Hannah up at the airport. She could almost not remember what Hannah looked like. Was that possible? Was that why she had propped a picture of her on the dashboard, or was it just to keep her company on the ride over? Things were going to be different now between them. Six months was plenty of time to think and feel and act on their own. Lily, herself, was in this for the long haul. Hadn't they both pledged that, long ago? Hannah said as much, again, on the phone. But things would be different. Hannah needed to talk with Lily about something serious, something that would change their lives forever. And on that thought, her heart jumped again.

Back at Sophia's, Lily knew, there was a party gathering. It couldn't be stopped or put off. And although Lily knew that the last thing that Hannah would want to do would be to socialize, well you couldn't fight family and friends. You especially couldn't fight Sophia. And so she had compromised. There'd be a party as long as it was not at her house. The space was too small in spite of the renovation, and anyway, if the party were at her mother's, she and Hannah could make a run for it, and everybody else could just keep celebrating. They probably would, since Sophia had gone out and bought herself a blender to churn up margaritas. She'd become quite adept at it, she'd told Lily. "After all, being way over there in Amsterdam, when do you suppose was the last time Hannah had a margarita?" As if margaritas were, somehow, a southern American fare, nowhere to be had but at OzGirlz.

Lily watched a little man on a cell phone talking and walking around in circles, one hand holding his phone and the other covering his ear, as if the noise of jet planes on approach were disturbing his conversation. He looked annoyed and got louder, forcing others nearby to get up and take seats across the waiting area. If Cat had been here, she probably would have grabbed that phone and tossed it into a toilet. Cat hated cell phones.

Then there was a popping sound like a vacuum releasing its hold, a snap and swoosh, as the door from which Hannah would emerge opened. A thickening began in Lily's throat and tears stung her eyes. Suddenly feeling dumb, since Hannah hadn't even appeared yet, she stepped back to let the family groups crowd forward. Small children were jumping up and down, shrieking at a glimpse of Grandma, throwing themselves into the arms of their weary business-traveling moms and dads. Some arriving passengers embarked without a glance across the awaiting faces, as if this was not the last leg of their journeys or as if it was their vehicles waiting out in the parking lot that really mattered. As people continued to pour from the tube leading from the plane, Lily caught a flurry of brown curls, far down the walkway tunnel.

Hannah emerged, her eyes searching for—and finally landing on—Lily. She moved toward her almost like a stranger or an angel, Lily couldn't decide which. Hannah's hair, much longer and a little grayer than Lily remembered, was piled in a messy knot. She wore jeans and sneakers and a light blue sweatshirt with Amsterdam printed across its front. She was burdened with a shoulder bag, a thick laptop computer case, and a plastic grocery bag that had come from the duty-free shop at an airport overseas.

Lily knew somewhere in the back of her mind that tears had started streaking down her face. She didn't care. In their embrace, the roses crushed between them, and she was vaguely aware of their strong scent floating around the two of them. Hannah would later say that the smell of roses would, from that moment, forever be a turn-on for her.

"Hey, babe," was all she said now, though. Her voice was husky-sweet, no change.

"Your hair got long," Lily managed, wiping a quick sleeve across her eyes against the tears.

"And you are too damn skinny," Hannah said. "I thought you said you were eating?"

Lily shrugged and then tugged at Hannah's shirt. "This new?"

Hannah held up the bag. "I have one for you in red."

"My favorite color," Lily said. "God, I have missed missed missed you."

Hannah's eyes searched her own as if remembering, as if it were all coming back to her now.

Lily retrieved the two large suitcases with wheels (thank God) from the baggage carousel, and pulling them behind her, herded Hannah toward the parking lot and loaded them into the back of Sophia's truck. It was the only vehicle, she explained to Hannah, that could haul all her stuff. "Unless you wanted me to pick you up in the work van?" She laughed.

Not until they had settled in the front seat did they hold each other, their lips drenched in mingled tears meeting, opening hungrily, tasting each other like new lovers. Desire rose in Lily in a thick flood of heat. She buried her face in Hannah's neck, feeling the soft curls sweeping her, feeling Hannah's hands on her, moving down her arms and body as if she, too, were trying to make herself believe that they were, in fact, together again.

Their ride from the airport was filled with chatter punctuated by touches and quick kisses and hands that only unclasped when Lily had to shift. Hannah had wanted to stop at the grocery store to pick up things that she hadn't been able to get in Amsterdam; peach bud candy and hominy grits, she said, were somehow at the top of her list, and did Lily think that she'd be able to find a green tomato anywhere in the state this late in the season? After they'd filled the shopping buggy with a lot more than grits and green tomatoes, Lily glumly told Hannah that next they had to return Sophia's truck.

"Now? But why not tomorrow?"

"You wouldn't believe my mother lately," Lily began. "She's the president of this and the chairwoman of that. She's taking college classes, belongs to a book group. Suddenly she's the new Jane Fonda workout queen of the seniors set. You can't pin her down for anything anymore. Tomorrow, she's getting up at four in the morning to go sit in a rowboat in the middle of a duck pond with her new friends, Joyce and Dianne, to catch a glimpse of a rare red-bellied pepper-pot sparrow."

"You're making that up."

"OK, I forget what bird, but she needs her truck too early in the morning for me to have to get out of the bed with you to bring it back."

Hannah grinned and brought Lily's hand to her lips.

"'Cause anytime's too soon after I get into the bed with you," she murmured.

There were no cars to be seen as they pulled into Sophia's driveway. Lily imagined them stacked bumper to bumper behind the barn and over the crest of a hillock near the back pasture where the Camerons kept beef cows. She grinned, imagining the guests sneaking along the back way from the pasture, balancing trays of cookies and Jello molds they'd brought, maneuvering around cow pies.

There was only the kitchen light on as she pulled up in front of the house. Hannah said, "Looks like no one's home. Good. I'll catch Sophia tomorrow. Let's just get the hell out of here." Her hand skimmed Lily's thigh, sliding high. If she could have, Lily would have jumped back in the truck and driven out of here like a madwoman.

"Awe, c'mon now, Han. Mamma's been nearly as anxious to see you as I have."

Hannah frowned.

"It'll be quick." Lily hopped out of the truck without waiting and leaped around its front grill, opening Hannah's door and offering a hand.

"What's going on?" Hannah wouldn't budge and crossed her arms.

"Whatdya mean?"

"I know you, Lily Cameron. I've known you *that way,* for fifteen years."

The way Hannah had said *that way* liquefied Lily even further. If she had allowed herself one moment to luxuriate in the image of where she really wanted to be right then, she believed that she would puddle, literally, like the Wicked Witch of the West, into a steaming pool of unrequited love at Hannah's feet.

Hannah reached over to tug on the edges of her collar, pulling her gently back into the truck, toward her and then into the embrace of her open, inviting thighs. Lily felt the soft denim of well-worn jeans skimming her ribcage as Hannah guided, wrapped, and moored her like a slender slip of a boat being taken into harbor. Nestling her face between Hannah's soft breasts, Lily breathed her in more deeply now than ever. The scent of roses was gone now. This was Hannah, the salt-sweet smell of her so familiar it sent a surge of desire through Lily that was so powerful it almost frightened her. But mostly it relieved her, especially since her . . . indiscretion (as she thought of it) with Arlo.

Hannah's fingertips were swirling prints over Lily's skin, at first tracing, skimming along Lily's collar, lightly playful; but then pressing, guiding Lily's hands to the snap and zipper of her jeans, quick fingers unhinging the jagged metal teeth, unfolding an envelope of denim into which Lily slid her palm against Hannah's soft belly. Reaching down through fine familiar curls, until the tip of her finger touched the tip of Hannah's torturous spot, already wet with her own rising desire; Lily began a slow descent with her mouth gliding below Hannah's collarbone.

A snapping click and sudden flash of light from behind jolted the pair apart. Lily pulled back; sliding out of the vehicle, she whirled around. She felt Hannah's arms reach to protectively encircle her shoulders. Squinting into the darkness, she saw a dim figure leaning against the wall of the house, in the shadows, but not particularly skulking. In fact, the person—a man—was laughing.

"What the fuck?" Lily demanded.

The figure walked out from beneath the eaves, into the moonlight. Kevin, Lily's brother, was pulling the tape from a Polaroid camera.

"You two are going to have to save that stuff for later," he said. "Mamma's waiting." He turned his back for a moment while the women righted their clothing and hair.

"You got some fucking nerve," Lily grumbled, buttoning her shirt. Hannah climbed out of the truck.

"I got it all right here on film," Kevin teased, waving the morphing photo in the air.

"Gimme that." Lily snatched it from him.

"What the hell is going on?" Hannah finally asked, looking from Lily to Kevin.

Kevin corralled the two, drawing them in on either side and guiding them to the back door. "Just look really surprised when you turn on the lights."

"What? Surprised?!" Hannah moaned. "Lily, how could you?"

"You try telling Sophia Wright Cameron that she can't have a party."

"Party." Hannah drooped. "Damn."

"We'll make it quick. I promise."

Sophia had gone all out. *The shindig of the year,* she later liked to brag. It was true. There were over two hundred people, Lily had guesstimated. Every Cameron brother, sister, aunt, uncle, kid, cousin, and granny had arrived; every Burns from here to the Tennessee border seemed to have come solo or in packs, no in between. These two families alone would have filled a McDonald's, but add in friends: the Hoods and the Marleys with their respective broods; Hannah's colleagues and a couple of recovered patients were laughing around the snack table. Lily was stunned to see big old diesel-dyke Ruthie from OzGirlz, her arm draping a cute little androgynous thing with a butterfly tattoo on a shoulder and a spike through a brow, in deep conversation with no less than Lily's brother James and (his generally prickly wife) Rebecca!

"Mamma, Ruthie's just bound to say something rough to Rebecca," Lily hissed in Sophia's ear as she passed with a tray of avocado dip and bluish-looking chips. "You're carrying this *diversity* thing a little too far."

But Sophia only shushed her daughter away, grinning broadly, as if she had captured the National Perfect Party award. She was gliding in and out of rooms like a fancy maitre'd, her face bright with an almost iridescent glow.

Apparently Sophia had even convinced her book club cronies and the students from her ancient Celts class to come say hi to the returned Hannah (whom none of them knew). They had clearly all found common ground on the screened-in porch off the big room Sophia had always called "the parlor," where Lily's Uncle Georgie and his bluegrass band were fiddling away.

There were trays of margaritas everywhere and cheese nachos topped with green olives stuck through with toothpicks—Sophia's idea of finger food. "Now, you let them have those . . . babies got to have greens, too," Lily heard her mother say to Will Hood, who was trying to keep one of his twins from devouring the olive Sophia had put in his little hand, in spite of the scrunching of Stryker's nose as he brought the stinky ball to it. Lily swooped over and rescued Mary Kate from her mother's next indulgence.

"Mamma, babies can't have olives," Lily reprimanded. "She's too little, for heaven's sake."

Sophia sighed and popped it into her own mouth, patting the toddler's arm. "Never you mind. I raised seven of my own; I think I know what I'm doing."

Lily was aware that she was holding the child and felt suddenly awkward. The little girl, who surprisingly looked a lot like her aunt Cat, was gazing up at Lily with a smile creasing her blue eyes in the same manner that Cat's did.

"Hey you," Lily said. The child snuggled up against her. She had wispy blonde hair that curled at its ends just above her tiny shoulders and she smelled of baby powder just like her daddy.

"She looks like Cat," Lily said, making her way over to Will. "She's got that smile that takes over her whole face."

"That's what Marce says." Will had scooped Stryker into his big arms and swung him up onto his shoulders. "This one, on the other hand, is no doubt his daddy all over again."

The toddler felt softly heavy in her arms, like something valuable and vulnerable at the same time. Lily pressed her cheek to the top of the little girl's head. She was warm and snuggled her own cheek into Lily's neck.

Across the room, Hannah was standing, watching her. One hand was holding a margarita raised halfway to her lips. She was not smiling, just looking. Confusion swept across Lily. What was the matter? She raised her eyebrows at Hannah, who only nodded slightly, looked away, and went back to sipping her drink.

It was hours before anyone let them leave the party. And they did not, as Lily had imagined they would, leave through the back door. Instead, Sophia orchestrated their departure. She'd had it all planned, complete with rice, which everyone was instructed to throw. "Never mind that stuff about it being bad for birds," Lily heard her clucking when her cousin Winnie (an amateur naturalist) protested. "That's a bunch of bunk," Sophia said.

Back in the truck on the way home, Hannah looked tiredly out of the window and said, "That must be what it feels like for straight couples, when they leave the reception earlier than everyone else." She held onto Lily's hand. "Can you believe your mother? Treating us like a couple of newlyweds off to copulate on some luscious Caribbean island. The whole party cheering us on, throwing rice and kisses, pretending as if it were for the first time." Hannah rolled down the van's window and breathed deeply of the moist mountain air. "Home. It has its own smell, and taste, and feel. I never want to live anywhere else."

"Are you sure?" Lily asked.

Hannah turned and took Lily's hand. "Why would you ask?"

"Well, seemed like you were having such a great time. Getting all internationally important, and all. Your friends . . . seemed interesting and more exciting than anybody around here."

"Remember that night you called?" Hannah now squeezed Lily's hand. Her tone had gone quiet, Lily noticed.

"You mean when you all were celebrating your award?"

"When we hung up," Hannah continued, "I felt so empty. Like it didn't matter. And then . . . and then, Heather . . . well, Heather tried to comfort me."

Lily's breath held and stilled.

"She had been interested in me from the start."

Lily interrupted. "Did you like her back?"

Hannah shifted, trying to find a more comfortable position, but couldn't. "I guess I did."

Lily nodded. Fear and then guilt about her own mild infidelity with Arlo rose quickly.

"But in those moments between hanging up with you and Heather hanging on my neck, I realized how much I missed you. Sharing my world with you. Missed your voice, your laugh, your smile, and *you* hanging around my neck. I understood how meaningless it felt with Heather and without you."

Lily wondered if Hannah had slept with Heather, then wondered if it mattered. Even if she had, she'd obviously made a choice and that choice was Lily. And so she, Lily, chose not to ask or care. When it seemed that Hannah might try to share some more about Heather, Lily thought of Arlo and how her feelings had risen and then again fallen, and so pressed her finger to Hannah's lips, quieting her confession.

"Let's not say anymore, then," Lily whispered. "Let's just be in this. You here, back home with me. Let's just be in that."

Hannah snuggled closer. "I love you, Lily Cameron. And every bit that comes with you."

"Even with all the crazy characters around here tonight?"

Hannah yawned, and then looked over at Lily. "My God," she said, "she even invited Ruthie from OzGirlz! How on earth did that happen?"

"Oh, you would not believe the things that have been going on around here. OzGirlz is now one of my mother's favorite haunts. She loves Ruthie's margaritas, she loves *womyn's* music, she loves all the girls at and behind the bar, and she most especially loves Ruthie who treats her like a queen, no pun intended, when she walks through the door."

"How funny." Hannah leaned into Lily's shoulder. She grew serious. "I missed seeing Jim tonight," she said. Her eyes glittered. "I wish I could have been with you while you were going through your grief. I'm sure you've been doing some of that, whether you'll admit it or not."

Lily didn't answer. She didn't want their reunion to be about sorrow. But she sighed, in spite of herself.

Hannah shifted closer. "Sorry, sweetie. I didn't mean to upset you."

She shook her head and wrapped an arm around Hannah's shoulders. It was over and the two of them were together again, better than before.

She turned the van into their driveway and pulled on the emergency break. The two of them sat looking at the house as if it was their destiny, itself, finally reached. Then, folding into her lover's lap, Lily began to cry from a place inside that she didn't know existed—a place so dark, so deep, she realized it had been unknown to her, till now.

Finally, Hannah led her into the house. And not until considerably later, when in exhaustion her sorrow subsided finally into a quiet, different place, did she understand how the tidal wave of aching had consumed her; only as she and Hannah drifted toward sleep wrapped together, their souls and skin and sweat merging, did Lily admit to herself that her months of terrible waiting were at an end.

Nineteen

"So? How's it going?" Sophia asked, as Lily sipped from her margarita. These luncheon meetings were now something of a weekly ritual for the two. Each Friday, Lily's mother had invited her for a margarita and lunch at OzGirlz. Every time Ruthie nearly jumped the bar and rushed to greet them, so impressed was she (still) by the big party.

Lily had confided to Hannah, "I hope Ruthie doesn't have some kind of fucked up kind of lesbian crush on my mother!"

"Things are slow," Lily said now to Sophia, referring to the turn in business. "Now that Cameron is out of my hands, getting Girls with Hammers back on track is taking some time."

"Trouble getting contracts?" Sophia asked. But she was waving across the room at a group of sports dykes as they entered the restaurant. One of them waved back, a slick young shellacked-looking thing, whose hair was stiffly sprayed in an outdated mullet, crisp white shirt tucked neatly into her pressed jeans.

"How the hell do you know them?" Lily demanded.

"Oh, that's Robin. She's my personal trainer at the club."

Robin was now making her way to their table. She bent over Sophia and gave her a big hug. Introduced, Lily shook her hand, but she was not happy with the interruption.

"Your mother is one tough cookie," Robin bragged. "The only seventy-year-old that I know who can run three miles on the treadmill and barely break a sweat!"

"That doesn't seem right," Lily said. She looked across the table. "Should you even be running three miles?"

"Oh no," the trainer responded, "Sophia is perfectly safe. She's the most physically fit woman of her age that I have ever seen. In better shape than a lot of younger women, too." She leaned over Lily's shoulders, placing her hands on either side, an intimate squeeze making her tense. "Maybe you should come to one of our spinning classes," Robin challenged. "You'll see how amazing your mom is."

Lily didn't like the feel of those hands on her and she shrugged them off, annoyed. Didn't this little yahoo know she was talking to a carpenter? Was she drunk? *There was a time, sweetheart, when you would have been pudding next to me.* But the softness of her biceps beneath her crossed arms reminded her that she'd better get back to work soon, or her mother really would be showing her up.

After the woman left, Lily leaned across the table. "What are you doing hanging out with all these dykes?"

"I don't see them that way. And you should be glad I don't. They are just nice women who've come into my life. We're all God's children, Lily. These girls are very kind to me. I like them."

Oh my God, Lily thought, *my mother is suddenly Betty DeGeneres.* "You're not gonna suddenly confess anything to me, are you?" she said.

"You mean like I'm coming out of a closet?"

Lily sucked the remains of her margarita and shook the glass over her head. Now that she was with Sophia this was the only signal needed. Another drink would magically appear before her. Sure enough, a small elfin woman with wispy hair came skittering across the room, carrying two of the frozen concoctions.

"Well, you gotta admit, this all looks a little suspicious."

"Oh, Lily," Sophia said, reaching across the table, patting her daughter's hand. "You know I could never replace your father. The man was a gentle saint. He gave me a fine life and many *many* children . . ."

The emphasis on the *many* made Lily wonder if that had been mutually agreed upon or accidentally concluded, and then she knew she didn't want to know.

"Look at my life," her mother continued. "I have a wonderful family. Lots of grandbabies to hold and cuddle, great old friends and good new ones, I'm enjoying all of my activities, many of which you have inspired me toward."

"Me?" Lily was confused.

"Honey, you are an amazing woman. You're strong, smart, loyal, dedicated. Why, watching you manage this whole mess over the last few months has really shown me what kind of person you have grown to be—what kind of woman you've become. . . . I'm so proud."

Lily was moved to swallow back the shy tightness that had filled her throat.

Sophia didn't stop there. "I think your father always saw this in you. From the moment you could toddle, he believed in you. I remember once you found your daddy's hammer lying on the floor outside on the porch. You were maybe two. Jim had been fixing a board and had gone to get some more materials." She laughed. "It was summertime, and all you were wearing was a sagging diaper. You picked up the hammer by its heavy handle and were literally dragging it around the house, calling out for daddy. When he finally found you, you'd got the hilt of the handle to your shoulder, and with all your might you were hefting it up for him to take. Daddy kept laughing, saying, *'There's my girl with her hammer!'*"

Lily swallowed.

"He knew how you were, even back then." Sophia's voice had quieted. "So now, you are my role model, honey. You're the kind of woman we all could be, if we were just a little more brave."

Lily sat back, half-stunned. "Mamma," she said, "what are you talking about?"

"I brought you out here," her mother went on, "with a business proposal."

Lily sipped her new margarita. She had thought all the business proposing had been finished last week in James' office, when they'd all happily signed Cameron Construction over to Pappy and his sons. The name was now Cameron & Pearson Construction, to reflect the new ownership, but not lose the Cameron reputation. Pappy had said, "The integrity stays. That's what Jim would want."

Now Sophia said, "The thing is, I want a job."

Lily drew back. Hadn't Sophia just described the nirvana of retirement? She frowned and braced herself for whatever wild hair had tickled her mother this time.

"Not a full-time job. Part-time. To keep me active."

"Mamma, you're active as hell. What are you talking about?"

"I want to work for you."

"What?!"

"Keep your books, schedule your estimates. Do a little marketing, sales, advertising for new help. Here, look, I've already written the ad for you."

She pushed a folded sheet of paper at Lily, who unfolded it and read.

> Female carpenters needed. Only the experienced need apply. Call for an appointment.
>
> Girls with Hammers.

Listed below were Sophia's phone number and the time to call.

"What do you think?" Sophia asked somewhat tentatively.

"I don't know, Mamma," Lily shook her head. "You want to be my *secretary?*"

"Office manager. That seems fair. Just like I was for your daddy, only on a smaller scale."

Lily was silent. She hardly had an office to manage right now. Maybe Sophia's coming on board would get things up and running again. That way, Lily herself could attend to things she'd been neglecting lately, like getting out and doing some estimates, and pulling a sorely needed inventory. Since the fire, she'd been too depressed to even look at her losses. But she needed to do it for the insurance. That was one thing that she could sure use some help with.

"You're not going to make your own mother beg, are you?" Sophia said in a somewhat subdued tone.

"No. I'm thinking of all the problems it could solve, actually."

Sophia brightened.

"Good! Then that's settled," and she waved her glass at the bar. "Ruthie," she called, "come on over here and celebrate with us! I'm a working girl again!"

At least it'll keep her out of OzGirlz, Lily thought. *Hopefully.*

"So, how do you feel about it?" Hannah asked, pushing a plate of chicken over to Lily.

She shrugged between bites and shook her head. "I don't know what I'm more amazed by—Sophia's damn stamina and all the trouble it could solve, or my own excitement at the idea of having Mamma and me working together."

Hannah smiled. "So, you're thinking maybe it's a good thing, then?"

Hannah didn't seem so *foreign* anymore. Lily's eyes had traced each angle and curve of that sweet face a hundred times since she'd come home. Yesterday, in front of the bathroom mirror, while foaming with toothpaste, Hannah had coughed and then nearly choked. With some irritation in her voice she told Lily's reflection behind her, "Honey, I know you love me, but I'm feeling a little tiny bit *stalked,* right now."

"You know, you haven't aged one bit since I first saw you," Lily had said, kissing the back of Hannah's neck.

She had thought Hannah Burns the most beautiful woman in the straight honky tonk bar, where she'd first seen her. They'd spun Merle Haggard and Tammy Wynette tunes on the battered old jukebox, and the clientele was mostly rough. But the fad of line dancing had made its way to The Texas Tea, and everybody had come to scoot boots. Straights and gays (although the straights were clueless) had come dressed in their best western gear: hats and fringed leather and the pointier the boot tip the better. Just then, the "side steppin' boogie" was all the rage.

Sheer chance had placed her a few feet from the hottest gay chick in the place. Hannah Burns was seated at the bar. Clean-cut and sexy in a white cotton shirt with shoulder boards of red and pearl buttons, Hannah had brightened her spot at the bar. Lily was dressed as she always dressed: tight jeans and a black tank top with no pretensions of home on the range. She wore her maroon Red Wings, polished bright.

She'd been watching Hannah out of the corner of her eye. Her instincts told her that the goon that was drooling all over the babe in white was not Hannah's date, but a monkey she was trying to get off her back. Lily sipped from her beer and watched to see how the piece was playing itself out. Hannah, twisting to shield herself from the big ape, was Lily's first clue that he wasn't wanted, but apparently he had missed the hint or viewed it as a challenge. With the tap of one gorilla finger on her shoulder, he'd had the audacity to distract her from a conversation she had then started with a cowboy to her right.

Lily had wondered what Hannah was saying to the cowboy. She watched from her distance, as the hulk's countenance suddenly sagged, as if the air had been let out of him. At that point he left Hannah's side and his empty seat. Lily had seen her opportunity in that moment and made her way to the bar, slipping unnoticed into the goon's vacated chair. Before Hannah put her next cigarette to her lips, Lily was ready with her lighter. The brunette in the white shirt leaned toward her, caught the flame at her cigarette's end, leaned back, and dragged slow and long.

"Come here often?" Lily's seventeen-year-old brain was working overtime.

Hannah swiveled again to take a second look at the person belonging to the Zippo. Her eyes had done a clean sweep of Lily's entire body, from tank top to steel toe. Then she had grinned. "How old are you?"

Sure, Lily remembered every second of that moment. It was like clockwork, sweeping again and again, around and around, a timepiece solely devoted to keeping track of those fractional seconds that had recorded for all time their first glimpse of each other.

Something about seeing a familiar face all over again, somehow new again, was like seeing it for that first time. And other things had changed too. A lot of stuff had happened to Hannah in those months that she was away. Good stuff. Lily had to admit most of it could never have happened had she stayed here in this little town.

Hannah was *notable* now. She had been named chair of something called the *International Caucus of Psychologists.* It was a pretty big damn deal. The phone calls alone that came with this job showed just how important it was. Shrinks from all over the world wanted to talk to Dr. Burns. And although the position might sometimes take Hannah out of the country, to Lily's own surprise this did not make her sad or jealous, just proud.

Hannah's innovative work in child development had received an award by a notable women's organization that declared, *Dr. Hannah Burns is the coolest shrink in the whole world,* Lily had pretended to read, studying the inscription on the base of the plaque.

Hannah made a grab for it. "It doesn't say that . . ."

"It may as well," Lily had said, swapping the plaque for a kiss.

Hannah reached a hand across the table, taking Lily's hand and holding it for a moment. "Honey, I have something to talk with you about." Her tone was quite serious.

So, this was it. Lily's heart jumped. She swallowed, and then quickly sipped from her water glass. Wiping her mouth on her sleeve, she took a deep breath. She'd been waiting now since Hannah's return to hear this news that would change their lives. She hadn't asked about it, or worried much; mostly she figured that Hannah would bring it up when she was ready. Now seemed to be the time. "Shoot," she said, braver than she felt.

"There's this woman . . .," Hannah began.

Lily felt herself go cold. She felt her heart slow, and sensed that the room had lost some of its light. Dining by candlelight—I can't even see her, she thought. As she reached for the wall switch behind her, she missed the next part of what Hannah was saying.

"She's a very young woman."

Was it Hannah's hand that was trembling in Lily's or hers in Hannah's?

"A teenager, actually."

No, Lily thought, feeling hurt and confused. This wasn't what she was waiting to hear. Things had been good between them.

"Hispanic. Are you listening to me, Lil? This is important."

Apparently Hannah didn't get that she was saying something terrible. Hurtful. Lily chose not to answer.

Hannah took a deep breath. "Anyway, she's pregnant," she said. Releasing her fork and scooting her chair toward Lily till their knees touched, she said softly, "I mean . . . she's giving the baby up for adoption."

She waited.

So Lily waited.

"We could adopt her baby," Hannah said.

Lily's heart stopped. This time there was no doubt. She was positive. Not even a slight pulse. Cardiac arrest: it ran in the family somewhere, maybe.

"Lily?" Hannah said.

Lily knew she was staring, her eyes locked onto Hannah's mouth as if it contained her very life. *Move, mouth,* she wanted to say.

"Honey? Did you hear me?"

"Adopt a baby?" Lily finally managed. "Us?"

"Honey, we've talked about it," Hannah reminded.

"Not for a million years," Lily sputtered. "I mean, not for a long time."

"I know," Hannah nodded. "It's been awhile."

"So long that I just figured, well, you know—that it was just talk."

"Was that all it was for you? Just talk?"

Lily got up from the table and began to pace the kitchen. "No, no, I don't think it was *just* talk, but I don't think I ever thought it could ever *really* happen, either. You know." She paused, pulled on her lip and looked at Hannah. "Like, we were fantasizing about it. When we were young. When we believed in stuff like that. You know?"

"I know. And then we got too busy, didn't we?"

"*Yeah.*" *But really what I want to do is grab you and tell you how bad you scared me and how much I love you and can't stand the idea of ever losing you—*

"Maybe," Hannah said. "Maybe too busy. Busier now than ever before. But when wouldn't we be? Everybody's busy, Lil. And they have babies *anyway.*"

Lily paced. It was what she did best in moments like this. Although she'd never *had* a moment like this.

She circled first the table and then wound her way around the living room and back into the kitchen. She had to think. Adopting a kid. Jeez, jeez, jeez. It had been hard enough keeping up with that old country dog she once had, till it ran away. A lot of responsibility. Could she be a parent? A good parent? What about the poor kid? Hispanic—white *lesbian mothers* . . . *Hello?* Kid goes to school in the rural south, Hispanic *and* has two moms. Seemed like a helluva thing to do to someone, if you asked her. Jeez, jeez, jeez. Could that be good for a kid? Bad enough to actually *have* a kid, any kid, and mess up its life. But to actually go out and *get* a kid, to deliberately throw it into that kind of a situation, well, that didn't seem right.

Hannah was looking at her. "The truth is, I hadn't decided whether or not to talk to you about it, until your mother's party when I saw you with Mary Kate. Aw, Lil, I *loved* seeing you with that baby. You looked so tender . . . so gentle . . . so I talked to Sophia about it."

"You talked to my mother before you talked to me?"

"It just happened. Or maybe I was trying to be sure. I don't know."

"What'd she say?"

"She said a family's made of love, not blood cells."

Lily let out air, and resumed pacing.

"Boyoboyoboyoboy."

"We don't have to decide now, Lil." Hannah stood and crossed the room. "One thing I've learned about myself in the past few months." She encircled Lily's waist and pulled her close. "I've learned how much I'm in love with you. How good we are together. I never want this to end. And I know how great it would be to share all this love with a child. To have a family together."

Lily pulled her closer. Pressing her face against Hannah's curls, breathing in her scent, for the hundredth time since Hannah had come home from Amsterdam. She whispered, "Do you want this baby?" She felt Hannah's body shiver against her and then relax. Lily knew she was crying, and her arms wrapped even tighter. The two stood together, as if waiting for this flood to sweep them away, as if they were willing to *be* swept away in it, as long as they could be together.

"What is it?" Lily whispered. "Tell me. Do you really want this baby?"

"Like nothing I've ever wanted before," Hannah said.

Lily wondered how you could live with someone, loving her more than you loved yourself, and still not know her. But it all made sense. Hannah's job was all about mothering the whole world. Her work with children was intense and overwhelmingly important to her. Often Lily had wondered what Hannah could see in a mere carpenter who had no sense of the deeper motives that drive us, that begin in childhood. But then she had decided to let such questions go—to just accept that Hannah found something as satisfying in her, Lily, as she found in her work.

And had she counted the number of nieces and nephews that Hannah had jumped at the chance to baby-sit, she, Lily, would have known something more about her love of children. But she had missed such signs. She'd taken their mutual silence on the subject for mutual disinterest; their immersion into their own careers seemed the thing they would pursue.

"When's this baby due?" Lily asked.

"Not for months. We have time. Though it would be a kindness to Maria to let her know as soon as possible. She doesn't ask much—just her hospital expenses and the promise that we will love this kid forever." Hannah laughed. Her eyes searched Lily's face. "That's what she said—forever. I told her you and I know all about *forever*, Lily. I did."

They settled together onto the sofa. Hannah curled under Lily's circling arm and picked up the clicker for the TV. It seemed like years, Lily thought, since they'd watched it. It was the opening story of the nightly news that stalled Lily's beginning channel surf. She and Hannah stared, mouths gaping, as an unshaven Patrick Shay, Malcolm Galway's lover, in handcuffs, was being escorted across the screen, up the stairs and into the county courthouse. The news anchor's voice in the background was reporting charges of arson against the man.

Lily turned to Hannah. "It was Patrick?!" She was astonished.

"Not surprising," Hannah said matter of factly. "Arson is usually committed for only one of two reasons, money or revenge, and this is clearly the former."

"I'll be damned." Lily watched the screen as another man, probably Patrick's lawyer, made an attempt to shield his client with a raised briefcase, and then the entourage disappeared into the building.

"At least now you know it wasn't Arlo."

Lily sat back against the couch. "Oh, I always knew it wasn't Arlo." She smiled. "I'm just glad now that everyone else will know."

Hannah patted her thigh.

"Change that channel and let's get drunk watching sexy HBO crap."

Instead they found themselves sucked into a rerun of *Leave It to Beaver*.

"I'll be Ward," Lily said.

"Of course." Hannah patted Lily's leg. "But don't be expecting that pot roast and mashed potatoes and gravy stuff. Tofu and veggie burgers, Ward dear."

"No turkey, June?"

"No turkey."

"Pearls? You will be wearing the pearls, though?"

Hannah barked a decidedly un-June Cleaverish laugh. "If that's what it takes, baby, I'll be wearing the pearls."

Twenty

"Whatever you two decide, dear. You know how this family feels about babies. We just love a good baby to hug on." Sophia was speaking to Lily between licks at an envelope. Placing a stamp in the corner and mashing it with her thumb, she slid it to the pile of others like it.

"Well, we're not deciding for sure right now. We've got awhile before we have to decide. The girl wants the baby raised only by women. That's pretty much what she told Miriam, the caseworker. I guess she took some abuse as a child."

"And she doesn't want to keep this baby?"

Lily shook her head. "She's just a kid herself. Miriam says she's smart and just wants the best for the baby."

"Well, that's good then. That's what you and Hannah can give her."

Sophia was sitting behind the desk in her office. She had upgraded the space once Lily had officially hired her. They'd moved the operations of Girls with Hammers from the extra bedroom at Lily's to Sophia's house, where there were lots of unused rooms, and had made it quite official-looking by converting the old dining room into a conference space where clients could come and lay out their plans on the big table. The sunroom at the front of the house was the perfect bright spot to do her work, Sophia had said. She even mastered a new computer program that could generate 3-D images of potential renovated space just by plugging in some numbers. She was anxious to show it to Lily, who shied away from that kind of newfangled-ness.

"The girl was so relieved and happy when Miriam mentioned Hannah and me that she called right away."

Sophia was mildly distracted by the images on her computer screen. After a few minutes she looked away from it, up at Lily. "You know, the idea of two mothers is nothing new. Whole families used to live together; even friends did. Why, back during World War Two, my Aunt Gertie and her friend May rented a house and raised both their sets of boys when their husbands went off to war," she repeated this well-worn tale.

"They never quit living together," Lily reminded. "Not till they died, the very same day." She knew the story by heart.

"They were the very best of friends. And when May's husband got killed and Uncle Dill came back wounded, well, they all just kept right on living together."

"Mamma, Aunt Gertie and May were lesbians."

"Now, Lily, that's just not true. Why, Uncle Dill was there the whole time."

"Think about it." Lily leaned toward her mother. "Uncle Dill had been *where* the whole time?" She slapped her knee. "I'll tell ya where—sleeping all by himself in that little room at the end of the hall."

"That was on account of his injury from the war," Sophia explained.

"And just exactly where *was* Uncle Dill's injury?" Lily asked, knowing full well that they both knew the answer. But she almost shouted anyway, "The groin, Mamma! I mean the guy probably hadn't had a woody since nineteen forty-two!"

"Lily!" Sophia fanned herself with the next licked envelope. She was sending out advertisements for free Girls with Hammers estimates with the *enclosed coupon*. When Lily had mentioned that they'd always done free estimates with or without a coupon, Sophia defended, saying coupons would make people feel special.

"Aunt Gertie and May in no way had that kind of relationship. They were roommates."

"Roommates, huh? Roommates who went on vacation together every single year since I could remember."

"Lots of women do that for the companionship."

"Right. And made yearly pilgrimages to Provincetown, even rented a winter house in Key West! Hell, they lived over in *Asheville*! For God's sakes!"

"So? They liked the beach and mountains . . ."

"Mamma, they slept in the same bed. Small towns like this would get wind of something like that right away. You know perfectly well in those days they would have been shunned like poison."

"All right, fine. They were *lesbians.*" Sophia lowered her voice. "But we don't talk about it."

"What's wrong with talking about it?" Lily knew her voice was rising.

"Just because you feel comfortable with your *sexual orientation*," (Sophia said the words as if like she was trying them out) "doesn't mean that being gay was OK for Gertie and May!"

"Mamma, you're rhyming." Lily laughed, breaking the tension. "You gonna be a rap star, now?"

Sophia waved her on with another coupon packet. "Or a poet," she said, flashing her daughter a wide smile.

Lily bent to write in the notebook she was holding, and chewed the end of her pencil. She was attempting a list of questions for the prospective hirelings that Girls with Hammers would be interviewing this morning. There were six on the list. Number one was due to arrive any minute. "I don't know what to ask them," she sighed.

"What'd you ask those other girls—your *Ah* girls?"

"Ask them? There was no asking—only beggin'. Remember, I was desperate. And look how that worked out for me. Every last one of 'em bit the dust. Including that Dolly who I thought was in for the long haul."

"Just think about what's important to you in a workmate."

"How about a writer, blonde hair, best friends since kindergarten . . ."

"Now, Lily . . ." Sophia warned. Not for the first time, either. After they'd begun getting calls about the job from the ad in the paper, all Lily could seem to do was compare the prospects to Cat. Sophia had finally put her foot down and made Lily stop. It was now a rule.

"Fine," Lily mumbled. "Hannah says she'd like it if it turned out to be a girl."

"I thought you were only going to hire girls, anyway?"

"I'm talking about that baby. Hannah said she'd love to have a girl. I think I'd be better with a boy."

"Sounds like you have already made up your minds."

"Not for sure. We're just tumbling around the ideas. I mean, it would be great to have a boy to teach carpentry."

"Not a girl to teach carpentry?" Sophia raised a brow.

Sophia's new college course, Neofeminism in a Postmodern World, was having an effect on her.

"I don't think many girls are like me, Mamma. I think I was something of a fluke, don't you? I mean, there ain't a lot of girls in this field, not even today. Too hard. I don't know if I'd want my daughter having to get dirty and all banged up every day of her life."

Sophia peeked over her glasses.

"What?" Lily harrumphed and then looked at her watch. "When's this parade of applicants supposed to start, anyhow?"

"First appointment is in thirty minutes. Settle down, you're making me nervous. You just remember to ask the field questions and I'll ask the work questions, all right?"

Lily tapped the end of her pencil against her front teeth.

"Eight hundred bucks," Sophia said.

"What?" Lily stopped.

"That's how much those teeth of yours cost. Eight hundred bucks worth of braces and you're beating on them like you can get some new ones tomorrow. You just wait."

"Wait?" Lily leaned forward. "For what?"

"You'll see. The minute that baby starts doing stupid things, like rapping on expensive teeth . . . well, you'll see."

"Nobody said we're adopting this baby."

"I'm just saying."

"There's a helluva lot to think about, you know! Criminy, you have no idea."

Sophia rolled her eyes as her seventh child continued to spout.

"Diapers and formula, college and piano lessons, and not to mention the teenage years. Boy howdy, I don't know if I'm gonna be able to manage all that. I remember how wild *I* was . . ."

Sophia cleared her throat and glanced sharply at Lily. "There are some things we *never* want to hear about. Understand? If you don't know now, give yourself about fifteen years, when she's off on a motorcycle with her equally stupid pal, getting drunk and getting tattoos at seedy biker bars on either side of the state line."

Lily sat up straight. She stared at her mother. How had she known?

As if reading her mind, Sophia answered, "Oh honey, you've got kin in nearly every county from here to Knoxville and over to Charlotte. Not to mention some that migrated down to Greenville and those that stayed up in Johnson City. Do you really think that Daddy and me didn't know exactly what you and Cat were up to nearly every minute you were up to it?"

Lily was awed. "Why'd you let us keep up those shenanigans?"

Sophia removed her glasses and rested them on the desk. "That's something else you're going to find out about when you become a parent. After six boys, I learned to pick my battles well. And your daddy said he wasn't about to start treating you any different just because you were a girl. Do you remember that time that you and Cat were out making mischief, down at the quarry?"

Lily's jaw unhinged.

"The cops busted up your little party and hauled the lot of you downtown."

"I called James . . . how'd you know?"

"You don't think that James told us?"

"But I spent that night in jail!" This came almost as a question. And, then nearly incredulous, the next was an accusation. "Everybody else's parents . . . well, except mine and Cat's, had come and taken them to their nice warm homes. But we sat up, huddled on a nasty cot in the corner, while a prostitute puked in the toilet all night."

"Yes," nodded the omniscient Sophia, "and finally James came and got you."

"Yeah, got us and made us do all that crappy community service, while the rest of those kids got off scot-free."

Sophia smiled, reminding her. "Trash pickup."

"I hated it. Cleanin' all those beer cans out of the park for a month. And all those kids tossin' them right back in every Saturday night."

"Tell you a secret, sugar. Daddy made it all up. There had never been any community service assigned by the judge. But it was good for you."

"No!"

Sophia laughed. "Anyway, we had our ways after that of keeping our own kind of eye on you. Daddy said one time, *'Let her go—she's a might wild right now, all right, but she needs to get herself both into and out of trouble. It'll save her in the end.'* "

"Probably did keep me outta jail permanently, I gotta admit."

"Think about your friend Arlo. Even though he was cleared of these current arson charges, too bad somebody didn't take care of him like that. Going to jail at such a young age—what a shame. Just shows you that with the right parenting, it *can* be prevented. You think about that, too. In case you do get that little baby, after all." Sophia turned back to her work. After a minute or two, still typing at the keyboard, she asked Lily, "What do you hear from him? Arlo, I mean?"

Lily knew her mother. She was prying, but trying to sound casual. She didn't want Lily to have heard from Arlo, Lily suspected, because Arlo had been a kind of aberration in Lily's life. And, by extension, he had disquieted Sophia's life, too. Even though he apparently had had nothing to do with the vandalism and the fire, things had seemed to fall apart only after Arlo had come into the picture. But Lily hadn't heard from Arlo. Not since that night in her house. She dismissed the image. Not since the note that had accompanied the books and journals that were now hidden away in her attic. Arlo Halsey had disappeared.

Lily hadn't mentioned the notebooks to Sophia or even to Hannah for that matter. She hadn't so much as peeked beneath the lid of the box, never mind between the covers of the tablets. It wasn't like she hadn't wanted to or hadn't been tempted to—she had. That's why she'd kept them secret. She wanted to be the only one wrestling with her conscience.

"I don't know, Mamma. He's gone," she finally said. "At least we know he didn't start that fire. But I knew all along."

Sophia nodded but kept silent. They heard the wheels of a vehicle crunching across the driveway and looked at each other, fluffing their hair and straightening their desks as if it were they, not the arriving stranger, who was about to be interviewed. They waited as the tentative knocks hit the door.

"Come in," Sophia said, rising. She opened the door only after saying it, and extended her hand to the young woman. Lily continued to lean back in her chair until her mother's eye caught hers and warned that she was verging on rude. Lily rose and extended her hand.

"I'm Roxanne Tumble," the girl said. She came into the room and shook Lily's hand. Roxanne, it turned out, had just received her master carpenter's license. She was also certified in finish carpentry as her specialty diploma.

Roxanne Tumble was well over six feet tall and looked as if she could have picked up Lily with one hand and twirled her above her head. Instead, she grasped Lily's hand and continued to pump it while she explained her credentials. Squeaking in time with her greeting, snugly wrapping Roxanne's hips was a new leather tool belt; each sheath and pocket equipped with its own gleaming instrument. Roxanne's dark hair was pulled tightly back, stretching her face, just enough for her to appear somewhat startled. Not one wisp dared an escape from that long braid, Lily noticed. The thick rope hung down the straight of her spine.

Her credentials were impeccable; Sophia had read the resume. She offered the young woman a seat and a cup of tea. "So—and you also, I see, hold a degree in structural engineering. Quite impressive, wouldn't you say, Lily?"

Lily was sitting with a copy of the resume on her lap. "Sure got a lot of letters hanging off the end of your name," she said, trying not to sound as annoyed as she felt. "What about your work experience? Got any?"

Sophia threw Lily a dark look.

"You'll see," the woman pointed, noting page three of the vitae, "that I've worked for Habitat for Humanity and I did a stint in the

Peace Corps." She looked at Sophia, whom she had clearly decided was an ally. "We built a hospital in the Congo. It's quite a beautiful continent, Africa."

"Yeah," Lily interrupted, "but have you ever worked on a crew? Done an apprenticeship on a commercial site? Like here, in America?"

Roxanne sat back now. "As a matter of fact, I helped build the Rutherford Center." She grinned—still at Sophia—as she named the newest biggest events complex in the southeast. "I was lucky enough to be asked to be on the structural design crew." This time she smiled at Lily. "And then, I ran the crew for the second phase of the project. Thirty-five men."

"On steel?" Lily asked quietly.

Roxanne smirked slightly and barely nodded.

Lily got to her feet, extended her hand again to the woman, and nearly yanked her out of her seat with a short strong handshake. "Thanks for coming in, Roxanne," Lily said hurriedly. "You sure do have a lot of know-how and experience. We don't need to hear one more word. You are by far our top candidate." Lily pressed her palm against the woman's back, gently urging her forward. "Let's not take up any more of your time." She ushered the woman to the front door and out to the porch. "We'll finish our interviews today and get back to you the first of the week." Then she closed the door on Roxanne Tumble, without another word.

"Whew!" Lily said, throwing herself into her chair. "That was a close one."

"What are you doing?" Sophia asked, removing her glasses and setting them down on top of Roxanne's resume.

"Saving us the trouble."

"Trouble? What trouble? The girl's a gem!"

Lily raised her hand. "I know, I know. Looks like that on paper, for sure . . ."

"Doesn't just *look* like that; she *is* that, Lily."

Lily shook her head and leaned back. "You don't understand about these things, Mamma."

"Then you better start explaining, missy."

Lily nodded at her mother, ready to clarify her position. "That girl walked steel," she said.

"So? That's a good thing, right? She won't have any trouble getting up a ladder then, will she?"

She could see the growing impatience reflected on her mother's face and tried to clarify. "Look Mamma, when you're up there, straddling cold rail, there's no room for two walkers to pass around each other. One of them has to back up. *Who* backs up? Well, that's determined by one of two things. Either someone's the boss or someone's got more balls. Kind of like a game of chicken."

Sophia folded her arms. "This is crazy," she said.

Lily thumbed over her shoulder. "That Roxanne? She didn't ever back up."

"How do you know?"

"How I know is how she answered me. She smirked."

Sophia scoffed. "Smirked?"

"And it told me everything I need to know. She's either always been the boss or she's always had balls. I can't work with that." Lily's tone had finality in it. She turned away from Sophia and pulled her notebook out.

Sophia watched as her daughter scribbled away. After a minute, she asked softly, "Lily? Did you ever back up?"

Lily bore down on the paper, making thicker the black lines of her marker, weeping ink through the paper to the next page. She threw her mother a side glance. "Never," she said with a smirk.

The next two candidates were washouts. Lily said she knew it before they even got in the door. Following them was a blonde named Michelle, pronounced *Mee-shell,* she said. She got as far as sitting in the interview chair. Lily took a peek out to the driveway and saw a silver Mercedes shining in the sunlight. If this wasn't clue enough, Lily knew the interview was over when *Mee-shell* confessed that her desire to be a carpenter stemmed from her love affair with anything and everything Martha Stewart.

"Martha Stewart," Lily echoed. "Isn't she a crook?"

Michelle dismissed that notion with a wave of her red-tipped fingers. "Oh, she's not. I watch her show every day. I have tried most of the crafts and I can even operate a drill now." Michelle paused, leaning toward Lily. "Oh my God, my friends would be so jealous if I actually had a job *decorating* and got paid for it. My boyfriend, Brent, thinks it would be cute."

Lily leaned forward, too. "Carpentry ain't exactly *decoratin'*, honey," she said.

"Oh, I know. But you know what I mean."

The next interviewee was a *lovely* girl, Sophia declared after Tiffany had left. She admired the butterflies that adorned the upper corner of Tiffany's resume, which listed nine jobs in two years. And although Tiffany seemed determined to *make this carpentry gig* a go, Lily couldn't take a chance on being Tiffany's tenth *disappointment,* which was how the little creature described her rate of turnover.

Lily was most surprised by candidate number four, who never showed up and didn't call until after she and Sophia had finished their lunch hours later. She did telephone with her excuse of having overslept her alarm, apologizing and saying to Sophia, "I swear this has never happened before and I swear it won't happen again. I know this doesn't look good."

"You're right about that, miss." This tone of her mother's surprised Lily, who was beginning to think Sophia had a soft spot for the unemployed, regardless how hopeless their credentials were. "It does not look good. Certainly not to Girls with Hammers. We don't take excuses. Good luck and good riddance!"

"Whoa!" Lily said, placing a cup of tea in front of Sophia.

Sophia smiled and stretched, leaning her head against the back of her chair and said, "I'm feeling a little cranky, I admit."

Lily suddenly saw her mother old . . . or older, anyway. Without Daddy, she had seemed to blossom. Especially with all that healthy diet and exercise, or maybe Lily was finally taking notice of someone who had been there all along. But right now Lily could see that Sophia was tuckering out quicker than usual.

"You okay, Mamma?"

Sophia rose and rubbed at her temples. "I'm fine, dear. Just tired." She looked down at the calendar. "We've got two more interviews, but they're not coming till tomorrow morning. Why don't we call it a day?"

"Can I get you anything? A sandwich?" she asked, trying to smile, but instead, awash with a feeling of helplessness. As if this woman, her own mamma, would ever accept anything like pampering from her daughter. Sophia's silence was her answer. Lily was suddenly saddened to be witnessing her mother's slowing. Covertly aware of the steadying hand on the desk top, the easing of her rise to standing, Lily watched through the moment of stillness as Sophia got her equilibrium before moving forward. She had glimpsed this before, noting Sophia's seeming acceptance of the necessarily slowed pace up the long flight of stairs to her bedroom, how she took those journeys with a kind of gathering resolution, one step at a time.

Just as Lily was closing the front door behind her, she heard Sophia call from the top of the stairs. She turned back into the foyer, recalling the location of each squeaking floorboard as she had maneuvered them in her youth, sneaking back in after a thousand rule-breaking midnight escapades. She detoured those boards now as she had then. Approaching the foot of the casement she looked up to see her mother standing, haloed in a soft early evening light, that flooded in from a hall window on the second floor.

"You called me?"

"Are you really considering adopting that baby?" Sophia asked.

After pause, Lily said, "I guess I am, Mamma."

Sophia nodded. "Your daddy knew you'd be a good person, and from the time he fit you in the hollow of his baseball glove and carried you around like he'd caught you out in left field, he even knew you'd be a great carpenter. I swear he did."

Lily waited.

"I knew something else. I just never knew whether I'd ever have a chance to say it to you, Lily."

Now Lily frowned. A strand of hair had loosened from her ponytail and she pushed it back. She waited for her mother to go on, half impatient with Sophia and half worried over the tired tone of her words.

"Anyway, just like your daddy always knew you'd be a great carpenter, I always knew that if you had the chance, or made the choice,
well, *I* always knew you'd be a great mother."

They stared at each other, Sophia smiling gently.

"Daddy wasn't the only one who kept the faith for you," she said.
She then blew a kiss and went slowly down the hallway to her room.

Lily sat down on the bottom stair, listening to the sounds of the
house settling in the dusk, while the old hot water heater chugged
and clunked familiarly. She listened for the sounds of her mother getting into bed; the drop of each shoe, the slide of the bedside drawer,
where Sophia kept her reading glasses, the quiet but distinctive clink
of her water glass settling back down onto the nightstand. When the
final familiar groans and creaks of her mother's aching bedstead had
settled and there was silence from above her head, only then did Lily
rise and make her way to the door, setting the lock and gently closing
it behind her.

Twenty-One

They were curled around each other in the bed, talking softly. Hannah's day had been no less intense and hectic than her own, Lily knew. Telling each other about what had happened today was nearly as exhausting as moving through the day itself, she thought. But now, quiet had fallen between them and Lily felt its weight. Of all the things that they had talked about, the one subject they'd managed to avoid was that of the baby. It hovered.

Finally Lily said, "With days like these . . . where would we fit in a baby, I wonder?"

Hannah shifted in her arms. "But people do it. We'd make the time, Lil. All these *things* wouldn't matter as much anymore. They wouldn't even cross our minds."

Lily wove fingers through Hannah's curls. "Seems like another whole person could just add to the chaos, though," she said.

"Or bring some peace. Cohesion." Hannah turned her head so she could look at Lily. "Babies do that, you know. They take your mind off petty details. We'd be a family—three people loving each other instead of just two. Think about that."

Lily thought of Sophia, how she'd grown older. A baby would be just one more person to lose. "But there's just other stuff that worries me," she said then.

Hannah nudged her, "Like?"

"Like, I'm still *a* Girl with a Hammer."

"That's about to change. And that's not what's bugging you." Hannah's voice became gentle. "Since you got home tonight, you've been . . . *gone* . . . a little distant. What's going on?"

There was a momentary pause and then Lily loosed her arms around Hannah and sat up in the bed. "My mother's getting old. I noticed it tonight." She shrugged. "Just some weird things."

"But Sophia is healthy, honey. She's active—probably in better shape than either of us . . ."

Lily shook her head. "She's tired. Slowing down."

"I understand, sweetie." Hannah held her closer and whispered, "but I don't think it's something that you can let yourself worry about. People get older. That's a fact we *all* have to live with. You can't go living your life around hypotheticals or eventuals; they only distract us from what's right here before us. Your mother is right here now. That's all we can know. Not the *what ifs,* Lil."

"I know, I guess . . . it was just a moment." Lily took a deep breath.

"Can't let fear get in our way, Lily. It never has before. Why start living afraid now?"

"Maybe it's me getting older. You think?"

Hannah laughed. "Losing people we love is scary. But you had no more control over your daddy falling than you did over Cat leaving. You won't have any control over anyone else's going away, either. That's just the way it is. But the one thing we *can* focus on is, do we want to be parents?"

Hannah's voice drifted. Lily was falling asleep—knew she was—and Hannah's voice was fading away. She let her body relax, feeling her legs pressed warmly against the curve of Hannah's body. Together they wrapped each other this way, and the rhythms of their breaths carried them off to sleep.

Lily was jarred awake by a dream. *Nightmare.* Clutching the sheet, she felt sweat running cold between her breasts as she searched the darkness for her bearings. In the next moment, Hannah's easy breathing soothed her, anchored her again, and the panic began to subside.

Lily squeezed her eyes tight, but the visions from her dream appeared, anyway. There was the deer carcass, more vivid now, as if the color had been digitally enhanced; another—surreal—repeating in fast-forward/rewind mode: Jim falling down and up the ladder over and over; then a frantic search at a baggage claim carousel for a duffel bag containing a baby, feeling herself wince each time another suitcase thudded onto the conveyor belt. Then Arlo, off in the distance, was walking away from her. She recognized the unmistakable slouch of his shoulders, the tilt of his head. She called to him, but he kept going. In her dream she gave a hard chase, but the distance between them never closed.

She crept out of bed, careful not to awaken Hannah. Grabbing a flashlight, she'd made her way up into the attic to the corner where she'd stowed Arlo's stuff. She flipped over an old wooden kindling box, and made herself a seat in a stream of moonlight beaming in through the dormered pane above. She pulled the plastic box in front of her and gently pried off its lid. The flashlight shone onto the contents. Pushing aside paperbacks, she reached for the notebooks. There were six in all. She arranged them chronologically in her lap. Youngest to oldest—*Fifteen* through *Twenty-three*.

The moonlight was enough for her to see and so she clicked off the flash. Smoothing her hand across the first one's surface, she traced Arlo's crude numbering. It was as if she could feel his touch beneath hers, his hand on these pages. There would be truth here. She was reminded of how Cat had found something of herself in some old diary of her grandmother's, and how the writing had changed her life—or at least had freed her to go do the thing she wanted to do—travel to Scotland, get the full story of her family. But Arlo was not related to Lily. Arlo was his own man, really only an acquaintance of Lily's. He had no power over her, no matter what the "truth" was that was contained in his diaries. And why, even, did she care?

Maybe she didn't want to know what was here. And yet, just as the thing in the middle of the road had become more vivid, more distinct in her dreams, so too had Arlo's elusiveness and she knew she had been drawn to that in an equally perverse sense. Something about Arlo and his life, she knew, was somehow connected to her own. She opened the book. In a very neat and precise handwriting it began:

Arlo Halsey, Age 15

My mamma always told me I was a gift from God. But I aint. Tonight, here on my fifteenth birthday, I come to know what I really am—the spawn of a demon seed . . .

She quickly closed the cover. He had pressed down so hard on the paper with his pen, he'd nearly torn through. Hard truth told in the hand of a young boy. Lily felt tears rising—she wasn't sure why—and then she was weeping, the tears falling and washing across the cover of the notebook, smudging the old ink, the innocence. She looked up and out of the window, toward the moon glowing high in the deep, unknowable sky. No child, she thought, no matter how old, should ever feel something like this about himself.

Quietly she went back down the stairs and lay down beside Hannah. Half in sleep, Hannah reached for Lily's hand.

"Where've you been?"

"Getting milk. Couldn't sleep."

"You OK?"

"Hannah? I think we should get that baby."

Hannah leaned back, facing her. "You mean that?" She brushed Lily's cheek. "You've been crying."

"Maybe."

"Why?"

Lily held her. "Because I'm happy," she said. "How classic is that?"

The next morning with the sun just peeking over the ridgeline, casting early shadows, Lily pulled into Sophia's driveway. Her mother was bent over in the garden, a straw hat on her head, yanking away at weeds.

"How long have you been out here?" Lily said carrying the cup of coffee she picked up on the way along with a couple of glazed Krispy Kremes.

"Oh, since about six, I suppose," Sophia straightened and yanked off her gloves. Reaching for the doughnut, she asked, "What's the occasion?"

"It's a carpenter thing. You know, doughnuts and coffee and all that. I thought we should do it every once in a while."

"Let's have it be that, then," Sophia said. "*Once* in a while. I'm not out in the field, like you," she said, patting her stomach. "I don't want to start packing on the pounds at my age."

Lily laughed. "Mamma, when I'm your age I'm gonna eat what I want, drink what I want, smoke cigarettes, cuss and swear, and lay on the couch channel surfing."

"No, you won't."

"How do you know that?"

"Your children always need you. You'll stay healthy for your child. Wait, you'll see."

My mother the psychic, Lily thought. She could go on *Oprah*. "You're a regular Kreskin, Mamma. Me and Hannah were up all night deciding. How could you tell so fast?"

"That little bounce in your step. Yesterday you were dragging. Come on up into the house." She went up the steps. "I'll wash up. That first girl is supposed to be here in about ten minutes."

"Hope she's better than the last five or we're sunk," Lily said, following.

"We're not sunk. That Roxanne Tumble is the perfect candidate and you know it!"

Lily groaned and sat down at the small desk in the corner. It was bare except for a notepad and a mug containing an assortment of pens and pencils. Her mother had bought her a nameplate that read *Lily Cameron, Field Manager*. It was mostly for show. The only thing she really did here was sit and doodle. Over her shoulder and across the room was the heartbeat of the operation. Sophia's desk was humming with purpose. A wooden plaque with brass letters reading *Sophia Cameron, Office Manager*, was propped at the front of it. Sophia returned, wiping her hands and carrying two mugs of steamy coffee.

"Give me that," she said, taking the paper cup from Lily's hand. "You and your father, I swear. Drinking gas station coffee and thinking it's good."

Lily laughed and then jumped, startled, at the quick rapping against the door. The next interview had arrived early, and they had missed the approach. Rather than rising, Sophia called out, "Come in," and stayed put.

Rode hard and put up wet, came to Lily's mind, seeing this one.

DJ didn't smile or say a word. She just shook hands. Lily had the feeling that she hadn't smiled in a very long time. Her face was deeply creased and her eyes squinted hard. A heavy smoker's face. She had black hair of varying lengths, some of it slithering in snakelike ropes along the shoulders of a worn black leather jacket.

When she did talk, her voice had the hum of a bass drum.

DJ explained how a bunion condition made her leave her job with the DOT. "Standing all them hours—cars a comin' and a goin'. Feet take a beatin'."

"Ever do any carpentry?" Lily asked. "Got any certifications?"

Then DJ held up her thumb—or half a thumb, more exactly. The top half had evidently taken leave. "This enough certification for ya? Miter saw, back in nineteen eighty-five—or was it nineteen eighty-six?" She barked a laugh. "Cain't 'member which; I was drunk for one of 'em."

Lily and Sophia exchanged glances. "Well," Lily said, rising, "we're really looking for someone with paper credentials and a more recent background in the field."

"Now you wait a minute, here." DJ got up and pushed her chest at Lily. A substantial blue-black spider tattoo was visible on her neck. "You ain't even gonna give me a chance?" She turned toward Sophia, as if she might reach across the space for her.

Lily slid in front of her mother's desk. With one swift movement, she hooked a finger around DJ's pinky, pulling it back, just shy of a snap. "You want to leave now?" she asked, bearing down on the finger. She was nose to nose with the troublemaker. Feeling the woman weaken, she shoved her toward the door and out, following and releasing the little finger only after DJ had begun to trip down the porch steps. Before slamming the car door, DJ turned and flipped the bird. "Cunt," she called as she roared away in a beat-up white car.

"Nasty girl," said Sophia standing right behind Lily, now watching the woman roar off in a beat-up white car with expired out-of-state plates.

"She ain't even from around here," Lily said. "A Yankee to boot. No wonder they got a bad reputation with us. They earn 'em."

"No kidding," Sophia agreed.

"When's the next one?" Lily asked, already and suddenly bored.

"Soon." But the hands of the clock ticked around its face for nearly an hour, and Lily began to get grumbly.

"We can already scratch this next one off the list. I got no need for tardy types," Sophia said and shuffled around some papers.

"Maybe she got confused about the time. Let's give her another five minutes. What's her name?" Lily wondered for lack of anything better to do.

"Wanda," Sophia looked down at the schedule. "Wanda Tompkins."

"Oh, for God's sake." Lily twirled a quarter across her desk. "Who'd name their kid *Wanda?* Almost as bad as you naming me *Nelda.*"

"Now that was your daddy's granny's name. You ought to be proud to be carrying it around."

"Yeah, well at least you didn't give it to me for my first name. Hannah wants to name this baby *Isabella.*"

"That's pretty."

"It's all right. I told her I'd call her *Izzy.*"

"I'm sure that made Hannah happy."

"Threw a shoe at me."

"Can't blame her." Sophia was buried in a pile of paperwork and was barely paying attention to Lily or the time.

"This sucks," Lily said. "I don't want to hire that big old Amazon, Roxanne, Mamma. She scares me."

Sophia laughed.

"What?" Lily looked defensively at her mother.

"She scares me, too."

"Ha! Well, then we ain't pickin' her. Run the ad another week."

Another twenty minutes went by before Sophia crossed Wanda's name from the list. She balled the finished schedule, and tossed it in the trash.

"OK, we'll give it another week," she agreed.

Just as the pair headed for the kitchen, there was a knock on the door. Both frowned at each other.

"Got a lot of nerve showing up two hours late for a job interview," Lily said. "Assuming that's Wanda wanda-ring in."

She turned the knob and yanked back on the door. Cranky words already half out of her mouth ended in a muffled gasp. She stepped backward, throwing open the door, and a quick breath stopped in her chest. As the figure came into view, it was the exhale she couldn't quite make. Things were somehow real and unreal at the same time.

The sun was bright behind the figure, creating a near silhouette. He was leaning against the door jamb, white T-shirt stark against his tanned skin, his jeans creased straight and his shy grin still, Lily noticed, just a bit crooked. In his hand he held the folded copy of the *Galway Mountain News*; a red pencil had circled Sophia's carefully penned job advertisement.

Lily turned toward her mother behind her, whose look she could see was a mix of surprise and suspicion. Sophia stood poised, teacup clinking just slightly in its saucer. When Lily's gaze returned to her visitor, Arlo straightened his form and took a step backward. Across his hips was strapped an old tool belt. He smiled, revealing the corner chip of his front tooth, his cowlick springing in his slight bounce.

"Well," he said tapping the newspaper, "I ain't a girl." He then yanked the steel head of the hammer from its holster on his belt. "But I do have a hammer." He held the tool in front of him. "Still hiring?"

About the Author

Although she was born and raised in New Jersey, **Cynn Chadwick** has lived in the South for the past twenty years. She now makes her home in the Blue Ridge Mountains of western North Carolina where she teaches writing at the University of North Carolina at Asheville. She received her master's degree in Southern Literature and a master of fine arts degree from Goddard College in Vermont. *Cat Rising* (Haworth) was the first novel in this series.